LOOK AT IT THIS WAY

MASAI DREAMING

IN EVERY FACE I MEET

LEADING THE CHEERS

Interior

JUSTIN CARTWRIGHT

SCEPTRE

First published in 1988 by Hamish Hamilton Ltd
First published in paperback in 1989 by Minerva
Sceptre edition published in 2000
A division of Hodder Headline
A Sceptre Paperback

10 9 8 7 6 5 4 3 2 1

A CIP catalogue record for this book is
available from the British Library.

ISBN 0 340 76761 8

Printed and bound in Great Britain by
Clays Ltd, St Ives plc

Hodder and Stoughton
A division of Hodder Headline
338 Euston Road
London NW1 3BH

CHAPTER 1

It was hot in Bangunes. Nothing much stirred except the guinea fowl, which roused themselves from their torpor from time to time to rush dementedly about before settling back into their dusty, backyard existence amongst the melon skins and corn cobs of the town's Victoria Road. There these schizophrenic birds would pretend to be chickens for a while, scratching in the dust unskilfully, or squatting comfortably in the shade of a burnt-out car. On a whim they would soon be off again at a mad, staccato gallop, giving full voice to their anxieties for a few minutes, before plumping themselves up again in the dust. There was no discernible cause for their anxiety.

Bangunes was a town which was supported almost entirely by Scandinavian aid. This aid found its way to the lively market of Victoria Road. Volvo marine engines were used as generators; high-protein soup mixes were taken as a medicine by infertile women; fat and virile bulls were eaten at presidential banquets; NATO arctic survival huts, donated by the Norwegians, now housed the President's bodyguard; surgical gloves, made in Finland, were used for washing up by the metropolitan sophisticates and as contraceptives by the slighter forest people; the new automatic telephone exchange, donated by Denmark, had left its crates (marked ambiguously GIFT OF THE DANISH PEOPLE COME IN PEACE) to reappear in the enamel basins of the market mammies as electrical components; circuit boards could be bought along with Bang and Olufsen television sets. Beside this transmogrified technology, the traditional products of

Banguniland were to be had: green edible monkeys in basket cages, scrawny chickens, spiny prickly pears, livid forest fruits, iguanas, the skins of medicinal animals, sacks of maize meal, powdered and shaved horn, beads of ostrich shell, feathers of the great loerie, the tails of cheetah and woven mats. Almost the only thing you could not buy in the market was the flour given by the German Federal Republic, which went straight to the Italian baker in Ndongo (formerly Speke) Square, to be made into croissants for the diplomatic community. This community had shrunk over the years as Banguniland's promise had failed to be realised. The truth was, there was nothing in Banguniland to excite the desires of the more avid consuming nations. Long searches of the interior by planes, trailing sensitive equipment in ovoids of plexiglass, had failed to find any minerals. When the taste for avocado dip declined in the West, the abandoned avocado ranch along the Banguni River had quickly turned itself into an avocado arboretum, producing giant trees and tiny dry fruits, sportive woods run completely insane. The game park, established by the World Wildlife Fund and opened by Prince Bernhardt of the Netherlands, had long ago reverted to its previous existence as a piece of wild scrubland inhabited by a small and fluctuating population of animals and nomads. Nobody visited it because it was inaccessible in the rainy season and in the dry season the animals, and the nomads, moved to a large swamp beyond the first row of the Malanja Hills. There had once been plans to turn this, too, into a game reserve, but the word at the World Wildlife headquarters in Geneva was that Banguniland had slipped from the first division. Bangunes was thus spared another invasion of bearded men in zebra-striped Land Rovers.

Although the Scandinavians and sporadically the European Economic Community still gave money and staples of one sort and another, the rest of the world had assigned Banguniland to the boneyard. No mineral wealth, no cheap primary products, and a succession of charmless presidents, the latest being President Ndongo, had proved all too easily ignored by the consumer nations. Strategically the country was useless, too, because the

Banguni River issued forth from the hinterland into a delta which was controlled by the Portuguese enclave of Puerta Nueva. The title deed to Puerta Nueva gave this natural harbour to the Portuguese in perpetuity. Since their own revolution, the Portuguese had been too preoccupied with the paperwork of quickly passing governments ever to reach a final agreement with the evanescent regimes in Banguniland. The river, once navigable by large lighters and steam tugs, was now a dangerous channel again which required specialist knowledge and powerful outboard engines to negotiate. In consequence Bangunes Port, with its sturdy and optimistic colonial buildings, was now suffering the sort of decay to which everything in Banguniland was subject. Schemes to dredge the twelve miles to the coast again had been abandoned. The last steam dredger had run aground on a sand bank when a boiler blew only three months before. Arab dhows with diesel marine engines sometimes made the age-old trip, taking out with them domestic servants, usually young girls, and bringing in transistor radios, Honda motorcycles and Porsche sunglasses.

It had not always been so. In 1959, when my father and Mrs Mary de Luth had made their trip for *National Geographic*, Mrs de Luth had described the country as 'Africa's promised land, and land of promise'. This was a reference to the small and secretive tribe of the deep interior, who were believed to be an ancient Israelite sect, famed for their work in brass and gold. On this expedition, my father had been drowned in an accident with an overloaded ferry. His foot, so Mrs de Luth said in her letter, had become entangled in the webbing holding one of the Land Rovers secure when the ferry struck a submerged object and the Land Rover fell over the side. 'I deliberated for some time before I decided to carry on our work. I believed then, and I believe now, that I owed it to the memory of your husband and to the readership of *National Geographic*. Richard Burton [she was referring to the explorer] once wrote "Travellers are mostly an angry race." This did not apply to your husband. A more agreeable man it would be hard to find.' At the time of my father's

7

last, and only, trip for *National Geographic*, Bangunes was regarded as a mysterious and seductive town, and Banguniland as a colourful and promising country. The fine artwork of the Israelite tribespeople, and Speke's testimony to the grace and courteousness of some of the tribes he had met in 1868, contributed to this lingering impression of a land of milk and honey. Mrs de Luth did nothing to dispel this illusion as she travelled energetically in her top-coat.

'The author finds it more comfortable to travel in the Tropics in a top-coat, a tip she learned from the Bedouin Arabs,' reads one caption as she stands, a dead ringer for Eleanor Roosevelt, inspecting a collection of intricately carved bronzes made by the *soi-disant* Hebrews in the interior using the tricky lost wax method. This tribe lived under a grove of enormous wild African fig trees. 'Rumour has it these trees were brought from the Jordan Valley nine hundred years ago,' she wrote. They had since been shown to be a fairly commonplace species known as *ficus capensis* whose fruits had medicinal powers. Because these fruits hang in huge, fecund clusters, goats and other animals are sometimes sacrificed beneath the trees in order to encourage fertility in women. Nothing much was known of this Jewish tribe since the troubles. They had been massacred and dispersed, and their treasures looted. A few survivors had been removed to Israel, where they were learning Hebrew and living in a special camp, their Jewishness hotly disputed, but somehow authenticated by the ghastly pogrom which had undoubtedly taken place in the interior. If ever history has footnotes, they will be in the finest type.

*

I was looking for a trader, named R. Patel, but nothing stirred in Victoria Road except the deranged guinea fowl. Patel, sensibly, must have retired from the uncertainties of an African afternoon. I could picture him in the cool interior of a rambling house, regaining his composure after a hot and comforting curry, perhaps with sweet mango juice from the Kelvinator, soothed by

8

the cadences, the puppy noises, of family life. The ambiguity of the African self, its lack of moorings in this world, he could perhaps explain to himself in the palliatives of the *Bhagavadgita*: the true self is unknowable, but realisable in a miniaturised way through knowledge of the self in man. Perhaps the 'R' in 'R. Patel, General Traders (Pty Ltd)' was Rabindranath. I had written to Patel for supplies and received his handwritten confirmation that they would be ready. Victoria Road ran absolutely straight for about a mile. At either end it gave up life and became a track quickly multiplying into a series of paths, leading off into the scrub. Victoria Road was bisected by Zwane Street, which led from the old residential quarter on a slight rise, down to the port, by way of the Anglican church. The Anglican church was surrounded by a grove of jacaranda trees. It was built of local stone, crudely dressed, at a glance giving the illusion of a church in Gloucestershire. Victoria Road was made up of low buildings, with shopfronts shaded by tin roofs, leading onto cement verandas. But many buildings were missing, perhaps burned out in the troubles, or perhaps simply decayed and collapsed, rotten teeth in an untended mouth. These gaps in the street had been colonised by nomads with their goats and dogs. The very poor lived there too in shelters of palm fronds and plastic bags and bits of wood. Some of these people approached me as I searched for Patel in the heavy stillness of the afternoon. Their faces had acquired a state of grace, of imperturbability, caused, I guessed, by the certainty that they were going to die soon. I gave them some money which they took without apparent excitement, before walking away, their long, thin legs almost too frail to carry the little bundle of bones and rags filling in the gap between their legs and their large, gaunt heads. I found Patel's shop. It was shuttered. There was no sign to say when he would be back from his repose. I wished then that I had never made the trip to this mortuary of a country. The people were dying; the fabric of the town was dying; hope and promise had long since died.

At that moment a pale green Pontiac pulled up beside me. It was a 1951 model, identical to the one my father had bought when we first lived in America. When he bought it, it was already, we reported anxiously and disloyally, old enough to raise questions among our neighbours. Yet here, nearly thirty years later, was the identical model, Indian chief stone-faced up front, plastic leather-look seats, stick shift on the steering column, sunshade over the windscreen. It had a rather insubstantial rear, which later models moulded into extravagant fish tails of chrome and steel. The driver rested one delicate arm, as muscled but fine as an antelope's, on the sill. His face, with its dark hair, sunglasses and even features, presented the blank gaze of a building by Mies van der Rohe.

'Are you lost, sir?' he asked.

'No. I am wondering what to do. I am supposed to meet a Mr Patel who is supplying me with some equipment.'

'Mr R. Patel is sleeping now, sir. He will open again at four o'clock.' He glanced at his watch. 'I will take you on a tour of Bangunes in the intervening hour.'

I wanted to ride in the Pontiac.

'OK,' I said.

'Where do you wish to go, sir?'

'What's there to see?'

'What about the People's Conference Centre, where the Organisation of African Unity met in 1979?'

'No thanks. Let's go down to the port.'

I watched him pull the stick towards him and down for first gear. We drove smoothly along Victoria Road and turned into Zwane, past the church. The driver glanced at me from time to time, smiling from within his disguise.

'My name is Frederick, sir. My African name is Ngwenya.'

'How do you do?'

'Fine, sir. I know who you are.'

'You do?'

'Yes, sir.'

'Are you a taxi driver?'

'No, sir, presently I am a student.'

The University of Bangunes, once a pet project of UNESCO,

had closed since the troubles. In Africa universities were seen, with some accuracy, as focal points for all the malcontents and ideamongers in the country. Along with the television station, they are the first to go in times of trouble.

The plastic seats were sticking to my back and the underside of my thighs. We drove past the embassy and aid district, a collection of compounds with a plentiful supply of Land Cruisers and official cars parked in the shade of woven reed garages, an ethnic touch adapted from the native architecture. These cars gave a sense of purpose and activity to the foreign missions. They stood there, material proof of their governments' wealth and technological mastery, admittedly stalled for the moment here in Banguniland, but serving an important totemistic function, nonetheless.

The old port, like those remnants of the past in our own big cities, had a comforting charm. The port had probably never been more than a series of wooden jetties poking out into the Bangunes River, but it was served by a cluster of Portuguese, tiled buildings, admirably suited to the dilapidation of the passing years, wooden shutters hanging on one hinge, stucco walls flaking and paving stones rising unevenly in the cool inner courtyards. The harbourmaster's house had lost its roof, but palm fronds and reed thatch filled the gaps.

Overlooking the largest jetty was Brannigan's Hotel. I had often looked at a picture of Mrs de Luth and my father with their porters ranged outside Brannigan's at the start of the journey to the interior. It is the last picture of my father.

He stands, half his face in deep shade from his solar topee. Next to him is Mrs de Luth, veiled like an aristocratic beekeeper, in her topcoat. The porters stand beside custom-made boxes and cases. They are at ease, but they have a purposeful look, fired no doubt by Mrs de Luth's zeal. She has about her a no-nonsense look, a gung-ho directness; my father, perhaps in response to this unspoken ethic, carries a clipboard. Because of the shade cast by his topee, it is impossible to see his expression. His chin, however, juts confidently into the sunshine. His forearms are hairless, but well formed. He is wearing long shorts, British naval style, which make the bottom half of his legs look somewhat puny. To one side of this purposeful group stands another white man in a very heavy tweed suit. I take this to be Mr Brannigan. If there was ever a Mr Brannigan, nobody had a recollection of him now. My student taxi driver, Ngwenya, pronounced it 'Brengun'. He suggested we have a drink in Brengun's Hotel.

There was a picture of the Wicklow Hills on the wall above the bar, gone yellow, with the edges curling up osmotically, which made me think Mr Brannigan was from there.

The bar was empty. We sat at a table with a view down to the muddy bank of the river immediately below, the jetty, to which a canoe made entirely of one piece of tree was tied, and to the opposite shore, a mysterious place from which some smoke rose lazily into the afternoon sky. The sky was not so much blue as white. The river flowed by towards Puerta Nueva in a thick, green brown. It was like seawater in mid-ocean, dangerously deep and powerful. The river bank immediately beneath us was, I now saw, covered with tiny scuttling crabs, going about their territorial business, in a way nature films (I know) can make interesting and exciting. From here, with a warm Mauritian beer in my hand, the mud appeared at a glance to be moving fitfully as a consequence, suggesting primal upheaval.

'I know why you are here,' said Ngwenya.

'You do?' His face was as graceful as his faunlike arms. Without his glasses his eyes were brown and bright, and his face had lost its inscrutability. I guessed he was about twenty-five.

'You are here to solve the mystery, sir.'

'You should not believe everything you read in newpapers. Particularly not the *Bangunes Times*,' I said. 'There's no mystery.'

But there was a mystery. Not, as the *Bangunes Times* had fancifully said, 'The mystery of his father's disappearance on an expedition to seek lost treasure'. The mystery was why this ill-assorted couple had set off together. Why had Mrs de Luth, with her unblinking, Lutheran gaze, taken my father (no traveller he) on this expedition? She was a redoubtable traveller who died in her bed in Georgetown in 1978, aged eighty-four, after many an expedition for *National Geographic*. She had visited Hiroshima in 1951 and written this caption: HIROSHIMA HAS ALL BUT RECOVERED FROM THE BLAST. THE AUTHOR BUYS GLASS AND POTTERY FUSED BY THE BOMB'S HEAT. In the picture she is not wearing her topcoat as she towers over the souvenir shopowner, presumably to avoid becoming too cool in the Japanese winter.

I could picture them, sitting in this bar, looking at the same smudgily typewritten menu which Ngwenya had so recently handled in hope. Oxtail soup, breaded lamb chops or *Wiener Schnitzel* with seasonal vegetables and steamed pudding and custard. The vanished Mr Brannigan himself would have held the menu in his pudgy, homesick hands; my father with his characteristic desire to impress would have demanded the wine list. Mrs de Luth would have fixed him with her pale, intense eyes, the Baltic blue of them as unreal as a U-Boat commander's in a war film. My father would have taken the wine from Mr Brannigan and poured it himself. He had a little trick of turning the bottle at the last moment, to avoid drops. Perhaps the police patrol boat would have tied up, disembarking a district officer and a police superintendent, fresh out from England, for a nightcap and a chinwag.

Frederick Ngwenya asked if he could come on my expedition.

'It's hardly an expedition. It's just a trip. This is the age of tourism, not travel.'

This second-hand aphorism did not deter him. He ordered us each another beer, smiling.

'This is the age of anything, sir,' he said.

The river outside, conscientiously carrying the last of the inland topsoil down towards Puerta Nueva and the open sea, was quickly becoming molten gold as the sun lowered towards the tops of the kiatt trees on the opposite bank, so that it matched the colour of the lager we were drinking. This was the hour of irrepressible madness and happiness in Africa, when sober missionaries turned lustful eyes on creamy schoolgirls in their congregations and planters sat gratefully on their verandas, porches and stoops, thanking God for not being in Europe. For the African it was a blush, a gesture of goodwill, before the uneasiness of the night, which closes fast after this technicolor interlude. I could see Mrs de Luth at this hour up country, sitting at a camp table, sorting out her rolls of film, perhaps making careful records of film speeds and exposures, sipping a drink based on an old Lapp remedy. Where is my father? Is he typing up his notes? No, he has never learned to type; it disturbs his flow. He is sitting on a rock, gin sling in hand, looking near-sightedly towards a pool of hippo whose tugboat sounds are starting up in earnest now. They remind him of fat and elderly clubmen on a night in town without their wives, as they set off lumbering and chortling into the gathering dark. Mrs de Luth goes early to bed; there is about her an equine directness which is, perhaps, beginning to irritate my father; he sits with his weak eyes no longer seeing in the crepuscular gloom. The rising noises of the surrounding scrub, with all their unfamiliar resonances, perhaps make him aware of his dependence upon the great traveller in this new life of his. Who is he, the erstwhile animal-feed expert, to harbour any ill feelings towards her? Travellers, she said, are an angry race, but not my dad. No, he would have been enthralled by the collaboration. The only mystery is what was in it for her.

Under the influence of two Mauritian beers, Frederick Ngwenya's eyes had lost their brightness. I had noticed this before in some Africans – drunkenness signalled by a colouring of the whites of the eyes. The Mauritian beer was very strong; I had forgotten Patel completely.

'Sir, I know what happened to your father,' said Ngwenya.

It was dark now on the river outside. A huge fire flared up on the distant bank.

Hold on. Let us pause for a moment. This student taxi driver, with his delicate forearms and cheddar eyes, was a fabulist. What happened to my father? How could he know? I had not even come to Africa to find out. That sort of quest happens only in journalists' imaginations, where outdated literary models linger on. Journalists attempt to impose a recognisable form, a comforting myth, on unrelated facts. Hence the article in the *Bangunes Times*, describing the mystery of my father's death. Here, where many of the other values of the western world were sensibly disregarded, the need to give fabulous qualities to essentially meaningless events was highly esteemed. President Ndongo's short and brutal military career had been invested with imaginary qualities. The government itself had long ago abandoned any practical function; instead it had taken the roles of shaman, witchdoctor and prophet to itself. In the years since independence, the bush had become a sort of netherworld from which the fortunate escaped to the city. They wanted nothing from this deadbeat zone; everything was in town. As Muhammed Ali said, 'Zaire must be great, I have never seen so many Mercedes.' When my father headed off into the bush all those years ago, it was regarded as an area of rich promise, the raw material of anthropology, topography, cartography and mineralogy all waiting to be assigned their rightful place in the order of things. But the heart of darkness was not merely asleep, as Mrs de Luth had written ('a slumbering giant, of infinite possibility'), but officially declared dead, along with the avocado ranch. So any idea that Ngwenya might have had of some substantive explanation emanating from the interior was absurd. Nothing much emanated from the bush now except nomads, wide-eyed and timorous, carrying woven coops of edible rodents and pathetically balding chickens. Fact was no longer hard currency in Banguniland. The purposes of things had been changed and the meaning of words to describe them had consequently had to adapt. The timetables in the airline office had only symbolic value; the President announced new five-year plans, which everyone knew could never be started; the chain of causation had been broken forever. So Frederick Ngwenya was certainly a fabulist, as susceptible as the next man to the sweet gases of magic and untruth which rose from the river outside.

'I know what happened to your father. He is still alive in the interior.'

His face had become slightly moist as, I could feel, had mine. But his now had highlights on the cheeks and the brow.

'Mr Curtiz, he is alive, sir.'

Skilful witnesses in police cases try to slip one or two lesser known facts into their evidence by the back door to lend credibility to their pleadings. My father had taken the name Lance Curtiz (after a Hollywood director) to give himself a more textured surface when we moved to America. No doubt the library of the *Bangunes Times* had this on file. I had worked in a newspaper myself during the school holidays. I amused myself by tracing the growth of lies, inaccuracies, myths and reputations. The original story in the cuttings could always be perceived, but invariably distorted with the passage of time. Frederick Ngwenya would have discovered my father's absurd *nom de plume* in a file marked BANGUNILAND, TRAVELLERS AND EXPLORERS 1861–1968 (INDEPENDENCE). Mungo Park had visited Banguniland. It had weakened his constitution fatally. Stanley, in his febrile courtship of Livingstone, had passed through the northern corner of Banguniland, and Livingstone himself had written of the Banguni: 'a people of such prodigious unreliability that it is said even the Arab slaver does not seek to practise his evil commerce in their country.' Livingstone had a curious attitude to slaves, similar to Jefferson's.

I looked closely at Ngwenya. He was smiling, but there was nothing sinister about his smile. He expected me to be pleased with his news.

'You are either a liar or an opportunist, and maybe both. Would you take me to Patel's now?'

'Too late. Curfew sir.'

'What curfew?'

'Unofficial. Since the President was assassinated.'

This is how you find hard facts in Banguni; the official channels are preoccupied with the occult.

'What about dinner?' said Ngwenya slyly. 'I like lamb chops very much.'

CHAPTER 2

When you are young, you do not see the strictures of life. If you did you would believe in some form of predestination. A man's existence is strung on fine wires between his mother, his wife and his lovers. What of women? What is their nexus? I could never really tell with my mother. She seemed to be connected to higher aspirations which she was unable to realise, but aspirations which left her in a deep, unfathomable, feminine anger for most of her later life. Her father was an Australian grazier who had fought in the Boer War and married a Boer. His life, sketchily perceived by me even now, was a succession of unplanned rushes and charges, not unlike the drowsy guinea fowl of Bangunes. There was some symmetry about his life, however; he was wounded in a shambolic rush by the New South Wales Highlanders at Matjesfontein and died under the wheels of the Garlick's delivery van almost exactly fifty years later, rushing out of our little front garden and into the street with an empty suitcase. The suitcase, too, was flattened. This to me as a small boy was more poignant than Grandpa's clean brogues poking out from under a grey blanket as he was lifted into an ambulance. It was the first and only time I saw my mother weep. I thought she was crying for the suitcase.

> I'm coming, Oom Paul Kruger,
> To have a talk with you,
> A word in your ear, old man,
> I am the kangaroo.

The kangaroo was cremated in accordance with his instructions and his ashes buried in a wall in a pathetically small pot.

My father's wanderings and his changes of tack were of little interest to my mother. If her eyes were fixed on the horizon, it was not in anticipation of his return. Her anger was never directed at him, indeed it was rarely expressed; it showed itself in a slight downward curve of the mouth and the tolerant smile with which she greeted the pretensions of politicians, priests, schoolteachers, traffic cops – almost anybody who allowed himself the delusion of importance. Where had she acquired this stubborn, independent frame of mind? It appeared to have come to her fully formed, the Olive Schreiner of the dusty suburbs of Potchefstroom, where she was born. She was of nowhere. She moved perfectly equably (although at this rumbling level of discontent) with my father. She never once asked us not to climb lunatically dangerous trees or ride our bikes in traffic or throw stones at the washerwomen passing with bundles on their heads, like huge, white pies for baking. She was detached. When we moved to America as children, she smiled her damning smile at the talkative taxi driver who got us off the boat; she smiled at the Empire State Building; she smiled at the expressways, as wide as football fields. She liked Howard Johnson's, however. She did not smile there. She saw Howard Johnson's as the expression of the American genius: anyone, anywhere in the whole of America, could have twenty-one flavours of ice cream; not for them the confines of vanilla, chocolate or tutti frutti.

'You're going to like it here,' she said to my father, 'this country is made for children.'

There was no irony in her remark.

'I like it here already,' he said. 'It's going somewhere, and we're aboard now.'

He could arrange anything: work permits; immigration; jobs; schools. There was a law in those days, designed to keep undesirable racial strains out, that allowed quotas of immigration based on the country of origin. He quickly discovered that Norway's quota was undersubscribed; we went in as

Norwegians. He made jokes about our Nordic gloom, which drove us into a genuine gloom as we set off for our new home in a rented car. He marvelled at the ease of hiring a car in America:

'Look at this. They have an open mind. They're eager to do business. A car is a piece of machinery at the disposal of anybody, not some sacred object of worship.'

'You're on the wrong side of the road,' said my mother coldly.

'You Scandinavians are very perceptive. The FBI needs people like you.'

'How long is this Groucho Marx persona going to last?' asked my mother.

'*Je suis Marxiste. Tendance Groucho,*' he replied cheerfully.

I could not speak French in those days, but this old joke has stuck. I like it still. But I was worried about this wisecracking, fast-talking American he had suddenly become.

'Look how beautiful it is. Just look at those barns. Those are called Dutch barns. They should always be painted that red colour. What do you call that colour? I call it Norman Rockwell red.'

My father devoured magazines. He had, I now realise, three pictures of America, different but overlapping. They were drawn from *Saturday Evening Post*, the *New Yorker* and *National Geographic*. Above all he loved *National Geographic*, yet he could slip easily from one mode to another in those early days. Similarly he had looked at Britain through the pages of *Punch*, the *Illustrated London News* and *Country Life*. We used also to get *British Movietone News* in South Africa. All these added up to a depressing picture of a civilised but cramped and sodden island, whose best days were past. Not so America; everything was promised and promises were made good. The vessel was moving. The journey was underway. We were aboard with our baggage stowed. Such is the power of metaphor. In truth much of our baggage had got itself wet in transit; in some mysterious manner, water had found its way into the hold where our stinkwood furniture (a priceless legacy of my Boer grandmother, carried by ox wagon over mountains and ravines and gorged rivers) was stored. It was ruined.

'I don't mean to sound callous, Ma,' he said, 'but perhaps stinkwood furniture, like Italian wine, was not meant to travel.'

Secretly I suspect he was glad, hankering after Scandinavian modern with spindly legs instead of the heavy ball-and-claw substructure of our heirlooms.

My little brother who had a remarkably pale face (and still does) stared silently out of the window at the mighty landscape unfolding: lakes, bridges, rivers, factories, forests touched with gold and red the colour of the Rockwell barns. We had never seen so many colours. My father loved the Kodachrome brightness of it all. I cannot remember what I felt: perhaps a certain bewilderment at the tangle of roads and buildings and sky that was New York; relief at the pleasant fall warmth of the valleys and towns as we drove out to our rented home on the Island. My brother, I now appreciate, was seeing real estate and commodities and industries. He's an analyst on Wall Street these days. He never talks of the old country. The closest he has come was to advise President Reagan on the likely effect of sanctions on the market, but it was done without dredging in the atavistic memory. He is an American, *tabula rasa*.

I, by contrast, have become less sure of my ordained place in the order of things. This is the natural state of the refugee. Yet we were not refugees. We were part of the baggage, in train to my father's whimsical conquest of America. He quickly settled into American life. His love of our new country and his unstinting praise of its energy and colour helped him to find a job as editor of cultural events for a paper in Huntington. This was when he began his courtship of *National Geographic*, sending them, with his bottomless ingenuity, articles and stories about Africa as evidence of his knowledge of the dark continent, and his love of *National Geographic* and his fervent desire to be a part of this great institution. One story was about a traditional way of catching monkeys, which involved a dried melon with a narrow opening; into the melon, corn was placed; the monkey would insert his paw, grab the corn, and be unable to extract his tightly clenched, furry fist. This improbable tale was sent off with another, about the sociable ways of the baboon, an animal so sophisticated, it seems, that it has extrasensory perception. My own observations suggest that this faculty has not done the baboon much good.

My father's courtship paid off. He was invited to Washington to a reception at the Smithsonian. There he met the great Mary Grosvenor de Luth and her husband General Reginald de Luth. He talked freely with owners of banks, at least two admirals, high government officials and presidents of whole railway systems. He conversed in French with a young Frenchman, Captain Jacques Cousteau, about his sensational underwater ('*sous marin*') exploration of a Greek cargo ship. He met people with superlatively American names, names which made Gatsby seem flashy and meretricious: John Oliver La Gorce; Nathaniel T. Kenny; Emory S. Land; Lyman J. Briggs; Leo A. Borah. He drew a lesson from this, I surmise: important people in America have a prominent initial or a boldly distinguishing second name, which denotes a direct connection with power, money and family. So he began to employ the pen name Lance P. Curtiz, the very name which an African taxi driver had vouchsafed to me here in crumbling Bangunes.

My father's reputation grew. He forgot completely that he had been the editor (and proprietor) of *The Countryman*, a failed farming weekly, in South Africa. He had never known anything about farming. He could not even mow a lawn. There was an undertow of chaos in his life which continually clutched and tugged at his ankles, making his enterprises unstable. This chaos he thought of as the vortex of creativity; it has made me suspicious of the connection between the artistic and the anarchic. I have a dishonourable belief that one follows from the other, but not in the commonly accepted order.

The magazine failed, but not without an heroic effort by my father in his guise as expert on feedstuffs, barbed-wire fencing, Hereford beef cattle, native housing, borehole irrigation, diesel tractors, strains of maize, merino sheep, foot and mouth, and Rhode Island Reds. I discovered all these things by reading, from a never-unpacked and watermarked trunk, back copies of *The Countryman*. My mother contributed articles on preserves and chutney, flower arrangement, seven interesting ways to prepare mutton, the boiling of drinking water, advances in oil lamps, the private lives of radio personalities and books of interest to farmers' wives. Could you detect a desire for a larger, more polychromatic world in the dingy photographs of disconsolate cattle with massive humps? Or in the comically awful sketches of dried flowers, which seemed to me (with the embalming effect of Atlantic seawater) to have all the vivacity of an Inca tomb?

It seems clear the magazine failed because there were almost no English-speaking farmers and those few were widely scattered. The farmers were all Boers, as my father called them. This fundamental piece of market research could have been carried out by a ten-year-old boy equipped with a school atlas and a ruler, I now think, with the advantage of hindsight.

Lance P. Curtiz was merely the last of my father's *noms de plume*. When he wrote on cattle diseases he was Dr Bill Hoofenbeck; when he wrote on religious matters, he was The Rev John Devine; his restaurant guide was written by Alain Forno. It was headed, 'A Steak in Your Country'. The letter page, also written by my father, betrayed a roguish sense of humour. A letter from a Dr Hans Jungfreud read: 'Much of the traditional lethargy of Africa can be attributed to the bilharzia-carrying snail. Surprisingly, very few farmers have bilharzia. We must look elsewhere for an explanation of their symptoms.' Perhaps it was fortunate he had no readership.

We had been in America only a year and a half when my father set off for Africa with Mrs de Luth. My brother had become a trombonist in his junior high band, with that jaunty, unmilitary swagger; there he was, a little pale-faced da Souza in a mustard-yellow hussar's outfit at football games.

My father embraced our first Thanksgiving enthusiastically: 'Look at these turkeys. Fed on a special diet. Plumped up just in time with hormones. Humanely killed. Self-roasting. Big turkeys for large families. Little turkeys for small families.'

He was thinking *National Geographic* already:

APARTMENT DWELLERS WELCOME BELTS-VILLE'S SMALL WHITE TURKEYS.

From egg to succulent roast fowl, Uncle Sam's scientists strive constantly to improve poultry. Housewives applaud the plump meaty turkeys, specially bred for small ovens.

It took me longer to adapt than my chameleon family. I kept thinking of my little black friend, Skep, and his freedom. Nobody asked him to go to school. He lived a dusty, backyard existence; sometimes he helped his father kill the turkeys, which he did by placing a broomhandle on their throats and standing on it. The chickens his father killed with a sharp twist of the neck. Skep laughed when the chickens, sometimes inadvertently decapitated, did a frenzied dance of death. *Poulets sans têtes. Alouettes sans têtes.* I never found this amusing but I watched the spasmodic bopping, wondering when precisely the chickens died: before the dance, during the dance or some seconds later when they lay in the dust, just a spasm or two racking their bodies as the last soft feathers, dislodged in the struggle, fluttered to the sandy backyard? This was at the house of our neighbours, the Mullers; Mr Muller owned a butcher's shop and a general store. His son Fred was a haemophiliac. Skep's father sometimes did a dance himself, on payday. Skep laughed as he told me how his father would chase him on those days with a leather strap.

Here in America we sat in front of our customised turkey; my father told us the origin of the festivity; my mother smiled; my brother, ever practical, asked 'What's the point of making them as small as chickens?'

'The turkey is part of this great country's history. Up until recently, the turkey was too big for people living alone, or in apartments. In America, it was believed, nobody should be denied their birthright, so science fixed the turkey.'

'Is it still a turkey?' I asked, thinking of the leathery and uncooperative monsters which Skep's father manhandled to the ground.

'Existential sort of question. In America existentialism has not taken root, because nobody has the time to ask if they exist. They're too busy existing.'

'Carve the bloody turkey before we all cease existing,' said my mother.

There were woods behind our house which had become swamps of deep snow. How odd we felt, gathered around the table in our new American clothes, our faces unnaturally pale, to match the snow outside, eating turkey.

'Is it Christmas, really?' asked my little brother plaintively.

'No, darling. It's Thanksgiving,' said my mother. 'We are giving thanks for snow and miniature turkeys.'

She said little else, but there was no need because my father provided a storm, a tempest, of folklore, history and hearsay. The truth is, however, that I cannot picture my father's face, except in the guises he left behind in photographs, which we, the bereaved, kept after his disappearance. They showed him at various stages of his life: naval officer fighting the Japanese (somehow he had found his way on to the *Missouri* when the Japs surrendered. There he stands, just behind Admiral Nimitz, ready to sign the surrender document on behalf of South Africa); newspaper reporter; newspaper proprietor; fisherman (in long khaki shorts, with his line characteristically in a tangle); transatlantic traveller (we are all in this one, at the bottom of the gangplank, about to board ship for New York). What lies photographs tell: arms thrust out to embrace near strangers; whimsicality sprung up like crocuses on a February morning; smiles burgeoning unnaturally; locals wheeled on like props in a movie; hats swopped jokily; donkeys placed in suggestive juxtaposition; the subjects frozen with wine or spaghetti en route to their mouths: the acts of achievement and enjoyment subjected to the cryogen of photography.

*

Mrs de Luth appears bigger than my father in the photograph of their departure from Bangunes. The porters are posed on the jetty in an informal but positive fashion, like a basketball team; Mrs de Luth wears her long coat and hat, an Eleanor Roosevelt lookalike, while my father stands beside her, a good head shorter, although he is a perfectly adequate five foot ten inches tall himself. I have often tried to pierce the deep shadow on the top half of his face to guess at his mood. Nor do the porters give a clue as to what they think of this stringy old broad with the mad, Lutheran eyes. Mr Brannigan has the look about him of a prosperous shopkeeper in Dublin, fat, content, puffed up like a hen for the photograph. Is my father buoyed up to be at the start of the great adventure? He must be proud to be on the trail with *National Geographic* at last; he is carrying the clipboard under his arm unconvincingly. My mother, who is now seventy-two, told me recently that he never owned a billfold or a watch in his life. So the clipboard, with its associations of a military efficiency, has purely symbolic value.

But where do they fit together? Why are they venturing into the interior? What links them? What is their nexus? My mother can offer no suggestions. She accepted his overtures to *National Geographic* without interest. She showed no desire to meet Mrs de Luth and her husband the general. She was deficient in curiosity, of that there can be no doubt. And now she has sunk into the quietism of old age; she lives in a home in Wiltshire in England, formerly a cider house, cleverly refurbished to give each of the residents a space of their own, so it said in the literature. In practice they seem to sit, constantly watching television in a large communal room – the images of war, death, rock music, soap opera and politics bathing them harmlessly from the giant TV in the 'day room'. There they sit, their knotted old hands busy crocheting, their journey through this vale of tears not so much done as run out of steam. Nobody is interested in them any longer. Their opinions, like their lives, are now as significant as the sharp chirps of the budgerigar in the corner of the television room.

My mother and Mrs Orme-Watson have formed an alliance. They have detected in each other a consanguinity which sets them apart from the other residents; they eat their meals together and sit next to one another watching television. A deep and immovable sense of unfulfilment binds them. The day before setting off for Bangunes, I visited my mother. She and Mrs Orme-Watson and I drove into Chippenham for lunch.

'I am going to Banguniland, Ma.'

'What would you want to do that for?'

'I am going to make a film, I think.'

'Oh, I love films about wildlife. Do you make those?' asked Mrs Orme-Watson.

'I have done, yes.'

'How did you get that picture of the lion eating the water buffalo?'

'I don't know which film that was.'

'Very well done anyway. The young are so much more clever today.'

'Margaret and I like wildlife and travel films,' said my mother.

'Do you think this has something to do with *National Geographic*?' I asked, always keen to make connections.

'No, I don't think so. Why should it?'

She meant to tell me that she, at least, needed no aids in her interests and aspirations.

'Anyway, I never really liked that magazine. Your father was taken in by it completely.'

'What's that, dear?' asked Mrs Orme-Watson.

'*National Geographic*. It's a magazine in America. Or was.'

'I like the Americans. Although their food is awful. They eat the most awful muck.'

'Jolly good food at the Copper Kettle, isn't it?' said my mother, 'though the chicken is tough.'

'Shall I order something else?' I asked.

'No thank you. I'll manage.'

Her eyes were slightly bloodshot. She ate heartily for an old lady – they both did – her big shoulders clad in a kind of checked jacket which was perhaps available to the residents of the Old Cyder House by mail order, because Mrs Orme-Watson was wearing something very similar. The two of them seemed to be clearly discernible but filtered, as remote as Santa Claus in one of those little glass balls with the snow falling noiselessly. I tried to discuss Banguniland and my father's fatal trip, but my mother gave me her wintry smile.

'I suppose Bangunes has gone to pot like all the rest. I can't think why anyone would want to visit.'

They were sitting watching children's television as I set off for the airport on the start of my journey to Banguniland.

I once met a cameraman who worked for CBS in the hotel bar in Namibia; he drove to the front in a hired car, recorded a unique interview with the leader of the guerrillas, bullets flying around his head, and was back in the bar the next evening. In this way we can get almost anywhere within a few days, from Madison Avenue to the Masai Mara; from the Faubourg to the Orinoco, and in my case, with happy assonance, from Bristol to Bangunes. The only people who have not been touched by the magic of mobility are the locals. They remain subject to drought, crop failure, disease, famine, necromancy, brutality, superstition and the synthesis of all these, which is called politics in their world. Previously these were not thought to be part of a compound.

In this way, I found myself in Brannigan's Hotel only a few sunrises later.

'Great chops. Delicious.'

'Frederick, who are you really?' I asked my dinner companion.

'I am your guide to the interior.'

'I thought you were a student.'

'I come from up country. My family home is up country.'

The uplands; up country; up the river.

CHAPTER 3

I liked Conrad's notion that the great rivers are part of the great oceans of the world; they connect London with Leopoldville and New York with Amazonia, all one glittering shard of water, jagged but unfragmented. Seen from this point of view, the mariner's point of view, these waterways and the oceans at the end of them are simple, uncluttered things, so different from the landmasses with their awkward mountains, jungles and deserts. All you need is passage in the right vessel and the whole world is yours. For Conrad the sea ended only at the first rapids; Livingstone regarded the Victoria Falls, for this same reason, as an infernal nuisance. The parochial aspect of the sea is lost to travellers now. We vault airly over continents, unaware and unconcerned about the minute life going on down there, scuttling as busily, and ordinarily as unseen, as the crustaceans on the river bank outside Brannigan's Hotel. The stenches and smells have been expunged, the journeys below on foot, by camel, by bicycle, by canoe, have been rendered meaningless because of the foreknowledge that they are doomed, because the people below are living in another era, so far away that their only contact with the planes overhead is a glint in the sky, a falling toilet roll, or the sun catching a silver sliver, always accompanied by a faint, ethereal whine, the mosquito noise of the winged classes as they hurry on their inexplicably mad missions.

National Geographic's mission was to make colourful and comprehensible the incomprehensible world over which we fly and which we will never ourselves visit. Even thirty years ago intermediaries were necessary; my father had volunteered himself as interpreter of this unmanageable world. To this task he brought his mercurial adaptability and his experience as naval man, journalist, self-taught agriculturalist and amateur of all things American. He read us a few lines of Robert Frost in that first, shockingly cold winter as we struggled with the unfamiliar press of deep snow, like sleepers with a pillow thrust over their faces.

> How the cold creeps as the fire dies at length
> How drifts are piled
> Dooryard and road ungraded
> Till even the comforting barn grows far away
> And my heart owns a doubt
> Whether 'tis in us to arise with day
> And save ourselves unaided.

He also read us these lines, by way of encouragement:

> The woods are lovely,
> dark and deep
> But I have promises
> to keep
> And miles to go
> before I sleep
> And miles to go
> before I sleep.

My father loved Frost. He did not live to see JFK endorse his good opinion of the old man by inviting him to his windswept inauguration. Recently in Paris I saw a Cousteau exhibition, '*Cousteau: images d'une vie*'. Perhaps my father would have entered the public consciousness in the same way: 'Lance P. Curtiz. A perspective'. If he had not caught his foot in the webbing.

Ngwenya had eaten his lamb chops and two helpings of steamed pudding with custard. Custard, as it exists in the Anglophone parts of the world, is a hangover from the days of dried egg and dried milk. With a little warm water it can be mixed up into a viscous mass and poured over suety desserts to give the illusion of a northern abundance of dairy produce. At Brannigan's the tradition was continued, unaffected by the fickleness of dietary fashions in the rest of the world. The custard was complete with a thick, elastic skin which Ngwenya found particularly appetising.

'You don't like steamed pudding?' he asked me with the deliberately patient tone you employ on the chronically obdurate.

'No, but have another. Have mine.'

'No thank you. I am keeping to two because of my training.'

'What are you training for?'

'World Cup qualifying round. I am the centreforward of the Banguni national soccer team.'

'You are a man of many surprises.'

There were not many people in Brannigan's but our meal was constantly interrupted by men coming to shake Ngwenya's hand in that particularly African way, two spatulas meeting and spreading goodwill. Perhaps he was a football hero; I did not care. I had a headache and could feel the unreality of Banguni-land and Brannigan's Hotel pressing acutely. Who knows what they put in the beer? I ordered a Coke, but even that tasted peculiar, as though the recipe had been adulterated in the local bottling plant. Probably by Ngwenya's brother. People began to sit at our table and order drinks on my tab. Ngwenya introduced me. They were all students and soccer players. ˙

'He's come to find his father.'

They nodded, these Africans in their sharp clothes and huge wrist watches. All those lumpy digital watches with tiny portholes for the numerals seemed to have ended up in Banguniland.

'Very nice, where is he your father staying at the moment?'

A great deal of African life is taken up with complicated family arrangements, involving long, dusty walks and even longer years of separation, so they were not surprised by the story.

Ngwenya slapped me on the back and winked.

'*Garçon*, more beer, over here,' he said.

This had turned into a party. The cheddar eyes were appearing all around me. These were the sons of the men in that photograph: their fathers were *askaris*, porters, trackers; they were the new generation whose only hope lay in a coup or a United Nations job if they were ever to join the Wa Benzi – proud owners of a Mercedes. That was it, the big one, a transformation which would come about when circumstances were right. The forest had traditionally been the spring, the source of magic and change, but the forest had all been burnt and robbed of its generative abilities, so that they were looking elsewhere. In the meanwhile they were partying and plotting and playing football to pass the time. All Ngwenya's friends had got word of the party. The bar was choked now. People shook my hands warmly; I was the host. I began to worry about paying for all this; the beer was not cheap. Bottles of South African brandy appeared; girls with strong hips and high heels began to dance. The whole place, overlooked by the aging picture of the Wicklow Hills, became a mass of bodies, drinking, dancing, talking. I sat at my table, a sort of totem, or perhaps Eisenstein's ideal spectator. My head was throbbing. In this detached, unhappy state, I could see with a horrible clarity; I was not merely paying for all this but responsible for it in some way; yet it had sprung up spontaneously around me, like the circus tents of Fellini's childhood, unbidden. Whatever they had all been about to do this evening they had dropped quite happily to come here. The partygoers, like most Banguni, were smallish people. The girls were thin, but with those very pronounced derrières; they would make great sprinters one day; the force was concentrated in the hips. They danced with their hips, opening their knees suggestively. The music was a sort of rock, but with an African lilt, endlessly repetitive and mesmeric. I had here a glimpse of timelessness. The men were good natured, not at all aggressive behind their dark glasses. They may have been getting drunk, but drunkenness produced a state of comatose good humour. A girl sat on my lap; she was surprisingly heavy and the inside of her happy mouth was langoustine pink.

At this point in my party, the army arrived. Nobody seemed surprised or alarmed. I had the feeling that it was expected. They picked out about ten people, including me. The barman spoke to one of the soldiers in his camouflage jacket, and I was politely asked to pay the bill. I produced a roll of dollars, intended for Patel's supplies.

'Nice party. Thank you, sir,' said the barman amiably.

'Keep the change.'

'Thank you, sir. Goodnight.'

The hand on my arm was light, as light as the grasp of a baby, as we were led away. Outside there were three waiting Land Rovers. An officer with a swagger stick, his face damp and broad, walked towards us. Our escort, who wore tin hats and carried those short, Italian machine guns, halted.

'Major Dubane.'

He saluted.

'How do you do?'

'Fine, sir.'

'What's happening, Major?'

'Just routine. There's been some trouble. I would like you to go back to your house.'

'What about these people?' I gestured towards my erstwhile guests, who were standing forlornly in the headlights of the Land Rovers, handcuffed together in a line, a scene which reminded me of the woodcuts of Arab slave convoys.

'Bad elements, I'm afraid. But harmless oafs, really. I don't advise you to mix with these people again, sir,' said the affable major.

'I wasn't exactly mixing with them.'

'I know what you mean. Bloody freeboots the lot of them. Take them away,' he said wearily.

Ngwenya was not amongst them.

'What were you doing at this old place? It's a dump. Why don't you use the Pan-African Hotel?'

'Well, you know I may be filming, certainly writing something, and I wanted to see the old port.'

Against a backdrop of my guests being bundled into Land Rovers, we walked to the major's car.

'I'll take you home. You chaps are so preoccupied with the past. All the old colonial stuff. Forget it. Forget it, my friend. Even our own people seem to keep harking back. We've got to get away from all this.'

He made a clicking sound of disgust. But how do you do this? How do you slough off the past? Nobody, except Americans, really lives in the present; the past is more real. For Americans the past is merely a charming fairy story.

'And you can forget any nonsense you may have heard about your father. These people' – he gestured at the departing prisoners – 'will tell you anything. They've got nothing to do. Sweet FA. So they make up stories.'

He looked pained. His soft face was perpetually damp, like a rock face on a mountainside, weeping from within.

'What do you know about my father?'

'Only what I read in the newspaper.'

'Everyone reads the paper.'

'Frankly, my friend, there's not much else to do just at the moment, for most of these poor devils.'

We drove off towards Zwane Street. I was staying in the house of an acquaintance, a zoologist trying to second guess the migratory habits of the African kwelea bird by preparing nasty explosions in the nesting sites of these apparently insatiable little avians. The major knew the address.

'Dr Gullikson's house. I like it. Goodnight,' he said as he let me out of the Peugeot. I paused in the front garden. God knows what time it was. My watch had stopped and my head was pulsing. This is how it must feel to have a stroke, I thought, as I tried to unlock the door. Gullikson, sensibly, spent most of his time in Tanzania and Kenya in pursuit of the kwelea. Even these voracious birds bypassed Banguniland now, not for fear of explosions, but for lack of nourishment. The night air was warm and dry, yet invested with that plangency peculiar to Africa. In every town you can still hear the bush crowding in, with its lively

33

and dangerous night life, the mighty weight of an existence outside the circle of the fire – or in this case of the flickering electric light strung erratically along Zwane Street. President Ndongo was no more, if Frederick could be believed. I let myself in and found in the massive refrigerator a jug of cold (but previously boiled) water. I drank it all. In the morning I would find Patel and at the same time try to lose Ngwenya for ever. As I lay in bed, in the suburbs of sleep, I remembered vividly what the major with the damp, amiable face had said.

'Forget any nonsense you may have heard about your father.'

A mosquito had found its way under the net and was sounding persistently. Sleep was impossible. I tried to think about Magda at her most sexually inventive, but the Mauritian beer had unmanned me.

In the morning I had the sensation, familiar to all drinkers, of not having slept at all and yet the sunlight when I lifted the blind was overwhelming and it was noon. Thanks to my encounter with Ngwenya, I had wasted nearly twenty-four hours and done great harm both to my finances and my brain cells.

I could hear the servants in the back yard. Deep in conversation, their voices had none of the urgent cadences of a conversation in my old home town on Long Island, where intentions to be up and doing things punctuate every exchange: 'I must cut my smoking. We'll meet after school. Get that transmission looked at, you hear? I'll bring my Wilsons. Dr Schmidt said to go easy.' Here the conversation, naturally quite incomprehensible to me, as I dare say it had been to Mrs de Luth and my father, was as open-ended as birdsong and probably serving the same purposes; this endless, soothing talk, this campfire camaraderie (which the white man can only recreate with his barbecues, safaris and boy scouts) is an essential part of the human condition. The planter mentality – rip up those bushes, plant these in straight lines, grow things you cannot eat, spray on chemicals and so on – has made little headway in Africa. Mrs de Luth had written: 'Banguniland, the breadbasket of Africa, predicts scientists perfecting a new breed of maize.'

Africa's ambivalence towards the West is based on a deep and understandable uneasiness about this get-up-and-go culture. And yet the idea that Africans are tuned to some inner harmonies which we have lost the faculty to hear is absurd. They have different harmonies.

My marriage had been a clash of harmonies. Magda had wanted constant reassurance about the harmonies she sought. Her anxieties and changes of mood, her exacting approach to my emotional responses, had drained me. The sly harmonies we had once enjoyed had gone on to be replaced by a bruising reproachfulness. Yet it still hurts me to think of her so young, so full of possibility, when we met in London and made love constantly on buses, in parks, in friends' kitchens, in cinemas and behind curtains. Even as we were playing Scott and Zelda, I knew it could not last. Few have the stamina for immoderate passion, and I am certainly not one of them.

These were the sorts of things I was thinking as I made a cup of coffee for myself. The conversation outside was stilled by a loud, harsh voice, speaking Banguni, but clearly a white's. A servant came in to the house; he was a thin, calm old man with hair that had become sparse and grey. Before he could announce him, a visitor, a big man with an enormous belly rolling over his khaki shorts, entered, waving the servant aside.

'Hello,' he said and sat down on a rattan chair. He looked round the room and waved his hands dismissively at the artefacts and ethnic gewgaws.

'Airport anthropology. I'm Monroe.'

'Hello there, Mr Monroe.'

'I'm Jumbo Monroe of Monroe Springs,' he said. 'Where's our feathered friend?'

'Dr Gullikson?' I said primly.

'That's the one. Amazing, isn't it, that you can spend five years at Oxford in order to learn how to shoot canaries? If they had asked me, I could have done it for them at half the cost. Do you know why Jesus Christ couldn't have been born in Banguniland? They could not find three wise men or a virgin.'

Monroe laughed bronchially at his own joke. His hair was thin and his face was puffed out unnaturally, like someone who had just been through serious surgery.

'He's in Tanzania at the moment.'

'And you've taken up residence at Casa Knick-Knack. Tell me something, you're a well-travelled sort of chap from what I hear, why do these academic types always collect the local junk and pretend it's art? Beauty is in the eye of the beholder. Behold a lot of crap.'

He waved dismissively at the gourds and carvings and musical instruments, cunningly fashioned from bits of wire and strung on rough-hewn wood with crude patterns of birds and insects. A beer was placed in front of him without his having to ask.

'The only art this country has ever seen has long since been stolen,' he said. 'I've just got out of jail, by the way.'

'What were you in for?' I asked, making an effort to keep my voice matter of fact.

'Nothing. Bugger all. I simply pointed out that the President-for-Life, whose father used to be our chief cowman, by the way, was a thieving opportunist. Everyone knew it, but it was considered impolite to say so. Luckily for me the President-for-Life has come to the end of his term. He died two days ago, and I was able to persuade the Chief of Police to release me.'

'Have you come to see Dr Gullikson?'

'No. I've come to see you, as a matter of fact. Do you know why they hate me? It's because I know them. I knew all our late President's little tricks. I was brought up here. I speak the language. I know when they're trying to screw the United Nations or your own gullible ambassador. I know which ones cheated at school, and I remind them as often as possible. My family have been here since 1891. We go back to when the wheel was a novelty in Banguniland. Of course, I understand nobody likes to have their failings pointed out to them all the time, particularly not in the exciting new Africa you see around you.'

'Why do you want to see me?'

'Because, my dear new friend, you have not understood

something about Banguniland: if you want to know the truth about anything in this god-forsaken, fly-blown dump, you have to ask Monroe.'

'And what sort of things would I want to know?'

'Come on now. You mustn't mistake me for a cretin just because I look as though I was dragged through a bush backwards. You want to know about your dad. I'm surprised, by the way, that you haven't turned up sooner.'

'Mr Monroe, everyone in this country seems to know something about my father.'

'And most of it is bullshit, if you'll excuse my French,' said Monroe. 'The truth about your father is that whatever happened to him up country in '59, whether his foot got caught or whether he was pushed off the raft, there was a hell of a rush by the leader of the expedition, a Mrs de Luth, to hush the whole thing up. None of the porters was allowed to speak to the DC about the accident. The inquest was a fiasco with no witnesses available and so on.

'Beer, Suleiman,' he shouted suddenly. 'Don't you want one?'

'No thank you. I'm not feeling so good.'

'You mustn't drink that piss down at Brannigan's. It's watered and then wood alcohol is added. Anyway, if anybody tells you that your late father is still alive, forget it. There was a white man living near the Malanja Marsh for a few years. I met him twice. He went completely crazy and lived in a small nomad village. He was Hungarian, a miner, who left Hungary in 1956 and tried prospecting. He could hardly speak a word of English, though he was upset to hear about Watergate. Not easy to describe in Banguni, I can tell you. Anyway, he's dead and he was Hungarian, so don't believe it when they tell you there's an old boy living in the bush. OK?'

'OK, Mr Monroe.'

'Look, everyone calls me Jumbo. I know it's a fucking silly name but I would feel happier.'

Monroe's knees were very brown, but when he pulled down one of his long khaki socks to scratch his huge shin, the skin exposed was as pale and dead as if he had pulled off a piece of elastoplast.

'OK, Jumbo,' I said. 'The point is I know that under the circumstances you must think I have come to find out what happened to my father, but I must tell you that that is not the case.'

There was something about Monroe that inhibited me; an importunate drunk on a city street has the same effect. Actually, what I was thinking was that for Monroe, sitting there heavily in his rattan chair, contemptuously fingering an elongated carved mask, the events of thirty years ago must seem quite real still, whereas for me they had never been real, and were no more real now that I was actually on site. Banguniland itself was as remote as Ougadougadou or Timbuktu. Meanwhile, Monroe – Jumbo – had been wondering why nobody had come out to get to the bottom of this business. While he had been wondering, Banguniland had achieved independence, toppled the monarchy, gone bankrupt, suffered three coups and gradually faded from the sight of the world, rather as though, by a strange reversal, the people of the western world had acquired the African river blindness, cutting off their peripheral vision. The periphery, the margin, was where Banguniland now found itself, irretrievably.

'You're thinking, oh shit, I've just fallen in with the local character, a frightful old pisspot who never stops talking,' said Monroe.

It was a low blow. Monroe, I was beginning to see, was a shrewd man. He reminded me of Madga's brother, another fat man doomed by his appearance to give a wrong first impression. Fat people cannot afford to look too unhappy or too clever.

'No, of course I'm not. I'm thinking, does it matter what really happened?'

'No, you're not. That makes no sense.'

Monroe said this without malevolence. His face was extremely large and rounded like a Henry Moore with real features super-imposed.

'What have you come to tell me, then?'

'I've come to tell you, old bean, that the treasures of Banguni-land were never seen again after Mrs Mary de Luth left the country, millions of dollars' worth of the national treasures of Banguniland, the only cultural heritage that might have distinguished this wretched country from the starving scrub all around. My father was the uncrowned king of Banguniland. It was a marvellous place, for all the wrong reasons, of course. We owned everything and ran everything. It was too cosy. We were brought up with the royal family. It could not last. Now what we have is a fully independent, sovereign shit house, an outside toilet with the door flapping.'

He stood up.

'The treasures of the Orefeo were gorgeous.'

'Gorgeous' was such an odd word to use that I was thrown for a moment. At the best of times I can often completely miss the point of what people are saying; there was no need to worry, however, as Monroe was going to spell it out.

'They were here to steal our treasures. They knew – or at least Mrs de Luth knew – that the treasures of the Orefeo rivalled and even surpassed Benin. Not only that, my friend, but ours were made of gold, not mere bronze. What do you think of that?'

He looked at me contentedly.

'I think I will have a beer after all.'

'Beer, Suleiman,' he called out happily. 'No, not for me, you'll be surprised to hear. It's for this gentleman.'

Suleiman was not surprised; he had lived in proximity to the white man for too long. Monroe was relentlessly cheerful. I wondered if he had had success with women; extrovert men usually do. Magda's tubby brother certainly had.

'What you need, my boy, is a good curry. Let's go down to the club.'

This reminded me that I was intending to see Rabindranath Patel to arrange my supplies but, as I would now have to send for more money, I gave in. The club was housed in a low, corrugated, iron-roofed house near the church. On the wall over the fireplace in the huge dining room hung a picture of Princess Diana and

Prince Charles. The walls were decorated with groups of stuffed animal heads – the wide open faces of Africa – alternating with poorly painted portraits of past presidents of the club. The former had, I assumed, been killed by the latter, although Monroe said that one of the club's ex-presidents had himself been killed by an elephant.

'The portrait was painted from memory. I had to go and pick up the remains; he was as flat as an ironing board.'

The club was surrounded on three sides by a huge veranda where members sat gazing out at the gardens. But the conviction had gone out of it; the lawns, once sweeping grandly down to a lake at the bottom of a small hill, were now as spare and worn as an old carpet. Squatters had taken up residence in the thicket beyond the lake; their washing could be seen drying on the far bank. Everywhere Africa was pushing in on the crumbling, flaking remnants of colonial Banguniland, that land of milk and honey and unrealised promise.

'Even the new hotel is falling down,' said Monroe. 'It was built by Rumania,' he added by way of explanation.

'Why was the President killed?'

'We have a saying here, which means, roughly translated, that the chief is chief by courtesy of the people. Let's just say that the traditional courtesy of the Banguni was exhausted. Shall we eat? I always sit here.'

Monroe had a great appetite, which I put down to the fact that he had just been in prison. The dining room was thinly peopled.

'The bloody vegetarians are here,' said Monroe, pointing at a group of thin, sun-blond aid folk in ethnic shirts. 'I hate the way they eat. Like spinsters.'

The Scandinavians ate slowly and mournfully, apparently conscious with every mouthful of the plenty on their plates while outside children were trying to catch grasshoppers to eat. No such irony troubled Monroe.

'The problem with them is they feel guilty that Sweden is such a successful country. No disease, no poverty, plenty of marinated salmon with dill seeds for everybody, nicely controlled birthrate, lots of terrific tennis players, Volvos all round. It worries them, because if they can do it in Scandinavia, why can't the Africans? So they are forced to conclude that the poor old white man has buggered up the natural order of things, which was all hunky-dory before we arrived. Pathetic, isn't it? That's why they wear those ghastly shirts without collars, and home-made sandals, as a penance. This is goat curry, by the way. There isn't a sheep left in the country.'

'Did you meet Mrs de Luth and my father?'

'I did. She was a terrifying old bird.'

'And my father?'

'He seemed, well let's say a bit . . .'

He was silenced by the arrival of Frederick Ngwenya, who sat himself down at our table amiably.

'Where have you been? It took me some long while to find you,' he said shyly.

His face was bruised, so that his left cheek was lumpy and saffron coloured, like a peach that has been damaged in handling.

CHAPTER 4

By the time I met Mr Patel I was mildly surprised to find that
his first name was not Rabindranath at all, but Ravi, like the
sitar-playing friend of George Harrison. Mr Patel, however, was
not surprised by my late arrival. He too had known all my
movements of the past four days. Although he was a supplier of
almost everything needed for an expedition to the interior, he had
never himself ventured past the Malanja Hills, visible from
Victoria Road as two purple lumps this side of the horizon,
beyond the bare, sandy outskirts of Bangunes and the small
villages of mud huts and reed fences which clustered diffidently
around the metropolis, edging fearfully closer to Gomorrah.

General stores in Africa are dark, cool places, shuttered and
verandaed against the glare and the heat. They smell of meal and
soap. Supermarkets in my old town now smell of pine forests,
insinuated into the air conditioning to produce a bucolic atmosphere in the controlled climate of the malls. What is this? Is it the
atavistic memory?

Mr Patel was king of his domain, speaking softly and gently to
me, but sharply, with a touch of malice even, to his African
assistants as they stowed my supplies in the Toyota Land Cruiser
he had procured for the expedition. I had planned a short trip to
Malanja as a dry run for my travels to the interior, wherever that
was to be found. Mrs de Luth had made the interior seem like a
place, a country or a large national park. Mr Patel, with a more
oriental cast of mind, depicted it as a realm of the imagination
rather than an actual place. She had written:

The desolate beauty of the interior, a land of inescapable grandeur where nature has sculpted the landscape in the course of aeons.

I had once visited Monument Valley in Arizona and that seemed to me to fit her description well, but Mr Patel, perhaps with the prejudice of his restricted ambit, suggested that the interior was simply that part of the country where decent people did not go. In other words anything beyond the first row of hills which had once marked the entrance to the defunct game park.

'There's nothing up there,' he said dismissively.

Mr Patel was dressed in a loose white shirt and dark trousers of a formal cut. He wore light grey shoes with a little chain on them. I judged him to be about fifty.

'I was a very young man when your father came through here. Beautiful expedition. Terrific organisation. They had everything, believe me. Radio equipment, scientific equipment, new maps, new outboard motors. The lot. They had it. Would you like some tea?'

'Thank you. Did you meet them?'

'Oh yes. I met them all. We supplied them with food for the porters and all sorts of things.'

'Did you meet my father?'

'Oh yes. Very nice gentleman. Not totally dissimilar to yourself, in looks, if I may say so, sir. Terrible tragedy. Terrible. Yes.'

He ushered me through the store into his back yard, where his daughters brought us tea and samosas under the shade of a dense avocado tree. His back yard had a chicken run in it and a large table covered in a plastic cloth of daisy pattern and rather unsuitable Chippendale dining chairs to sit on. His daughters wore silk trousers and their hair hung down in straight plaits. They looked very cool and cheerful, perfectly attuned to this hot climate. It was hard to believe that it was very cold up country during the nights, as Mrs de Luth had written:

Hot clear days give way to chill nights when the expedition members value their new kapok-stuffed sleeping bags, the product of army scientists' research drive for a lighter, warmer bag for GI Joe.

Back in the kitchen of Mr Patel's house, I got glimpses of an older, plump Indian woman in a saree orchestrating our supply of domestic comforts, sending out the girls with a plate of round Marie biscuits or tea, glancing anxiously at the contented figure of Mr Patel. His face was unlined and smooth, but he had dark rings under his eyes which were perhaps the product of years of struggling with the impermanence of Africa. Rajiv Gandhi, I have noticed, developed these too after a few years of being Prime Minister of India.

'Did you talk to my father at all?'

'You know, those were different times. My father was in charge of the business then. I wasn't allowed to speak to your father or anybody, except to fetch something for them. I did take some snaps. But I do remember that he seemed very cheery, full of jokes. As you say, the light and soul of the party.'

The chickens made a drowsy, domestic sound in their run and a lizard dashed up the avocado tree behind Mr Patel's head.

'Do you know anything about the treasures of the Orefeo?'

'Now or in those days?' he asked.

'Both, I guess.'

'They're lost. Nobody really knows where.'

'How?'

'I never saw the treasures. Very few people had actually clapped eyes on them. There was no museum or crown jewels or anything like that. The treasures were kept by the Orefeo and only brought out on certain occasions.'

I knew this much from Mrs de Luth's writing.

'What happened to them? Who took them?'

'That's a difficult question. I honestly don't know. I don't think anybody knows, sir.'

'Was the expedition involved? Monroe says they were.'

'Mr Monroe knows more than most people in this country. His family were brought up with the chiefs, but he's not reliable.

Have you heard his latest joke about Bangunes? Anybody driving in a straight line on our roads must be drunk.'

He laughed in a decorous, controlled way and flicked his fingers for more tea.

'The roads around here are getting worse. I got my brother to weld a steel plate under the Cruiser to protect the sump. No extra charge.'

'Thank you. You have been very helpful, more than helpful.'

'It's a pleasure. You know, to tell the truth, we miss the old days. Business isn't so good. There doesn't seem to be much going on at all. May I ask you a question, sir, if you will excuse me? Why did you come here?'

I made an answer. The truth was the reasons I had come to Banguniland did not bear explanation. Certainly not here in the shade of Mr Patel's convivial avocado tree.

Magda told me that she had once offered as blind man her arm to cross the road in London. The blind man had asked if he could feel her tits and she had led him into a small park and placed his hands under her shirt. 'Thank you very much,' he said after a few seconds of feeling them alternately, the way a seal plays the horns in a circus, 'that was very nice,' and tapped his way back to the road.

'Why did you do it?' I asked Magda.

'I had to do it. I wondered what he was thinking, never having seen a boob in his life.'

'How do you know he was blind from birth?'

'God you are so literal sometimes.'

'OK, how do you know he was blind at all?'

'That's a point. I never thought of that. He looked blind.'

That was why I fell in love with Magda. She possessed a spontaneity which is so rare in our self-conscious times. She also had a thrilling sexuality. But the problem with Magda, which led to my coming to Banguniland, was that in close counterpoint to her exciting unpredictability went a dangerous inconsequence. Perhaps because of the circumstances of my childhood, I have always looked for a certain domestic order and calm. With

Magda there was none. She regarded time spent at home, and domesticity – after all is said and done, the normal activity of countless millions – as time utterly wasted. Nor was there any pattern to her inconsistencies. In our four years together I loved her with an intensity which was unbearable, but her childish embrace of sensation and experience, her demands to be emotionally sated, her avid, kleptomaniacal collecting of new friends, seemed to me to be dangerously aimless. There was no end in sight. The journey, the travelling hopefully, was the whole ball of wax for Magda.

'If I may give you some advice, don't believe a word Mr Monroe tells you,' said Mr Patel. 'He's a charming man but a complete rogue, I'm afraid. That's why they locked him up.'

Magda seemed to be institution-bound herself, if the Scott and Zelda principle has any validity; life simply does not allow people to carry on the way Magda did, heedless of home, bank statements and careers, particularly my own. Her fat brother had tried to warn me before we got married about Magda, without wanting to be hurtful. The way it came out was that I was perhaps not man enough for Magda. He placed some hope in the stabilising effect of having children, however.

'Not that anyone would be right for Magda. I know she's twenty-six, but she's still young. There's something missing. I don't know. Maybe kids will do it. You know what they say.'

Magda's brother, Carl, was proud of his sister and a success with women. This conversation with me, two days before we were to approach the registry office in the King's Road, must have cost him a big effort of will and I should have taken more notice. We sat awkwardly over a pint as he tried to tip me off.

'Have you ever looked at the back of a tapestry? Millions of little fucking stitches which create the illusion of a landscape? You know, huntsmen and hounds and maidens with baskets of fruit, all that? Magda can't pick things out from the background. Everything has equal value. She doesn't know the illusion from the reality. Do you know what I'm getting at?'

'Not really, to tell you the truth.'

'OK. You will.'

Magda and her brother were from a family of East Prussian nobility; their father had led a colourful life after reaching the West some years after the war and eventually had made a reputation for himself as a journalist, although there were many who hinted that this was merely a cover for more interesting activities. He had married their mother, a ballerina with Sadler's Wells, when already a middle-aged man, but she had died soon after hanging up her ballet shoes. Magda and Carl were brought up as adults, shielded from nothing, taken everywhere by their father, doused in a kind of harum-scarum, old-fashioned, bohemian world. Naturally, the exotica had appealed to me. I wanted to live closer to the eye of the hurricane, not merely on the gusty periphery. Magda spotted in me some imaginary qualities as I was kneading her beautiful breasts; she had the illusion of giving herself to a man of depth and character; happily for me she was able to translate this misapprehension into a genuine sexual passion, a passion almost vertiginously crazy in the early days. I have often wondered about the disturbing nature of sexual encounter and its purpose, but I can't say I have come up with any new answers.

'You know the Empire, what they now call the imperialist exploitation, was a damned sight better than this lot,' said Mr Patel gravely, as if he had given the matter a lot of thought in the intervening twenty-two years.

Magda came to think of me as having an overdeveloped sensibility. Sensibility to her was an obsolete virtue, quite out of tune with the world she wished to live in, a world of whirling dervish sensation, enjoyed for its own sake but never questioned. Magda knew people who were planning to do things – interesting things – in rock videos, fashion, experimental theatre, herbal medicine, consciousness-raising, even drug dealing. All of them received her uncritical attention. They liked us: the enthusiastic, beautiful young wife and the more solid, but by no means boring husband. Somehow, my achievements appeared to become less interesting to Magda (perhaps because they were actual rather than imaginary, I told myself) than these other people's. None of these other people ever invited us anywhere. They weren't, of course, that sort of person: no fixed abode; always just about to leave for somewhere; always about to do some deal; always suntanned; always smiling. I see them now on planes, but they have forgotten me, or perhaps they do not recognise me without Magda. For a while they all wore Rolex watches and Lacoste shirts. Now they dress in squares of calico from Japan, all complicated ties and bits of tape, like stunt kites before you assemble them, and wear antique watches. Next year it will be second-hand safari clothes and cheap pink watches from Korea. How do these busy people, always on the move, have the time to agree the subtleties of international fashion? Perhaps there is a convention somewhere each year, somewhere truly international like Gstaad or Schipol Airport, where they all get their heads together. Magda herself believed that her craving for sensation, for gratification, was in some way a creative urge. She believed, too, that I had fallen into the trap of attributing my own short-comings to her. It was a nicely circular argument.

'Things have really gone to hell in a basket here,' said Mr Patel, eating a samosa carefully. 'At least when we had the paramount chief and that system there was order. Then after independence they introduced village and regional councils, which were supposed to run all the rural districts. The only problem was that the people appointed did not like the bush. They came to live in town. The whole thing went up the Swanee. Heaven knows what goes on out there.'

He called to one of his daughters. She came and stood expectantly by his side as he explained something. She soon returned with an old copy of *National Geographic* and a shoebox of photographs.

'Do you want to see these? These are my pictures, taken with my old camera, and the story of the expedition, which I am sure you have looked at many times.'

'You took pictures?' I asked hopefully.

'Yes, I'm sorry they're not much good.'

He showed me a picture of Mrs de Luth talking to his father. I scanned the background for evidence of my father, but there was none. Mrs de Luth stood at least a head taller than Mr Patel Senior, and she appeared to be wearing a holster, but the pictures were all of the same uninteresting variety, shot from too far away to make out any of the detail. The pictures were printed on brownish paper, dimpled like an orange skin. Mr Patel, while apologising all the while for his lack of skill as a photographer, wanted nonetheless to show me that Banguniland had once been a more ordered, more purposeful place, and adduced Mrs de Luth's prose to support this claim, although in truth it would be hard to imagine a place with less purpose than present-day Banguniland. The young Patel had taken pictures of his uncle's mechanical repair shop the day the governor's plump English limousine, a Humber, had paid a visit; he was there at the opening of the new road out to what was known as the 'aero-drome'; he recorded the unveiling of the new water-flushed sewage works, fêted by the *askari* band in tarbooshes and army boots. His interest was in progress, not human weakness, alas, and I learnt nothing of the relationship between Mrs de Luth and my father.

'Did you ever hear anything about the accident?'

'Nothing really. There was some complaint about official procedures, you know, not properly observed. To be honest, there are no official procedures any more, but in those days things were better.'

He did not seem to be desperately worried about the dis-integration to which he referred. His back yard, his shop, his cool house, these were his world and order prevailed here. Every corner shop in England is owned by a Patel now, driven out of Uganda by Amin, but here in Banguniland, perhaps because of the lack of official procedures of any sort, he and his family seemed to me immovable.

Magda was constantly on the move. She now lived in New York with an art dealer. He had lawyers who had given mine a pasting. I no longer owned my flat in London and they were busily on the track of the little money I had accumulated. It was particularly hurtful that Magda had not only walked out, but had been carrying on in her frenzied fashion with a cocaine dealer, now in jail, and a maker of rock videos, while I was working on a film about the social life of the baboon. Admittedly, there had been an element of deceit on my part, the baboons being second-generation suburbanites in a private zoo near Scottsdale, but I had wanted to bring the intuitions of Eugène Marais in on budget. And yet Magda had assembled a troop of reasons to excuse herself and accuse me of desertion, neglect and cruelty, and was now making good her threat to strip me bare. So an expedition to Banguniland was a better way of spending my money than handing it over to Magda's lawyers. They were a long way from here.

Mr Patel's soft face and gentle demeanour, accentuated by the dark rings under his eyes, which looked as if they had been underlined with kohl, reminded me of the postmaster in Ray's film of Rabindranath Tagore's story, and so we had come full circle: the sensitive, moral man, living amongst an alien people of a different culture, with rings under his eyes.

One of the girls came respectfully forward and spoke to her father.

'My brother is here. Shall we try out the Land Cruiser? He's made many extras for you.'

This was the vehicle to carry me to the interior. It was not new, but it had a sturdy, no-nonsense look about it, with its water cans, roof rack, ladder, tarpaulins, radio, shovels and all the other things the Patels deemed necessary for a trip to the unknown. There was an arrangement for allowing the front wheels to operate independently, and a winch for tying round a tree to haul the vehicle out of trouble. Mr Patel's brother, who had a more lively manner and a thin, wolfish face, showed me the rifle case, just behind the driver's seat, with clips and foam-rubber padding to hold two rifles secure.

'Do you think I will need a gun?' I asked.

'What are you going to eat?'

'Well, the supplies, obviously.'

'What about fresh meat or guinea fowl?'

'I don't eat much meat.'

'What about the bandits or rebels?'

'In the Malanja Hills?'

They were silent, significantly.

'Can you get me a rifle?'

'Very expensive at the moment. Why don't you ask Mr Monroe? He's an expert.'

I was reluctant to become enmeshed with Monroe again, although at his suggestion, I had agreed to take Ngwenya on the practice run to Malanja. Ngwenya had a home in the bush somewhere, up past the little trading post of Ngame, where my father and Mrs de Luth had stayed briefly, courtesy of the District Commissioner, a man whose district stretched away into areas of such elastic vastness that he would leave his office for up to three months on safari, by camel. This region, to judge from the photographs taken by Mrs de Luth, was very arid, but watered by the tendrils of the Bangunes River. The water took so long to reach the vast plain from the cool, inhospitable uplands, which were comprised of a vast and unexplored mountain range, that the scrubland had water when the rest of the country was dry. 'It was a region,' Mrs de Luth had written, 'of ancient caravan and slave routes from the historic east, of nomadic tribes of primitive hunters and gatherers, and of vast, teeming herds of game, whose migrations are a mystery.' A plan to study these migrations by means of radio transmitters attached to the antelopes' necks was proposed by her.

The rains had failed in the uplands for many years, leaving the rivers like old surgical scars on the landscape, and the remains of the vast, teeming herds had gone off to find refuge in the game parks in neighbouring countries. Of the nomads, there was no news since the troubles. The missionaries had pulled back for lack of custom and the sprawling capital village of the chiefdom had been burnt to the ground, dispersing the ruling clan, whose regalia were made by the Israelite tribespeople of the even remoter interior. Tsetse fly and malaria made these regions uninhabitable in the wet season, but the Orefeo had lived in a valley, which was really (Mrs de Luth pronounced after consultation with geologists back in Washington) an ancient dry lake. In this valley grew sturdy bushes which contained a natural chemical inimical to tsetse fly, and the Orefeo had been able to cultivate their unique, humped, blotchy cattle very successfully there, while spending their leisure hours under the giant fig trees making the figurines, stools, masks and headrests for which they were famous, artefacts which to amateurs were as good as anything knocked out by the craftsmen of Ashanti or Benin. Their favourite motifs were the spider and the praying mantis, both creatures of discretion and wisdom, but they also fashioned the likenesses of crocodiles, snakes and chameleons, less prudent animals, but all with qualities that served as exemplars to the rulers of Banguniland, and for that matter to Magda and her lawyers. (It is curious how far lawyers have gone down in popular esteem in my lifetime, and almost as fast as doctors.)

Nobody appeared to know where this valley of African figs and prophylactic shrubs was, although Mrs de Luth's map has it clearly marked with a precise longitude and latitude. Perhaps, like so many other things in Banguniland, it had slipped into the netherworld of unreality, the way a drowning person slips waterlogged and exhausted beneath the waves, silently, resistance at an end, into what Cousteau improbably called 'Davy Jones's locker'. Banguniland had ceased to accept exact distinctions between the perceived and the imaginary worlds, in this way not only reverting to African custom, but giving a boost to Descartes, who maintained that physical objects were not perceived directly at all, but through the medium of ideas. Do we get a real fright or an imaginary fright in a horror movie? Is the amputee really feeling his lost toes? These harmless puzzles did not trouble the Banguni.

The difficulties which lay ahead revealed themselves when the Land Cruiser, driven by me, ran over an enervated sheep and we were immediately surrounded by the dispossessed as I made the mistake of stopping. These people inhabited the cracks and gaps in Banguniland's crumbling self-esteem; they pressed round us, quietly insistent. The Patels wanted me to wait for the police, who would accept a small tip for flailing this insubstantial lot back into their nooks and crevices, but I paid handsomely for the sheep; we had not yet left the Victoria Road on my induction course. Mr Patel's brother was disappointed by my lack of resolution, but the faces of the poor, eyes unnaturally round from starvation, smelly bundles of bones, leather and bits of clothing, were too vivid to be ignored. As we set off, the sheep was already being butchered by the side of the road and skeletal women were waiting with their enamel bowls or old jam tins for a share of the pitifully small animal. These people, if they had strength enough, would have agreed with the Inuyit shaman who said that the Eskimo people do not believe, they fear. What was there to believe in here? Freedom from fear is surely the greatest freedom.

Magda's blithe acceptance that a lot of things were owed her by virtue of her youth, upbringing and some less easily identified attributes was at the other end of the scale from this. Many people have noted the fragility of our assumptions about security, happiness and material well-being. Nobody in Banguniland suffered from this complacency. Everybody here knew that the whole pack of cards could fall down, because it already had. And yet, in the rubble, like those survivors of air-raids in newsreel, some people were picking and scratching to survive, while others, like the Patels, had barricaded themselves into little private worlds of order and security.

Mr Patel's brother wanted me to test the vehicle's 'off-road' capabilities, a quaint term as most of Banguniland was without recognisable roads. We drove out to the last traces of the road, where it split like strands of thread being unwound from a spindle into the surrounding scrub. Already, the bush had a dusty, olive-drab sameness, stretching away in all directions, away from the river, away from Bangunes, away from the sea. It was easy to understand why the people of the interior were ignored: to live out there in the blind vastness was a wilful act.

We practised operating the winch at a small outcrop of brown rocks, piled randomly and precariously one on top of the other, a place which had once been a picnic site for the colonial masters because it gave a view back to Bangunes and off to the Malanja Hills. These hills were becoming a warm terracotta colour as the sun softened. An old man, apparently the guardian of some rock paintings and graves, approached us, wearing a khaki greatcoat and carrying a stick. Mr Patel gave him two cigarettes and he shuffled off to watch us from the shade of a drooping pepper tree as we drove the Land Cruiser up gullies and down banks, testing the four-wheel drive, the low ratio, the differential gearing, the packing of supplies and so on. Very soon we were all powdered by red dust.

'Custer's last stand,' said Mr Patel's brother as he looked at our faces, and we all laughed.

In the cool box there were Cokes and beers; we sat under a huge overhanging rock and watched the smoke rising lazily above Bangunes, the river glinting deceitfully in the lowering sun. The old man took me to see the Bushman paintings which were pictographs of giraffe and small antelopes pursued by small ochre men with bows and arrows. There was a warm musk about the caves, the smell of human habitation.

As we drove back to town past the flimsy villages, cooking fires were burning and the air was thick with the opiate pungency of Africa. I suffered a sharp pang of loneliness as the darkness rolled over us, whether because of Magda's inconstancy or because of the possibility that my father had been out there for thirty years, I could not tell.

CHAPTER 5

Perhaps I was harsh in my judgment of Magda. She had never promised to give up her restless way of life just because we were married. I had taken for granted that she would display some sort of domestic skill, but this soon proved to be a mistake. I have never had any experience of office or factory life, and excuse myself these blanks by making my little films and writing articles and so on; in the same way Magda had no knowledge of everyday life, as her brother had tried to warn me in his clumsy, circuitous fashion. Around the camp fire out in the cool night air of Malanja (Mrs de Luth was right about the chill) with the hyena whooping it up in the middle distance and Ngwenya smoking a suspiciously aromatic cigarette, all that heartache and soul searching, all those foul words and ludicrous overstatements, all those desperate recriminations could be seen for what they were: mere pinpricks on the leathery hide of the cosmos.

She said to me, 'You're too bourgeois to be a creative person,' a remark which set me thinking. I replied, 'If by creative you mean staying up all night snorting coke, you're right. And if by bourgeois you mean having a belief in the fundamental tenets of hygiene, you know, simple things like eating off clean plates and buying lavatory paper occasionally, yes, I'm guilty.' 'You know what I mean,' she said without rancour, 'and you're also pompous.'

In the bush a stick was commonly used instead of lavatory paper, but Mr Patel had thoughtfully packed a box of Andrex toilet tissue.

As we ate our meal that night, I felt at one with the implausible

55

poet, Roy Campbell, awash with the stars. These were the same stars which entranced Mrs de Luth and my father: 'The farthest reaches of the universe are unfolded here in fantastic brilliance.' We had arrived at Malanja with difficulty. The map took no account of thirty years of erosion and neglect. There had been a road to Malanja which was confidently indicated by a huge painted stone. 'Malanja 90 miles. Elephants have right of way.' There was no sign of the road now, nor of the elephants. Ngwenya said that there were still elephants in the interior, presumably on sentimental journeys to their ancestral homes from distant game parks. Ngwenya was not daunted by the unfolding emptiness. I did not tell him that Monroe had given me a shotgun and a box of heavy cartridges.

'Stop anything at ten yards. Even a charging game warden,' said Monroe as he handed over the gun.

'What should I do about the rebels?'

'Are you a religious man?'

'Seriously.'

'Try and pay them off. Take lots of tinned milk and tobacco. Ngwenya will talk to them. Anyway, you may not see them at all. They've been quiet for months.'

Ngwenya sat with his back against a stone and I sat on a folding garden chair, watching the fire and drinking Nescafé flavoured with wood ash. It had taken us three days to reach Malanja. We were camped at what had been a waterhole with a cluster of huts, each one with a view of the marsh and the hills beyond. The huts were crumbling, being absorbed back into the soil. Five or ten years before something had gone wrong with the water supply from the distant highlands. Whatever it was, water no longer reached the marsh, once five thousand acres of lush grazing for elephant, buffalo, waterbuck and strange, semi-aquatic antelope called sitatunga. Yet when the sun set, the former marsh gave off a cool, gaseous richness as though it had not yet given up hope. A few small impala could be seen hunched together timidly out on the plain, which had been the marsh, as the hyena began to call in their disturbing fashion. It is almost impossible to avoid being anthropomorphic about hyena; serious studies show them to be brave and intelligent social creatures, but the evidence of the eye and the ear is against them. They are in a constant state of psychotic disagreement, seriously disturbed slum dwellers, perpetually undernourished, always on the very edge of desperation.

I had been to Africa several times since my father uprooted us all as children. My mother had never wanted to come, not even to see her own family; she had decided that England was her spiritual home and set off there as soon as she decently could, which was as soon as we left home. She sold the saltbox and took the QE2. She longed, I now suspect, for the world of Nancy Cunard and the Mitfords, a life of cultured ease in the English countryside, surrounded by dogs and kind, undemonstrative, middle-aged men in old tweed jackets.

*

Magda and I had been to Kenya together. She had a French friend who had taken photographs of vanishing tribes; this interesting person was supposed to meet us and put us on the inside track. Unlike the tribes, who persisted, it was the friend who vanished, leaving us waiting at the New Stanley for days until I hired a car and we visited some game parks, rather lamely in the company of other tourists. I took every opportunity to return to Africa, and in fact my professional life revolved around my supposed acquaintance with Africa. In this way I had taken up my father's mantle, but I had never before visited Banguniland. Very few people visited Banguniland. Only slightly more people realised it still existed, in the way that old actors can simply fade from the public mind so that nobody knows if they are still alive. Yet Banguniland, because of its very ignorable quality, was the sort of place which might yield some interesting stories or a documentary. Nobody knew what had happened after the troubles in 1984. Nobody knew what the fate of the chiefly clan was in the new society. And obviously nobody knew, or nobody was telling, what had happened to any surviving Orefeo and their treasures.

Ngwenya had proved to be a good travelling companion in the

adversities which had befallen us on the interminable ninety miles. He still wore his grey Italian shoes as we dug out the Land Cruiser from a dry river bed (no trees, alas, for the winch), but his urban sophistication hid a gritty quality, so that he was always ready with a solution to our problems. He also had a magisterial command over his fellow countrymen; he had only to see a tribesman in a remote village to engage him in conversation and then in employment. In this way we were able to repair a broken radiator, obtain a scrawny chicken for dinner, visit some nomadic Bushmen and repair six punctures. It became clear to me that in the apparently empty bush around Bangunes life was carrying on unobtrusively, probably much as it had done before the appearance of the confused Portugese and the energetic British, and certainly much as it had done before President Ndongo's short and squalid reign. Calling yourself 'President-for-Life' was anyway giving too desirable a hostage to fortune.

'Where's your village?' I asked Ngwenya, as the chill rose out of the marsh, numbing our backs.

'It's quite far,' he said.

'North?'

'Yes. By the main tributary of the Bangunes River.'

'How far from Ngame?'

'Something about fifty miles.'

Africans are reluctant to give straight answers about distance, knowing full well that the circumstances of travel are very unpredictable.

'Look at the map. If it's right, and let me tell you that *National Geographic* is famous for its beautiful maps, we've only done ninety miles. How long do you think it would take us to get to the Orefeo country, here?'

'Your father is not there.'

Ngwenya was smiling. I had noticed a curious thing the previous day, as we drank beer in the uneasy company of some armed men: my shins were shining. It had been a cause of embarrassment to me as a boy that my father's thin, hairless legs seemed to shine as though they were made of wax. As Ngwenya

58

told the tribesmen a long story, which soon had them in rapt attention, I looked at my legs. In the pictures of my father with Mrs de Luth and with Admiral Nimitz, the tallow legs are clearly visible. For years I had avoided shorts. Magda liked my legs. No women, in fact, had ever complained about them, although looking down on them, they did seem to me to be rather unformed. I had long since grown out of this childishness, yet as I tired of watching Ngwenya practise his charms on these bandits, my shins, stretched out on a rock, were gleaming, just as I remembered my father's when we had all gone to swim in the Mullers' pool, which was really only a round concrete reservoir for watering the alfalfa and the turkeys. My mother had done her sedate, powerful crawl for a few laps, trying to avoid the dead and moribund insect life, as my father stood on the edge to dive neatly and – even to my young eyes – rather primly into the green depths, his legs gleaming, his dive, like his swimsuit, very Jantzen.

'He's not there. These people yesterday, they say he's in the mountains. They say he's got shiny legs, just like you.'

'They probably think all white people have shiny legs.'

'No, they don't think so. Some white people have furry legs, like cats. Mr Monroe has got furry legs.'

Ngwenya laughed again. He had become very relaxed out here under the stars; he was enjoying exercising his many talents on our expedition.

'Look, I don't want to go on some wild goose chase to the mountains. For a start it would take us six months if this little trip is anything to go by and secondly my only object is to get to Ngame and the valley of the Orefeo. Even that is only a thought.'

'Those people have gone. Some have gone to Israel. They were Jews. The Israelis sent transport planes for them.'

'I know all that.'

'Would you take some more coffee?'

'Yes please.'

I had no way of knowing whether Ngwenya was inventing the story about the shiny shins. It was becoming clear to me that he had a strong manipulative ability – I had seen it at work – and he was not above trying to persuade me that somewhere in this vastness an old white man, seventy-six years old to be precise, with iridescent lower legs, was living. I could not bring myself to imagine, although I had tried, what sort of existence that might be or why he would have chosen to live out there, or how he would have survived twenty-nine years of flood, famine, genocide, malaria, civil war, sleeping sickness, bilharzia, witchcraft and good old-fashioned human wickedness. This mythical person Ngwenya wanted me to accept may well have been a symbol, a totem, or a tribal memory. Many African tribes have in the repertoire prophecies of the coming of the white man, a bizarre creature with hair like a horse's tail and a mentality like a horse's arse, a sort of murderous and malevolent Cortez, unspeakably horrible but at the same time equipped with strange powers and a stick that thunders. (Now, of course, all Africa has the stick that thunders, not just pointed at a passing giraffe for fun, but, with the catch on automatic, sprayed long enough to wipe out a whole village, men, women and especially children.) The Benin bronzes show white men with guns as far back as the seventeenth century. Plenty of African art and folklore concerns the white man in this way, so I was taking a balanced view and attributing Ngwenya's extravagances to the rich, folkloric heritage of Banguniland, supplemented, perhaps, by the desire for a more colourful life. What could be more fun and time consuming for Ngwenya in his present state of *ennui*? White people, he had probably noticed, needed objectives. They invented them freely. Aimlessness was abhorrent to them. Life was a journey, and a journey without a destination – as I had many times tried to explain in less exalted terms to Magda – was no journey at all.

'Why do you think we're all going somewhere?' she asked.

'It's the way things are set up.'

'Who set them up?'

'It's the capitalist system. It depends on motion. This whole thing needs constant motion. You can forget about profit, as a matter of fact. That's low down on the list. It's all motion.'

'Like a hamster. Pointless motion.'

'The difference is that a hamster doesn't have financial commitments to worry about.'

'It all comes down to financial commitments with you. Experience means nothing; friends mean nothing; at the end of the day it's the cash flow.'

'I was only trying to explain the dynamic of the capitalist system: minor achievement, major rebuffs, insecurity, angst, giving way to madness and death, in a ceaseless cycle of motion.'

'Exactly. You're not as stupid as you sometimes appear.'

It was hardly surprising, I thought, that Ngwenya had picked me out as the sort of person who appreciates a goal; he was happy to be able to provide one.

We were settling down to our sleeping arrangements, Ngwenya under a canvas lean-to and me in the back of the Land Cruiser on an air bed, which was surprisingly comfortable, when we heard a lion roar. The sound of a lion roaring is so gratuitously full of menace, so clearly designed to intimidate, that I was not surprised when Ngwenya knocked politely, if a little urgently, on the back door of the Land Cruiser, carrying his bedding. I moved over. He was a man who slept with no regrets, absolutely still, the life in him merely flickering. There was hardly a pause between lying down and a little chuckle and a sigh which indicated he was asleep. I listened out for the lion, but it was moving away on its restless patrol, and roared only once more, like the noise of heavy furniture being dragged in a nearby apartment. Next to me Ngwenya breathed evenly, and outside the crazed insect life was at full volume, but it all blended into the night and I slept.

Now that we had arrived at the turning point of our shakedown trip, I had to have a plan, both to satisfy Ngwenya and to justify what I was doing here. Ngwenya had made breakfast and packed up his tarpaulin; he was clearly waiting for some pronouncement as I brushed my teeth the African way, with wood ash. It made the teeth shine and the taste was pleasant. The smell and texture of wood ash and woodsmoke figure very prominently in the African consciousness – the eternal fires, the wispy clean smoke and the piles of ash around villages and camps. So rubbing one's teeth with ash seemed to be a useful and appropriate act. Ngwenya had provided a washing-up bowl of warm water – this too was scented by the fire – and a small towel so that I could shave. God knows where he had acquired the small, ingratiating skills he was putting so effectively to use.

*

My mother met Magda only once. In the very final manner of her opinions, confirmed by removal to England and the haven of the Old Cyder House, she said: 'Basically, of course, she's mad, but good in bed, I suppose.' True, Magda's skills were sexual. This is not to say that she performed feats of athleticism in bed, rather that she knew how to make a man comfortable sexually. In the beginning this more than made up for her lack of mundane skills. She would always be ready for sex at unexpected moments, half-dressed in unlikely locations. Once she displayed her parts for my benefit behind a statuette as we were having a drink in the St Regis. I was intoxicated with this mayfly madness, this convincing imitation of Scott and Zelda, but fearful of the outcome, hinted at by my mother.

Her remark had set me wondering if my mother's widowhood had been belittling, even frustrating. Children never think such thoughts until it is too late. Perhaps her rather abstracted air and her resolute blotting out of the past had been a reaction. After all, my father had gone off into the unknown with another woman, got himself killed and left her in a strange country with very little money and two boys to bring up. She did not complain. Somehow she was never thinking about immediate problems, the little things in life; her eyes were cast elsewhere. She had only once spoken about Mrs de Luth, in dismissive terms, as someone who was not to be taken too seriously, a person of no significance. Was there any jealousy? As I turned the mirror of the Land Cruiser to catch the little hairs under my nose, I could not remember any single hint of it.

I could see Mrs de Luth and my father together at this spot. In those days it had not yet been proclaimed a game reserve, but it had been a hunting camp for friends of the Governor. It had been an easy day's journey from Bangunes, a stopover on the way to Ngame, which was really the start of their expedition. Ours had started at the end of Victoria Road.

'Frederick, I have been thinking.'

'Good. Well done, sir.'

One lens of his dark glasses had been cracked by a flying pebble as I gunned the engine in our unequal struggle with the terrain, but he still wore them so that his monochrome exterior had a slightly sinister look, his left eye hidden behind a perfect spiderweb of fractures in the expensive glass.

'Are you getting headaches?' I asked.

'No sir, not one. I don't get them very often. I never get the hangovers, either.'

'I can believe it. Anyway, we must go back to Bangunes for supplies and I need to send some messages and so on. What I am saying is we should set off today and get ourselves ready for a trip to find the valley of the Orefeo. Look, it's here on the map. If we cross the river here, I suspect it will be about a day's journey past Ngame. I'm going to get some proper map references, spare tyres and a better radio. What else do we need?'

The truth was that I needed to get back to speak to people, to wrap some substance around these insubstantial ideas. If I could speak to television companies in London and New York about following up the Orefeo massacre and exodus (with perhaps some references to my late father to add poignancy), the oppressive indifference of this vast country might be cracked open, like one of the clay ovens the Banguni had used in more plentiful times to bake the aardvark and vervet monkey. History does not exist until it is recorded; without a commission, without interest from television, I could neither justify nor consecrate this trip, even on the admirable grounds that it was depriving Magda and her lawyers – men I had never met – of my money.

Ngwenya was disappointed, but renewed the offensive.

'Don't you want to go all the way to the mountains?'

'No, I haven't got the time or the money. Maybe I'll be able to come back next year, for a film.'

'He's an old man, your father, sir. He may not be alive next year.'

I had finished shaving. I turned to look at Ngwenya who was crouching by the remains of the fire.

'Please Frederick, this business is beginning to tire me out. The mountain is a million miles away. It's in disputed country. Nobody – if you'll excuse a western bias – has been there for years. This Land Cruiser has a range of about five hundred miles, max. I'm no explorer. I'll get some money, do some research and then we can fly in during the dry season, always assuming there is a wet season of course, and see what goes on there.'

Frederick's eyes were invisible. He put our blackened kettle carefully back on the powdery logs of the fire. These African thorn trees burn with a fierce heat, even when the flame is barely visible, wraithlike.

'Frederick, if you are insisting that there is some old white man living in the remote bush country, give me some facts. Give me something to go on. It's not just as simple as setting off in a Jeep. I don't have limitless amounts of money. In fact, to tell you the truth, I don't have much at all. Your party set me back a bit. Our party,' I added.

I was trying to downgrade myself in his esteem. I did not want him to think I was a one-man *National Geographic*.

'You write in the newspaper,' he said finally.

'Frederick, newspapers in the biggest countries in the world tell lies every day. They make up stories. They emphasise trivial details. They try to make unimportant things, things to which no ordinary person would give a moment's notice, significant. They try to make connections which don't exist. The *Bangunes Times* naturally made a connection between my visit and my father's disappearance. This is the function of all newspapers.'

Was I being completely ingenuous? I was thinking of my father's heroic efforts to make connections on his farming newspaper back in South Africa. The farmers had refused to buy his vision of a new, colourful, dynamic world, a world of self-improvement and fulfilment, and above all of the knowledge that technology and science were on their side in the struggle with stones and trees and soil erosion. These natural things exercised a tyranny from which he wished them to break free. I saw it clearly now. *National Geographic* was the triumph of this progressive thinking. I saw now that it was a natural move from *The Countryman* to *National Geographic*, for *National Geographic* had reduced the natural world to its proper place. The motives of the founders of the Society – the 'increasing and diffusing of geographical knowledge' – were to understand the natural world around them and, more important, to capture it and render it intelligible, interesting, colourful and tractable. These men were not pure scientists, if there is such a thing, but captains of industry, journalists, military people, bankers, educators and explorers. Among them was Gardiner Green Hubbard, who had financed Alexander Graham Bell's experiments.

'OK,' said Ngwenya, 'we have to see my brother; he will tell you something. He will give you the facts.'

'Where is your brother?' I asked wearily.

'He's at his village. We Africans all have a home in the country,' he said smiling.

'Is it far?'

'It's not far. One day, maybe two days if we have bad luck.'

'Two days. Is there diesel there?'

'Oh yes. There's a road through to Ngame. We've got plenty of diesel.'

'Your brother is not going to tell me our family all have shiny legs, is he?'

Ngwenya laughed so hard, he had to take off his battered Porsche sunglasses to wipe his eyes.

It occurred to me after we had been driving for a few hours, painfully slowly in the crushing heat and choking dust, that perhaps he had laughed so hard because his last, desperate, ploy had worked.

CHAPTER 6

Finding before seeking. That is the principle great scientists employ. (Einstein was particularly prophetic.) They find the answer when they are musing idly; or they know intuitively what the answer is and then set out to prove it. We accept this now and no longer try to hide it as unscientific. This is a shot in the arm for the creative person – the writer, the painter, the musician – because for a while our trades seemed to be flim-flam in the face of the real business of life, which was science. Now even the most dyed-in-the-wool scientist acknowledges that you have to have an end in sight, a socially acceptable and useful one by choice. This is old hat now. *National Geographic* has taken steps to give a more caring image to its work in the last decade. Everybody wants to be seen to be caring. The word is as threadbare as the purposes behind it. Enthusiastic, unscientific Ngwenya wanted to fabricate the evidence. As the miles passed slowly, I questioned my judgment in going along with him. On the credit side it could be seen as a recce, a scouting trip, for the bigger trip to the Orefeo by way of Ngame. On the debit side, each passing mile provided me with new doubts.

The country we were passing through was sandy with scrubby little trees called mopani, and completely waterless. By the time the sun was fully up the life of this landscape had gone into hiding. Very occasionally a ground squirrel or a hornbill could be seen, but it was tricky country, with a deceptive, repetitive pattern to the mopani, so that you had the illusion you had passed this way before, past these little clearings in the scrub and arrangements of dried watercourses, each teasingly similar to others you had seen a few miles back. I could imagine a hunter or an explorer, lost in this stuff, quickly going mad with false hope. We were following a track of some kind, which Ngwenya, before falling asleep, said was the road through to the river and eventually Ngame. He lay sprawled like the victim of an assassination in Beirut. I checked my compass and the map from time to time; there was no question but that we were heading in more or less the right direction.

*

We had had a small memorial service in the Old First Church back in Huntington. My mother responded to some deeply heard chord of propriety and asked the Episcopalian minister if he would arrange this. She did not tell him she was an intuitive atheist. He was eager to please. It seemed that in Episcopalian vestries *National Geographic* cut some ice. Also, there was the link with the Church of England. We had all been baptised Anglican, except for my mother, who has somehow escaped religious instruction. Her father, the Aussie grazier, had mixed feelings about religion. Ever since Lord Kitchener had had one of his friends, Lieutenant Morant, shot during the Boer War, he had an Antipodean gut feeling that religion went hand-in-glove with the ruling classes. Anyway, my mother passed muster with the minister and so three months after the news came back we assembled a few of our new friends, the Wichts, who owned a successful lumber yard, the Cmerzyks, whose eldest son, Jim, became a congressman a couple of years ago, and the Staffords. Mr Mike Stafford went to jail shortly after for passing forged bonds. We said a few prayers, and the minister said a few words about my father – remarkably gracious, considering he had never met him. The gist of his little peroration was honour by association with *National Geographic*. Mrs de Luth did not come, as she was on her way to view *Zinjanthropous Boisei*, the skull of a prehistoric humanoid, uncovered by Dr Louis Leakey and his wife Mary in Tanganyika. This skull was believed to be nearly two million years old, give or take a hundred thousand years either way. What was the rush after all this time, my mother asked, without hope of an answer?

Far from feeling deep grief, all I remember was the sense of surprise that this priest, with his young soft face and Norman Vincent Peale glasses, should talk about my father's character in what seemed to me the most intimate terms:

Although I never had the good fortune to meet Lance, I have received a letter from his friend and associate in *National Geographic*, Mrs Mary de Luth, which makes me wish I had known him as well as you, his family and friends did. Let me in conclusion, read you a line from that letter: 'Lance Curtiz had an enquiring mind. I am sure that wherever he has gone, he will take with him that lively intelligence and warm good fellowship, which I so came to appreciate.' I can say no more, except that our country was built by people, by immigrants, with lively and enquiring minds. God bless him and keep him, and God comfort those who are left behind.

Mr Stafford was in tears. Perhaps his nerves were gone because of the risky nature of his business. Afterwards we all stood awkwardly outside the tall white church, with its colonial spire, but I knew that my mother had done the right thing. You could not simply close the book on a man who had disappeared in a crocodile-rich river without some mark of respect, some act of acknowledgment. She sometimes pointed out that just because you were an atheist, you were not absolved from a knowledge of right and wrong. She got a job the following week on the woman's pages of the *Nassau Enquirer*, and rose to be women's editor, sticking to it just long enough to see us safely out of the nest, as she put it. My rich brother and I support her now, but she made some money by selling the house at the right moment, as the suburbs began to engulf our little village. A shopping mall now occupies the site of our house and the snowy woods beyond. The house itself was moved intact to Southampton. There was also a small insurance policy, which involved many months of paper-work to claim.

Ngwenya, naturally, knew none of this. All this finality – this intricate structure of emotions and rituals and adjustments could not be unglued just like that. I had lived nearly thirty years without a father. What good was a deranged old man, living in a remote mountain forest, to me or anybody? When he had gone missing the term 'senior citizen' had hardly been invented. If there was an old white man living in the interior, he would be paramount chief of the senior citizens, a man who had truly understood the notion of the sun belt.

At this point in my reveries we hit an antbear hole and the sleeping Ngwenya was thrown on to the floor, where he became entangled with the low-ratio gear stick and smashed the Porsche sunglasses which he wore on the top of his head while sleeping. Although the Cruiser came to a complete halt and slewed right round, wrenching the wheel out of my hands, there was no other damage.

'Would you like some tea, sir?' said Ngwenya after he had found his badly damaged sunglasses.

'Why not? Let's go mad and have some tea in the middle of this enchanted wood.'

'*Midsummer Night's Dream*. I like Puck very much.'

'That figures. I'll get some firewood.'

A scorpion stung me as I picked up some bits of dry mopani. It was a large creature, a negroid version of the langoustines Magda and I had eaten at the Brasserie Flo. The book said that the big black scorpions were not dangerous, but that the affected limb would ache and possibly swell, and in most cases headaches would follow. Ngwenya killed the creature with a stone, which I thought was unnecessary.

'Why did you kill it?' I asked, as I waited for the onset of the symptoms.

'If you don't kill it, she will give his mother your blood.'

Little creatures are invested with amazing powers by Africans, and who is to say they are wrong? I took two aspirin and drank lots

69

of water, and counted my blessings that it was not the small brown variety whose bite, it said in the first-aid book, can cause paralysis of the respiratory muscles, leading to cardiac arrest, in ten minutes. I suspect it would have to bite you in the testicles to achieve that, which suggests a bizarre way of collecting firewood.

As we set off with Ngwenya driving, the day seemed to be becoming unbearably hot, and the dull, oppressive mopani, without even a hill to relieve the tedium, were closing in on the track. My hand and then my arm began to ache, as though they were being filled too full, like a balloon or a sausage skin. My vision became blurred by a soft, unfocused spot in the middle of my eyes.

'Could you stop, please? I want to lie in the back.'

'You must sleep, sir, it will be gone when you wake up again.'

I lay on the air bed, bouncing about like an erotomaniac in a highly specialised bordello, my hand feeling as though it would burst, and the dust which always got into the back of the Cruiser coating my mouth, fast drying mucus membranes and eyelids. I became drowsy, thinking that perhaps I'd been bitten by an outlandishly large specimen of the deadly dwarf variety after all or, worse still, by an unknown variety. So much was unknown about Banguniland, it was quite possible it harboured an undiscovered, deadly scorpion. SCORPIONS: LIVING FOSSILS OF THE SANDS as *National Geographic* described them. I was entering a state of narcosis, a sort of pre-med, induced by a living fossil, little changed for four hundred million years. The vision of a sprightly senior citizen, who now appeared to me in plaid bermuda shorts with shiny old legs poking out below, convinced me that I was dying. It also convinced me Ngwenya could not possibly give a moment's credence to this absurd story. No white man could survive thirty years out here alone.

Once in 1968, I had taken LSD in a sugar cube. At the time I had been unable to identify the awful, weightless, disorientated feeling. It had, I thought airily, no connection with the material world. In fact the sensation, part physical, part neurological, was just like being driven through a featureless wilderness on a plunging air mattress after being bitten by a scorpion, plagued by dreams of a grinning geriatric with alabaster legs.

Dreams are often couched in the most banal terms. But now Magda appeared to me, sitting on a beach in Greece, eating a warm fig, the little creases between her thighs and her hips just moist with sweat. This vision was unbearably erotic. Surgeons have noticed that patients under anaesthetic develop erections and dying elephants sometimes resort to sexual behaviour as a last hopeless gesture. What's the connection between sex and death? Is it as obvious as it appears, simply the act of creation in opposition to the act of extinction? 'Magda,' I thought. What an extraordinary name, what a violent grunt of a name. After she had eaten her fig she lay back on the sand. I seemed to be in a rather privileged position, my head not far from the damp sandiness of her thighs, which were, of course, much browner than my own. Or am I inventing this last detail? Anyway, we were as drowsy as wasps at summer's end. I am deeply suspicious of dreams and find all the explanations for them unconvincing. Yet I am sure that they must have some chemical provenance. Certainly this one, a dream of high anxiety, had a chemical origin in the sharp, venomous bite of *Buthidae Leiurus*, the living fossil.

When I woke I was quick to appreciate that I was alive, although my surroundings were puzzling. I thought perhaps I had reached the interior, the non-world of which Mr Patel had spoken so slightlingly, because I was lying on a mat, on the ground, in the dark. Although my arm still hurt and I had a monstrous headache, I could feel that I was recovering. Light of great intensity played upon me, in little dots and comet tails, as on the dome of a planetarium. It demanded an effort of the will to keep calm and wait for my eyes to sort out the details. I was lying in a hut, with a circular, woven reed wall, and a roof of grass and reed thatch. There were no windows and the door was covered over with a reed flap. I felt something cold beside me; it was an enamel cup from our Cruiser filled with water, which I drank. Beside that were some aspirin, my shoes neatly laid out, and a small plastic plate of cream crackers. I could recognise the hand of Ngwenya in these arrangements, and felt greatly relieved. I stood up.

'Hello,' I said loudly.

The noises outside the hut, chickens scratching and clucking, the low murmur of voices, children playing, a sort of African muzak, always fused with the African smells of woodsmoke, maize meal and earth (earth which has different smells for different seasons and locations), stopped abruptly. There was a whispered conversation and then the reed door was lifted back. A tall, stout man entered, followed by Ngwenya who stood just half a pace behind him.

'Good day, sir,' said this man.

'Hello, how are you?' I replied.

'He is my brother, Patrick,' said Ngwenya.

'Would you like something to eat? Simple fare, I'm afraid,' said Patrick. 'You are probably hungry.'

'Yes, I think I am. How long was I asleep?'

'Too long,' said Ngwenya.

'Horrible little creatures,' said Patrick.

It took me a moment to realise he was talking about scorpions.

'Come, let's go over to my house.'

'Where are we?' I asked, for this was a very peculiar village. There were Jeeps and camouflaged tents, a small encampment of makeshift huts, like the one I had been lying in, field guns, and a few armoured carriers.

'This is my home,' said Patrick. 'For the moment.'

He was wearing a camouflage jacket and matching cap and, round his broad middle, a British Sam Browne belt, to which was attached a holster in a canvas cover. Underneath he was wearing jeans and Timberland boots. We entered his house by way of a cochlea-shaped windbreak of woven reeds, an extended mat of a type which used to be popular in my day with students of the homespun variety; crumbs and bits of food became embedded in the cracks, and cheap red wine and the butts of joints soon made

72

these mats appropriately organic. His house was a bigger, more comfortable version of the one I had slept in for unknown hours. Next to it was our Land Cruiser, newly cleaned, up on blocks with a mechanic underneath.

'We found, in conducting our campaign out here, that low technology is the answer. Wherever possible we use local skills and time-honoured traditions. The windbreak arrangement is used by the local tribes; it keeps the bloody dust and the snakes out, and it keeps the house cool.'

Patrick Ngwenya was an urbane man. I was expecting him to say he'd been to Eton and Oxford. It turned out that he had studied for a law degree in London, but quit. Frederick Ngwenya offered no explanation for all this. He watched the great man, his brother, leader of the Banguni National Liberation Front, with such affection and so much admiration, that it was clear he regarded it as reward enough for me to be in his presence. In truth he was a very likable man, with a broad, princely face and the bulk that suggested, correctly or not, the physical strength of a wrestler.

We sat round a collapsible table and food was brought to us by young girls in uniform. They smiled when they saw me and I could believe that I looked comical, still dirty and sweat-stained, my nose peeling, one arm held tightly to my chest, and my hair, whose vitality had anyway given out some years before, streaked reddish with dust and stuck to my head. We had roast chicken and some root vegetable, with a large amount of maize meal.

'This is not simple fare.'

'This is specially for you. We killed a couple of old hens. You haven't eaten in thirty-six hours. But let me tell you we had a spell of nearly three months of living on worms and lizards. Mopani worms are full of protein. We carried them with us, dried. So far we have tried not to think about the nutritional value of lizards. We've got Mauritian beer. Do you want some?'

'No thanks, I've already got a headache.'

'After lunch, we'll fix you up with our special shower. The water's being heated now. It's a great arrangement, officers only

I'm afraid. We started out being very democratic, you know, "comrade private" and "comrade major", but I got bored with it. A lot of being a soldier is simple obedience. They understand the notion of chiefs better than the notion of officers.'

'My brother has not told you,' said Frederick Ngwenya. 'He is the paramount chief of the Banguni. It was our village which was burnt in the troubles. Our family is now dispersed, but the Banguni National Liberation Front is led by the Ngwenya clan.'

'Why did you bring me here?' I asked Frederick of the Ngwenya clan. I was angry at Frederick's deception; once again I had been put upon.

'Because, sir, to tell you the truth, you are the first important foreign journalist to come to Banguniland for nearly two years.'

'I've got bad news for you, I'm not a proper journalist, I write features and make extremely uncontroversial documentary films, and I'm far from important.'

'Yes, but you have connections,' said Patrick, 'in Washington and London.'

'Not many, I have to say.'

'Look, nobody has written about us, nobody cares about us. We need the publicity in the outside world. We need a lot of help when we get rid of the madmen in Bangunes.'

'The President-for-Life has gone,' I pointed out.

'We know all about that,' said Patrick significantly. His brother laughed loudly.

'Unfortunately, he was only a puppet.'

I could see their plan now. I had been lured here by some cock-and-bull story about my father to write nice things about them which they hoped would find their way to the eyes of the CIA or Whitehall, or wherever these things are decided; a cornucopia of automatic weapons, cash and supplies would be despatched, followed by an influx of agricultural, social, birth-control and veterinary experts.

The shower was a petrol drum with holes punched in one end. It was filled with hot water, pumped directly from another drum, which was warmed on a fire of logs. The shower was behind a

74

screen of reed walls. A new bar of Lifebuoy soap lay in a chrome dish, nailed to a wooden post.

'Ready,' I shouted as instructed, standing completely naked under the petrol drum.

'OK, sir,' came a voice followed by the noise of a hand pump squeaking emptily. After a lag of about twenty seconds – during which I wondered, my mind still somewhat confused by the scorpion venom, if someone were taking nude pictures of me holding the pink bar of soap – water suddenly cascaded down; very soon I was feeling more cheerful and thinking that perhaps there was something in this for me after all. A colourful article or an exclusive documentary, behind the lines with the London University-educated paramount chief guerrilla leader. I flexed my wounded arm and it felt better.

I was disappointed in Ngwenya, however. I had hoped that somewhere in the folk memory there might be some new facts about my father and Mrs de Luth; or perhaps he would know of a local chieftain who was there when the Land Rover went over the side. I had not thought that Frederick Ngwenya was telling me the literal truth, of course, but I hoped he could lead me towards something unexplained, the central relationship in that drama of twenty-nine years before: the relationship of Mrs de Luth and my father.

'You look much better,' said Frederick.

'I feel better.'

'Would you like to come gathering honey with me?' asked Patrick Ngwenya when I returned to his house, spruce in clean clothes, my walk across the parade ground watched by hundreds of eyes.

'Honey?'

'I'm going out with a tracker to find some honey. I love sweet things. I used to eat a lot of Cadbury's Fruit and Nut when I was in London, and Hershey's Kisses in America. Do they still have those?'

'I think so.'

'Also it will give us an opportunity to talk.'

In my father's stock of African stories, there had been one about the African honeybee. According to this harmless hokum there is a cosy relationship between a certain bird which likes honey but does not have the means to disinter it, and the honey badger, which likes honey just as much, but does not have the brains to find it. So the bird would lead the honey badger to the tree or cleft in the rock and the badger, the honest journeyman, equipped with thick, bee-proof fur and strong, irresistible claws, would get to work. So the story went. Sometimes these birds would form liaisons with groups of Bushmen to the same effect; according to my father, these bees could not be domesticated, just as the African elephant was too unreliable for domestic work. He wrote these articles in a folksy, rather whimsical style and, judging from the papers I found, managed to sell them all time and again. This was in his Rudyard Kipling mode. There was also a story about a rain queen in South Africa, who lived in an inaccessible gorge and survived many attempts by the Boers to prise her out of this fastness. At the bottom of all these stories was the mystical, wondrous aspect of Africa. Africa was a continent pregnant with meaning for mankind.

'Let me quickly show you around the camp. To tell you the truth it's more to show you off to them. They probably think you are an important hostage,' said Patrick Ngwenya smiling.

Frederick Ngwenya laughed loudly. I felt uneasy. We did a tour of inspection: the field hospital and the communal kitchen (simply a large tent with beer crates supporting planks for tables). The actual cooking was done outside on fires. There were children and women, as in a mediaeval army, and hens and other small livestock. Most of the men wore a uniform of one sort and another, but only the officers carried weapons. I was introduced to a group of officers who smiled and shook my hand, while clasping their right hand at the wrist with the left, a mark of respect in Banguniland. I could see a family or a tribal resemblance in them, the lean, gazelle-like look of Frederick Ngwenya repeated often. Apart from the chief, who had a positive obligation to be large, these men all looked delicate, dusty and slightly timid, with large, startled eyes.

'Natural fighting men,' said Patrick, as if he had been anticipating some doubts on my part.

'They look fit,' I said.

'OK, let's get in this Jeep. Freddie will bring a weapon and the tracker is ready. Let's go.'

The bees lived in a cleft in some rocks a few miles from the camp. These rocks formed a small hill. It seemed a look-out was posted up there, and the commander-in-chief's Jeep was expected. From within this cleft in the rocks came a deep, subterranean humming, like the string section of the Boston Pops tuning up off stage.

'How do you get at the honey?' I asked.

'This man,' said Patrick Ngwenya pointing at a tracker, 'is a nomad, a River Bushman. They are famous for honey gathering. Sometimes they follow little honeyguides, the bee-eating birds, to the nests. The birds actually call to them.'

The tracker, a smaller, lighter coloured man, with a Chinese face, said something to Patrick Ngwenya.

'He says, run like hell if they all come swarming out. He's completely immune to their stings.'

'I've only just recovered from being bitten by a scorpion,' I said.

'True, my friend, true. Watch this, he speaks to them, if they don't respond, which between you and me they never do, he lights a fire using a special wood, which usually makes them drowsy before they get angry. This is the art. If the little buggers get angry before they get drowsy, watch out. Freddie keep the Jeep running.'

The Bushman tracker knelt in front of the cleft in the rocks and spoke into the depths a quick, clicking recitation. He cocked his head to listen to the response. It was obviously unsatisfactory, for he placed his bundle of twigs and leaves in front of the aperture, lit a match and set fire to his pyre. Then he quickly stuffed it into the hole and fanned the thick, acrid smoke back into the depths. Patrick Ngwenya watched this eagerly.

'Now,' he said, 'if there is another entrance, the fun will begin.'

Nothing much happened. A few bees escaped and flew haphazardly around us. As I drew closer I could hear that the bee orchestra had dried up. The tracker crawled into the hole, so that only the nicotine soles of his feet were sticking out. Then he began to crawl out again, backwards. In his hands was a huge piece of honeycomb, dripping honey and drugged bees on to the ground. He handed it ceremoniously to Patrick Ngwenya, who offered me a bite. I took a waxy, warm mouthful and Patrick finished the rest. Patrick intended me to see some meaning in this, but he couldn't possibly have known of my father's interest in the Bushmen and the African honeybee.

'While he's getting it all out, will you come for a walk with me?'

'Of course.'

We walked up the hill, hopping from boulder to boulder. At the top there was a little look-out post, carefully camouflaged with grass and branches. The look-out saluted smartly and Patrick sent him away.

'Sit, my friend, sit here.'

I sat on one rock, Patrick on another. What's going on here, I thought? I must take stock. I've always had this feeling that my father, whom I only knew until I was ten years old, was a naive, eager person, the sort of person the world takes a delight in disillusioning, in wising up. The truth was the world took a delight in trying to put upon me too. I was forever being held in emotional bondage by women (Magda was not the first) and in financial bondage by agents, television companies and all the other people who are closer to the centre, of whatever it is, than I.

And here I was, my fingers sticky, with nothing to wipe them on, being used – I could see it coming – as a sounding board by an African chief turned guerrilla. He would probably keep me hostage until I delivered CBS, the BBC, the *Washington Post* and *The Times* to his compound.

'Bangunes is that way, two hundred and sixty miles. Our

village, our capital city lay over there' – he pointed towards the setting sun – 'about sixty miles. We control everything from here to the outskirts of Bangunes, and northwards behind us, right up to the mountains. We never believed in the ownership of land. One of the reasons I chucked in the law was this continual emphasis on ownership of land. God knows what the lawyers would do without it. But now we are forced to try and control the whole country to restore some sense and decency.'

He talked fluently and charmingly, filling me in on the background: the tribal jigsaw, the power vacuum left by the departing British, the crumbling economy, rising oil prices, falling commodity prices, the final, disastrous assault on the chiefly family. But I was wondering why it was that I, despite my lifelong attempt to do serious, or at worst semi-serious, intelligent work, and to live in a more or less ordered, unexciting fashion, was always being singled out. What was it about me that moved other people to unload their fears and hopes on me? Patrick Ngwenya was foraying skilfully and nimbly through the politics of Third World countries, and their dependence on Europe. What he wanted, it seemed, was a forum for his views. He did not want to walk into Bangunes and the Presidential Palace, formerly Government House, to be greeted by the United Nations and the Western Powers as just another crackpot African dictator.

'In return, I will personally direct you to find your father.'

Oh, Jesus, here we go again, I thought: finding before seeking.

CHAPTER 7

I spent more than a week with the Liberation Front before setting off for the Orefeo country.

Patrick Ngwenya said that the offensive after the summer rains, if there were any, would be decisive. For all his urbanity, he was not a decisive man. He would get drunk, don flared trousers and boots with high heels and listen to soul music most evenings. I was not sure he wanted to be President of Banguniland. Perhaps the enormity of the task – the retreat to the old ways of magic, of small wars, of wild predictions, of endless discussion, of ritual acts, of the encircling darkness, in short the complete decay of hope in Banguniland – may all have been too much of a burden to take on. He reminded me of a school friend, who desperately wanted to be a success in business but had no aptitude for it. Marx is wrong, one individual cannot be all things in a day. Patrick Ngwenya wanted to be somebody, in the circles where it mattered: in Paris, in London and in New York. The possibility that he might be seen to be as ridiculous as Amin was abhorrent to him. He wanted to be seen on the international stage, not as an African, with all the polite condescension that entails, but as a statesman. He wanted to be famous, and serious. Yet so far, his Liberation Front was hardly known. Only Israel and South Africa supplied weapons and cash, not the company he wanted to keep.

He was a superb motivator of his people. He loved them, and he basked in their affection, like a huge bull sealion with its harem. Just to be their chief was, perhaps, enough. It was against his inclinations to run a bankrupt country with no natural resources, a country which would have to invite in the Club Mediterranée and the World Wildlife Fund and Hyatt Hotels in order to re-enter the international community, even on a pro-bationary basis. Somehow I was to mobilise world opinion, get him on the best kind of TV chat shows, fly out journalists for exclusive, fireside interviews, and send in the networks and ace war-correspondents for the final assault on Bangunes. He would do the rest. He was suffering from a very contemporary affliction, the belief that you only exist through the flickering image of publicity.

We drank Mauritian beer and listened to his Lionel Richie records as we discussed the feasibility of his plans. We never talked about my father. Yet one night, by which time I was sure that his account of my father's disappearance was simply a ploy, he did produce a local chieftain, who had been one of the expedition's headmen, the man who delivered the necessary porters, cooks, traders and guards. This old man seemed to delight the Ngwenyas with his quavering but unbroken account of the expedition, a sort of declamation, a local odyssey. He had not actually been present when the accident occurred, but he knew for a fact that my father had been taken by a crocodile, a friendly crocodile, to an island lower down the river. There he had been put gently ashore, the way crocodiles do with their young, and there he had lived in a forest for some time learning the arts of the sangoma, the diviner.

Patrick Ngwenya translated for me, as the old man, the skin stretched taut on his face, sat in the dust in front of the three of us. Once or twice he drew with his fingers in the grey dust. Patrick found his story full of delight and significance, but I longed to be somewhere else. There was something unbearably tedious and misguided about all this. The old man unexpectedly reached inside the pocket of his torn jacket and produced an envelope which he handed to Patrick. Patrick handed it to me. It was a treasured possession, bearing the stamp of the National Geographic Society. Inside it was a letter, which read simply:

Motsemai,

For a true and faithful servant, a memento of our journey.

Yours

Mary de Luth

With the letter was a photograph. I took it with trembling hands. There they are, Mrs de Luth, my father and a young Motsemai, caught by the self-timing device on Mrs de Luth's Leica, examining a large iguana. My father has it by the tail; he is laughing, although the iguana is thrashing about in his grasp. This is obvious because it is blurred. My father is not wearing his solar topee and he looks, despite the period effect of the aging photograph, shockingly like me, a fact which the old man has apparently pointed out to the Ngwenyas, who crane over my shoulder to see this amazing relic, although I am feeling shaky, the way one does after a minor car smash. The old man clasps my hand; I have the impression that a character in a painting has seized me by the hand as I stand in the Rijksmuseum or the Metropolitan. I give him back the envelope, which he puts carefully in his pocket. But I keep the picture, transfixed. I feel as if by a sight of this picture I have strayed into the dream world.

The bush around is screaming with insect life. The heat is shimmering and baking. The small trees, bushes really, are drooping wearily. The old man never stops talking. They continue to translate his nonsense. It is about birds which whisked my father into the air. The old man saw war service; a medal is thrust into my hand. The old man fought in the Northern Desert against the Germans. He produces another photograph, of himself in uniform. He carries a .303 and wears a bush hat. He moves on to a story about a river crossing and hippo, whose onomatopoeic name is kubu, which he repeats several times – no distinction here between the sign and the symbol – 'kubu, kubu', a tug-boat noise. Have these hippo, too, been involved in my family history in some way? I will never know. His own family are dead. All his many wives, sons and daughters have perished in a variety of improbable ways. He feels isolated and alone; although he has taken a new wife he is unable to give her a baby. He is too old.

'Please ask him about Mrs de Luth and my father,' I say.

They ask him but his answer is completely nonsensical, about birds and elephants. How can so much of the world go on in this incomprehensible way? They appear never to have heard of the simple laws of logic, which have been around since Plato. They confuse the appearance for the substance. They are unconcerned that there are mathematics and science and even systematic philosophies of these subjects. We're not talking here of airy-fairy things, like literature and psychiatry, but of the demonstrable things like engineering, microchips and gravity. To these people they are all one; all nothing.

'Mrs de Luth,' says the old man, 'is a relative of the she-elephant.'

To me she looks more like a relative of the she-giraffe; now he is saying that my father is a relative of the heron. Again I can think of better comparisons, but it seems that these analogies are based on perceived qualities rather than physical attributes.

'Where are they now?' I ask – a trick question.

'Mrs de Luth, the she-elephant, has gone back across the seas. The other one, your father, the one with the shiny legs, has gone to live in the mountains. He is sangoma.'

I look at myself in the photograph. My mother confided in me, in her particularly direct fashion, that my father preferred my brother. She feels compelled to say these things. At one time she used to approach people in the street and ask them their age, when she was approaching sixty.

'I want to know how old I look; I can't picture myself, exactly, that's why I ask.'

We used to take evasive action whenever she accosted a stranger. A pair of Mormons came to our house and bade us all kneel and pray.

'How old are you?' she asked one of them in the middle of the Lord's Prayer. He was twenty-one, with a face undisturbed by doubt, or life, or even the hot sun of Utah, like a piece of pottery which has not yet been fired.

'I'm nearly sixty,' she said. 'I've lived three times as long as you, and I still have no faith whatsoever, so please get up off your knees, have a cup of tea and get on your way. I'm nearly sixty, you know.'

'Yes, Ma'am,' they said without waiting for a drink, disturbed by this implacable sceptic.

My mind was wandering. The old man continued to talk. They were no longer translating. I stared at the picture. Now even Patrick, who had time in excess, was growing impatient. The old man was given some beer and meat, his party turn over. But he did not want to return to the boring eternity that awaited him, nor to his demanding young wife. I pictured her sitting outside a house, childless, her thighs dusty and full, her breasts aching for a son to gorge himself; a little crease where her thigh meets her hip. The old man stood up, saluted and walked away saying, 'Left-right, left-right, left-right.'

We thought he had gone, but suddenly he about-turned and came back and saluted again with his free hand, and sat down in front of us. Patrick said something to one of his men. He led the old man away, holding his plate of meat and his bottle of Mauritian beer, still saying, 'Left-right, left-right, left-right.' I watched him go. He reminded me of the mad beggar in Tagore's story of the postmaster. I still had his photograph; I handed it to Frederick and went to rest in my hut. The heat was intense. The insects were outraged. All of Africa lay around, hot and dusty and living by its own rules. These rules are very complex.

I shut my eyes; the sockets were burning behind the eyeballs. I wondered how long the scorpion venom could linger in the system. My abused brain was goaded by images. I could not sleep. But in that uneasy twilight the images began to multiply, out of control.

I saw Admiral Byrd and his dog Igloo.

I saw the riderless black horse at President Kennedy's funeral.

I saw the world's tallest tree.

I saw Jane Goodall embrace a chimpanzee.

I saw Magda's thighs part on the billiard table.

I saw Snowflake the albino gorilla.
I saw Neil Armstrong reflected in Buzz Aldrin's gold visor.
I saw pollution on the Cuyahanga.
I saw the waiter's face of Captain Cousteau.
I saw the cheerful forges of the Orefeo.
I saw the Dead Sea Scrolls.
I saw a humming-bird in flight.
I saw a bright shoal of hawkfish.
I saw a huge stone head unearthed in Mexico.
I saw the floods in Florence.
I saw a humpback whale leap from the water.
I saw Louis and Mary Leakey on their hands and knees.
I saw starving children in Bangladesh.
I saw the Temple of Angkor Wat.
I saw Mount St Helens erupting.
I saw Sir Edmund Hillary and Sherpa Tenzing on Everest.
I saw an Inca child frozen for five hundred years.
But above all this I heard the fearful piston thump of helicopters and the cry of children.

*

When I finally slept, I saw the old man with the shiny legs. He looked just like me.

CHAPTER 8

When I arrived back in Bangunes with Frederick Ngwenya, who presumably was some sort of Trojan horse, I felt an urge to make contact with old friends. I had been neglectful. I had turned down invitations to stay in all sorts of places. For six months I had been enjoying my own thoughts and company in an unhealthy fashion. I had also been far too preoccupied with money. All my life I had been concerned about money, to the detriment of achievement. I wrote immediately to Magda's lawyers, conceding defeat unconditionally. I wrote to Magda herself, a high-toned and conciliatory love letter; and I wrote to other friends to arrange meetings, to observe birthdays, to blow air on to the embers which provide essential human warmth, and to weave myself back into the fabric of life. My father had shown me how to eat a Dover sole; he demonstrated how neatly the bones lay exposed on the plate. In the same way, I felt, the basics of social life are starkly exposed in all their skeletal simplicity, out in the vast bush country under the stars.

It was Mr Patel who had suggested going to look at the District Commissioner's report of the accident. In such an insubstantial place, the idea of records and papers and a government archive had not occurred to me. The termites would surely have eaten them, or the last president but one would have burned them all symbolically, or the colonial government would have taken them away, like the Elgin Marbles, to a safer place. But no, they were stored in an annexe of the cabinet office. Here all was drunkenness and cheerful confusion. The doorman still wore a neat uniform but his job had apparently changed from its original specification. He seemed to be running some sort of concession, a minor racket which allowed him to keep live chickens in crates inside the building. They were his tribute from supplicants who wished (I could only guess from a love of the works of Franz Kafka) to get into the building. Behind him was a reception desk, which was now used as a lunch counter. Curry and rice and half loaves of bread were being eaten there by the secretaries of the cabinet office, slim but strong girls who had probably been at my party. It was not yet ten o'clock in the morning. There was a large notice on the wall, written in fine bureaucratic language, which warned that drunkenness and lack of punctuality were not expected of civil servants. Underneath it was a crate of empty beer bottles. In order to get into the archives I had to fill in a request form. There was nowhere to write as the reception desk was now occupied, so I wrote on my knee while standing up. This form was taken off by one of the secretaries, dragging her feet along behind her, in pink bedroom slippers, down a long corridor. She came back eventually; I would have to wait one hour. It seemed the stamp for my form was busy elsewhere, validating documents of national importance. She asked if I was preparing to have another party.

I explained to the porter that I'd be back and that I had no chickens, and that I would give him a tip when I finally left. He saluted and then rushed out of the door, shouted at a small boy harshly and held the door open for me with one hand, while trying to seize the boy's throat with the other.

The DC's report betrayed a certain anti-Americanism. Friends of my parents, before we left South Africa, used to talk of 'the Americans' in this way. The Americans had only come into the war after it was all over. The Yanks had a hamburger every day when Europe was starving. Not my father; his only quibble, after his stint with Chester Nimitz in the Pacific, was that Yank ships were dry. In the Royal Navy by contrast the officer class got smashed every evening. 'Down the hatch old boy. Sun's over the yardarm,' they chanted.

The DC's main complaint was that the leaders of the American expedition had failed to go through the proper channels. They had recruited their own labour. They had brought their own maps and they had neglected to check in with the thin network of colonial police and district officers. All in all they had been far too well equipped and organised. By their lavishness and independence, it was hinted, they had disturbed the natives and the carefully balanced system of tribal antipathies. They had dealt directly with the chiefly family, ignoring the protocol officer, and they had not waited for permits before setting off for the Orefeo country. The misfortune that had befallen them, it was suggested, was a direct result of this travelling circus. No doubt the DC's office would be blamed, as it was understood that the expedition had friends in high places. However, as to the question of the inquest, the expedition's leader, Mrs de Luth, had refused to attend and the subpoena of witnesses had been impossible, because none of the labour had been registered with the district office, so was unknown. The coroner, who was also the writer of the report, had had to return an open verdict under protest, which verdict he was herewith appending to the above special note. Death of Lance Patrick Curtiz, as far as could be ascertained, was by drowning. Two further deaths, also by drowning, of unknown native porters were believed to have taken place. No further facts had come to light, although a police sergeant was questioning witnesses whenever he could find them. He would file a report in due course. I was able to find this second report with surprising ease. It was written on an old typewriter with smudgy characters in the sort of language I had imagined had been invented by Ealing Film Studios. The sergeant had done a lot of interviewing of subjects, translation appended, and a lot of proceeding on various compass bearings to various villages and outposts.

This peculiar document, filed away, unread, for thirty years, protected by the inertia of girls with thighs as round and rubbery as piglets', filled me with a strange, nostalgic sadness. My weeks in the bush had left me with a nagging uncertainty about where the boundaries of unreality began and ended. This Sergeant

Huggins, now probably sixty or seventy years old, maybe living in a bungalow in Eastbourne, believed, thirty years ago, that the elaborate paperwork, the statements, the evidence, the careful observance of correct procedure had some eternal value. What an assumption to make! Ten years later, independence for Banguniland, small pension for Huggins, the whole system stood on its head, to be observed only in the breach.

Huggins's documents contained the accounts of a few witnesses. They were all different in certain respects. One said that my father had slipped and fallen overboard. Another said that the ferry barge struck a rock, and one of the Land Rovers had been overturned, pulling my father with it. And the third said that my father had been trying to lash something to the deck, the waters being rather high for the time of year, when a securing rope had broken. The report made little mention of the two porters whose deaths were of no account as the expedition had failed to recruit its labour through the correct channels. No contact had been made with the police outpost at Ngame to assist with enquiries. Only the American consulate had been informed. Sergeant Huggins had obviously been subjected to some pressure to support the DC. Patrick Ngwenya's father, the paramount chief, however, had taken a direct hand in the search for the missing traveller. The police department wished to record its appreciation. It was evident what strain the two men had been under, the integrity of their respective services impugned by these over-equipped Yanks. This sort of thing had gone on for over a hundred years all over the Empire, endless writing of reports – this mountain, this Everest of papers, now of no interest to anyone except sneering Marxist historians. What was the big illusion these servants of the Empire were under? I am always surprised by the ease with which people are duped by the big idea. Every decade, every election year, every day, new illusions and new causes – all of them with as little foundation in reality as Sergeant Huggins's belief in the sanctity of administrative procedure – spring up to colonise the popular attention for a while.

*

Bangunes's attention was wandering. It appeared not to have heard of the offensive planned by Patrick Ngwenya and his Liberation Front, indeed the Liberation Front was as significant to the town dwellers as the Vietcong or the Kuomintang. I had been making discreet enquiries since my return to prepare myself for the stories I was going to write. Despite the President-for-Life's recent death, nothing much had changed. The soldiers outside the Presidential Palace stood, bored, and menacing, because they appeared so vacant, their Italian machine guns at ease. The dwindling force of aid workers and relief agency people still bought fresh croissants at the bakery on Ndongo Square (not yet renamed) and my friend, Dr Gullikson, was pursuing the troublesome kwelea bird in faraway places. Monroe, however, sought me out; he pointed out a significant change: the refugees, the dispossessed, had taken over the ninth hole of what had once been the little nine-hole golf course. They were creeping ever closer to the club house. No one had the energy to chase them back down to the damp patch, which was once the ornamental lake. Even Monroe seemed dispirited. Only Frederick Ngwenya, who had slipped back into his cosmopolitan mode, driving around in his old Pontiac, was cheerful. Monroe, however, wanted to know every detail of my trip. After reading the Commissioner's report I realised that Monroe was conducting a one-man mission to keep alive something of the spirit of the old days in Banguniland. He, at least, was anxious to find out about the rebels. He knew that my guide, Frederick Ngwenya, was from the chiefly or royal family, as he called them. It seemed pointless to deny that we had met the rebel leader himself.

'Bag of wind, I'm afraid,' said Monroe. 'Dreadful gas-bag. Too long as a big chief. All talk and no do. Did he mention me?'

'No, but then he had no reason to.'

'Typical. Our family supported his through thick and thin. My father actually got him into London University, though God knows how. He never passed a single exam or test in his life. Lazy bugger, but very charming.'

'Why didn't you tell me about Ngwenya before I set off?'

'My dear fellow, I'm the one who sent Ngwenya to find you. Once you get a mile or two out of Bangunes, you need one of the family or you're lost. Did you find anything out about your father?'

'Nothing that made much sense.'

'What are you going to do now?'

'I haven't decided. I'll do some stories for the papers, and maybe a story on the Liberation Front.'

'Good.'

Monroe tucked in to his curry, which he decorated with dried coconut, slices of banana and little mounds of chutney.

'Jumbo?'

'Yes.'

'What the hell's going on here? What's your interest in all this?'

'In all what?' he asked, chewing suspended for a moment, knife and fork held at the ready.

'Don't mess about, you know what I mean.'

He started to smile; this expelled a small amount of yellowing rice on to his lips as he put down his knife and fork.

'It's goat, you know.'

'I know. You told me last time.'

'I'm bored here. It's like living in a permanent dream, where you're moving but not getting anywhere. Do you know that dream? One of Jung's classics. Something's got to be done; we need the royal family back in business, we need the treasures back. We need investment, publicity and some continuity. I've watched the place – I'm a citizen you know – go steadily to the dogs since independence. But a white man, citizen or not, can't get actively involved in politics against the power-grabbing, self-seeking, murderous deadbeats, who have managed, financed entirely by foreign governments of the left, to get control of this country. They went too far when they sacked the royal capital in the name of equality. The tribespeople really are uneasy.'

'Why doesn't Patrick Ngwenya attack?'

'He's been on the verge of it for three years. I don't know. He feels that the world doesn't appreciate him. And the massacre of the Orefeo has disturbed the balance of life in some way. He's a strange man. Perhaps he prefers his present position. Anyway, nobody in town believes he's got the will to take Bangunes. What's happened, really, is a kind of division: he has the countryside and the fat bellies have Bangunes. Present company excepted. It's almost an unspoken arrangement between them.'

'Why me? What am I supposed to do?'

'You,' said Monroe, 'are a "media person", perhaps you can be the torch that sets the whole thing alight.'

'Forget it. You must be desperate to pick on me.'

Monroe looked hurt. He was one of those people who bubble with schemes and self-importance but somehow never get anything done. I've met lots of them. His meddling, his political views, his dislike of contemporary Africa, even his shrewdness were all out of step with the times and with the country he professed to love. Like many white men, he had a vision of Africa as it was before the white man arrived. The way things were going in Banguniland, his ideal might well come to pass without any help from the media or anybody else, for Banguniland was returning to the bush.

The interior was annexing more and more territory, a process replicated by the squatters who even now were picking flying ants off the pock-marked fairway for their dinner, where once mashies and niblicks had swished. Monroe had failed to understand what, I now saw, Patrick Ngwenya had grasped: there was absolutely nothing worth fighting for.

'You think I'm sort of bloody ridiculous old dinosaur, don't you? A woolly mammoth who hasn't cottoned on that the earth's warming up, I suppose.'

'No. Nothing could be further from the truth.'

'I imagine that Patrick told you that your poor father was still alive.'

'Yes.'

'Did you believe him?'

'No. There's obviously some sort of myth grown up around the expedition. That's all there is. It's the folk history.'

I didn't tell him about the old man with the letter from Mrs de Luth. We were eating tinned South African peaches now; outside the sun had left bands of colour in the sky which picked out the bodies of the hundreds of thousands of flying ants, like a dust storm, flying on their Icarus wings to new nesting sites. Behind them scavenged the starving nomads and hungry birds, until the light faded; at last the weak and flickering lamp on the club's veranda, pulsing in mute sympathy with the generator at the back, shut out the darkness with a finality which was not entirely believable.

'I feel like a bloody stiff brandy and soda, don't you?'

'Yes, I do.'

Monroe had nowhere to go in the evenings. Frederick Ngwenya was having a party, but I had declined his invitation, so there we were sitting on the dilapidated veranda in wicker chairs drinking brandy and soda, trying to ignore the noise of hungry children crying hopelessly on the ninth fairway, only a few hundred yards away.

I did not tell Monroe that we had gone to the country of the Orefeo, described by Mrs Luth as

> that blessed valley where craftsmen have wrought works of great beauty, for the ruling family of Banguniland, for centuries. So prized are these, the crown jewels of the Banguni, that the exact location of this valley has long been a closely guarded secret. Only with the blessing of the paramount chief, one-time student of George Washington University, were we able to visit the craftsmen, believed by some to be descendants of a lost tribe of Israel.

What I had heard about the troubles, the genocide, would not satisfy Monroe. He would want the last word. He pretended to know how the Israelis had airlifted the survivors, a state secret in Israel itself. He would dismiss the lost-wax method of casting the jewellery, medallions and figurines. He would have a tedious theory for everything. Also, I had begun to suspect that the fanciful accounts of the Africans were perhaps a sort of code I should endeavour to understand, without Monroe's translation.

*

Mrs de Luth's description of the valley, even allowing for the devastation of the forges and houses of the skilful Orefeo, was highly coloured and the photographs misleading. We crossed the river, the tributary of the Bangunes into which my father had disappeared, by a shallow ford. The water barely reached half way up the wheels, and the rocks which lined the river loomed above us when we reached the middle of the river bed. It was difficult to imagine anyone drowning in this trickle.

The Orefeo valley was blessed with a spring, which had never dried up. The valley floor was lower than the surrounding countryside and had to be approached by a difficult track of loose, sharp stones. The Orefeo had built small towers with these rocks along the track, from which they had been able to watch out for their enemies. Of course, this simple precaution had been useless against the Aérospatiale Alouette helicopters sent in in 1984 by the new President-for-Life. The huts, which were also of stone, were square rather than round. Their roofs had been burned. Soldiers always do this. In Africa many tribes burn a great man's village when he dies and the family moves on, so it had a special significance in the valley. The kilns, forges and important huts were set slightly apart near the famous grove of fig trees, which sadly were not producing their bulbous, sexually charged fruits at this season. The lost-wax method, to tell the truth, looked pretty simple stuff. The moulds that had been used to make the figurines lay in a pile, curious, crude shapes like the cardboard bottles that protect real champagne bottles, with all the detail on the wrong side. There were spent shells everywhere, all sorts of ammunition; it was clear the killing grounds had been just outside the village. The Israelis must have brought a rabbi along with them, for the mass grave was marked by a stone tablet bearing a short inscription in Hebrew. This token of a minor holocaust, miles from anywhere, was deeply moving.

The fig trees were waiting for the return of the Orefeo, spreading uxoriously over the little broken settlement. Only a few dogs remained; it was hard to guess how they had survived the years without their masters. The older dogs approached us cautiously, cringing and nervous. The new generation, which had taken possession of the empty huts, ran for a small hill, turning to growl fiercely. Patrick Ngwenya sent a guide with us, an Orefeo traditionalist, who held some sort of hereditary rank in the royal village and had been spared the massacre as a result. This man crouched in the dust while we looked around; he seemed to be oppressed by the place, to such an extent that he could barely move. I questioned him about the massacre, but I realised that I was asking questions at entirely the wrong level. He dealt in potions, roots and snake skins, not in dates, times, troop movements and numbers of bodies.

'He says there were a lot of people killed. We think about two thousand with another five hundred taken away by the Jews,' said Frederick.

I could not make out what Frederick thought about this dreadful place. I took a few pictures, trying to recreate the valley as depicted by Mrs de Luth, a bustling place of craftsmen. She had stood – Snow White with the industrious dwarves – in front of a kiln, holding a priceless gold chameleon, just as she had once held a piece of glass fused to a piece of pottery by the heat of Hiroshima; our guide did not understand the technicalities of casting in bronze and gold, but he had been involved with the choice of subject matter; it was his job to see that the chiefs and the nation were supplied with all the necessary articles to prevent famine, encourage new crops, keep the male birth rate up and so on, and it was true that since the Orefeo had been massacred, Banguniland had hardly seen a drop of rain and its troubles were not so much piling up as avalanching down. The connection was too obvious to need elaboration. He shook his head sadly, as he crouched in the shade of the giant fig grove. Actually, it seemed that many of the country's troubles had their origins a few years back, in the time of the previous chief, who had allowed some of the treasures to be sold. Some had been stolen by white men. The waters from the mountains had been slowing down ever since, he added. I didn't know what to say to reassure him. For Frederick, who had a very sunny personality, the secret of the restoration of his country's fortunes was straightforward. The Liberation Front must march on Bangunes itself. This would be the only symbolism required to bring back the rains and restore the pastures. He was respectful of the old Orefeo, but it was a conditional respect.

Also, I had not told Monroe of our trip because I was sure he would repeat the allegation that the expedition had stolen the treasures of the Orefeo; nobody else appeared to believe it. I was planning to consult what I guessed were a limited number of experts on African bronze and gold work and see where the stuff had got to. Monroe wanted me to believe there was some connection between my father's death and this crime. The most important article of the royal regalia to have disappeared was an ornate footstool, made in the shape of a spider, which the paramount chief had traditionally employed to deliver judgment. Perhaps the erratic and vacillating Patrick could become more consistent by resting his feet on the golden stool.

The relationship between the vanished Orefeo and the rulers of Banguniland, it seemed to me, had been far more ambiguous than Mrs de Luth had made out. By her account they were royal jewellers, the Garrards or Fabergé of the interior; everything was busy, industrious, fulfilling activity, an African version of a state fair, in return for which a tribute of women and livestock was sent over the hills from time to time. But, I now saw, the relationship was much closer to that of a mediaeval king and his archbishop, or King Arthur and Merlin. The Orefeo regarded themselves, in the airy matter of the mind, as superior, possessors not merely of manual skills, but of the intuition, the clairvoyance and the shamanic abilities that artists claim for themselves in all societies. They held the Ngwenya clan in thrall, I guessed, just as much as they were bound to supply the necessary magic articles; their curious hand-me-down Judaism, particularly if it were monotheistic, perhaps made them contemptuous of the multiplicity of spirits, ancestors and places to which their rulers were mortgaged. Perhaps this relationship was like that of the Rothschilds to the French court of the Third Empire.

*

Monroe and I were driven inside eventually by the furious biting insects. Under the portraits of the past presidents and their trophies, we drank a lot more brandy and soda. Then we played billiards. I had only done this once before in the Hill Club in Nuwara Elia in Sri Lanka, watched by a portrait of the Queen, her frosty half-smile perhaps a fair assessment of our skills. Magda was stoned on what she said was the best grass in the world; she always said whatever she was smoking or snorting was the best. She was beautiful, ecstatic, in the gothic billiard room, which was also decorated with trophies, the delicate heads of leopard and deer.

Monroe was good at the game. His aim was excellent despite the seven or eight brandies he had drunk. He gave me lots of advice, but I found it impossible to snick the balls in the required fashion. In Sri Lanka a marker had stood impassively by long into the night watching us fool about; when we went to bed another servant was waiting outside the door to see if there was anything more we required.

'What does one need at four in the morning?' I asked Magda.

'What about some tea?'

'Good idea. Tea for two, bearer.'

After drinking our tea under a lazily rotating fan, we sneaked back to the billiard room and made love on the green baize, watched by the stuffed and impassive heads. I was half expecting the marker to appear at any minute to award points.

*

Eventually Monroe tired of my clumsy efforts.

'We used to have great evenings here. The booze flowed like billyo, but these Swedish chappies prefer carrot juice and tennis. I am the last of the old soaks.'

He stood with his cue tucked under his arm remembering those days sadly.

'I must get to bed,' I said. 'I'm off tomorrow.'

'God willing.'

I left him putting his cue away in the rack in a special holder with his name on it. All the others were empty, although some of the names were still legible.

CHAPTER 9

If he envied me my travels and my different class of anxieties, which I used to believe had an artistic provenance, my brother gave no hint of it. Since those far-off days when he had stared pale-faced and calculating out of the window of our hired car, piloted by my exuberant father towards our new home, he had always given me the impression that he had inspected life's limited possibilities and decided to be rich. If you were not rich, you had simply failed to understand the elementary, even crude, mechanisms of western society. To him, being rich was like knowing how to play the piano or tennis, skills which those who have them naturally take for granted. He worked from home, linked to his wealth by computers in the contemporary fashion. Not even a secretary crossed his threshold. Beyond that threshold his family practised a closeness of the Sicilian order. The two children, a boy and a girl of seven and six, were watchful, like him. They made adults feel frivolous. His house, children, wife and dogs always gave me an opportunity to think about the nature of family life.

So my brother Tim's wealth was not of the visible variety. It was kept downtown, electronically. Although he owned buildings in Manhattan and resorts in Sardinia and even, he once told me, a golf club in Arizona, he had no contact with these things. Owners of real estate no longer had anything to do with their property; this was an outmoded idea belonging to the museum economies of the past. He laughed when I asked if they ever called him to complain about the heating or the colour of the carpets in his properties.

He had no sense of the past at all. To him, like all Americans, the past exists only in terms of comforting mythology. *National Geographic* viewed the past in much the same way: 'Buffalo Bill and the Expanding West; Lincoln, Man of Steel and Velvet; Athens: her Golden Past Still Lights the World.' The past was purchasable in handy sizes.

When I made these sorts of points, he smiled bleakly which reminded me strongly of our mother.

'You know how things are, really,' he said to me.

'What does that mean?'

'You know that what most people do most of the time has nothing to do with history or art or literature.'

'That's just not true. Every thought, every action, every gesture you make, or the kids – why don't they make more noise, by the way? – every single one is merely part of a huge tapestry of belief, of superstition, of art, of religion and of history. Americans are not exempt from participation in history. What you do is a form of arcane ritual, by the way.'

'On a certain theoretical level, OK, you could argue that. But it's the old argument of does the table exist when I leave the room. I mean, do they directly influence our daily life, all those connections with history? Which are easy enough to make, by the way.'

He enjoyed our little discussions. It amused him to find me still preoccupied with things which he regarded as fodder for students. The real things in life were what he had: money, valuable holdings and a close family. At this juncture I had even less of these than I had had before. He was disturbed to hear that I had thrown in the towel in my contest with Magda's lawyers. He had often explained to me the advantages of dragging the whole thing out for as long as possible.

'Why did you do it?'

'In Africa I realised that my feelings towards Magda have been poisoning me. I want a truce on any terms. I can't live in this state of conflict.'

'What you really want is to climb back into the sack with her. I would have thought that history teaches us that conflict is the motive force of life.'

'All right, you win. Your brief analysis of history, which by the way is Marxist, is the final word. I want to tell you about our late father.'

'What did you mean in your letter about him entering the folk memory?'

'The story of the expedition has achieved the status of legend in Banguniland. He was eaten by a crocodile but disgorged on an island without a toothmark. He's a sort of totem now.'

I loved his face, so solemn, so like the little pale child's face which had peered out of the window of the car.

'But they're not saying he's still alive?'

'Some are, some aren't. They don't distinguish as clearly as you or I do between myth and reality, spirit and body. Incidentally, that's probably why Wall Street can't get the repayment of interest from them.'

'Luckily for Wall Street the national debt of Banguniland is about equal to what this lovely state of Connecticut spends on schools for the deaf. Do you take them seriously, the ones who say he's still alive?'

'Lunch is ready,' called Josie, his wife.

'Something very strange happened in Israel. I'll tell you after lunch.'

Josie is a wonderful woman, in her early thirties, the granddaughter of a Portuguese who emigrated to Gloucester in Massachusetts. Josie was in tennis clothes. She played tennis with American concentration and verve, but her body was Southern European, round and soft, her legs just a little too short, each of her fine, dark eyes thatched with an arch of dark hair. I knew exactly what my brother loved in her. She is always intrigued to hear about Magda; the only time they met they got on surprisingly well.

'Come,' she said, 'tell us what you are doing now. I know the children can't wait to hear. They're so proud of their uncle.'

She liked to bring the children into everything; she didn't want them to miss a thing. So I told the story of my trip to Banguniland, watched by the dark, wise children, and I threw in some useful information about the lost-wax method of casting, employed by the late lamented Orefeo. I made it sound like a travelogue.

What I could not tell them *en famille* was what had happened in Israel. That was the reason I had come to spend a weekend in Darien. I had arranged to see Magda, too, in my new, understanding mood. Strangely this state of mind had not worn off in the six weeks I had been back from Banguniland working on the Orefeo and Ngwenya stories for various publications and trying to summon some interest in a documentary. This research led me to Israel to see the surviving Orefeo and this is what I had to tell my brother.

I arrived in Tel Aviv ('Israel: Land of Promise') with all the necessary permits and introductions arranged for me by the cultural attaché of the Israeli Embassy in London. The lady from the ministry who met me was quick to admit that the Orefeo were not assimilating. She herself did not regard them as Jews. She believed they were a Nilotic people with vestiges of an earlier, Semitic culture, which she called a 'passenger culture', presumably something like the cargo cults of Borneo. They were learning Hebrew and agriculture and they were being encouraged to update their Judaism, although she was not sure they felt the need. There was some hope that they would start producing the wonderful artefacts for which they were famous, but it was feared all the craftsmen and artisans had died in the Holocaust. The survivors had been out in the bush gathering wood and reeds at the time of the attack, and numbered only just over one hundred. Their family tree was being drawn and the oral records preserved. In fact, a whole industry was springing up around them: doctoral theses, comparative religious studies, semiotics, semantics, art history and so on. She believed that this was the way the world was going – vicarious experience, academic Disneyland and so on. She spoke fast, every sentence loaded. In the middle of this circus – she wanted me to know her personal opinion – were a few rather confused Africans, longing for their distant, lost valley.

I told her tentatively what the valley looked like and the desolation I had experienced there. Even a minor holocaust is not an easy subject to discuss with Jews; you don't feel qualified. But she was eager to help me. In that fiercely conspiratorial way of Israelis, she offered to introduce me to a man who knew a great deal about the airlift. The implication was that something funny had gone on. My guide had been born in Israel and had none of the essential Jewishness. I find this one of the ironies of Israel: in a nation of Jews, all the Jewish roles have been allotted.

We arrived at the camp. I have visited quite a few of the camps where the displaced of this world fetch up; psychologically they are wrong, usually prisons or army barracks or derelict parcels of countryside, which only emphasise that their inhabitants are the unwanted wreckage and spillage of the world's conflicts. This one was different. It was more like a progressive school than a refugee camp, with a central administrative block, basketball courts, handicraft workshops (so far unused) and three dormitory buildings, each with its own subtle arrangement of facilities designed to correspond (on anthropological advice) to the complexities of Orefeo society. The food supplies were not simply dished up in a canteen but were provided to individual families with their own stoves. The preparation and serving of food was encumbered with taboos and was still of spiritual importance to these people, said my guide. The staff were brisk and cheerful, but the Orefeo were not responding to this reasonable establishment as well as could be hoped. I saw a classroom where girls were learning Hebrew. In a playground three boys were kicking a football, wearing yarmulks and tracksuits, and the noise of the ball clattering hollowly on the playground had an institutional sound.

As a special privilege I was allowed to tour the private quarters. It was there that a young man came up to me and my guide. He spoke halting Hebrew.

'He says he knows your father.'

She was smiling, but I was choking.

'Stay well,' I said to him in Banguni.

He extended one hand, clasping it by the wrist with the other.

'Come', said my guide, 'I want you to see the workshops and kilns.'

The young man would not let go of my hand. He held it lightly but insistently, his long, dry fingers clasping mine. He was of a lighter colour than the Banguni, more wiry, more Ethiopian or Egyptian in appearance. He was wearing a thick parka against the cold of a January morning, and a woolly hat, so that he looked like Sherpa Tenzing in SIEGE AND ASSAULT, THE CONQUEST OF THE SUMMIT. He spoke to me directly in Banguni, but I could not understand. He tried Hebrew again. Still he held my hand.

'He wants to look at your legs.'

She was laughing now, but I felt extremely uneasy.

'Why does he want to look at my legs?'

'Because he says your father has beautiful legs and he is sure you have them too. Do you?' she asked, skittishly.

'Ask him where my father is now,' I said sharply.

It was an age before she resolved the difficulties of comprehension and translation. All that time the Orefeo was holding my hand; as children in South Africa we used to catch chameleons, and they had the same gentle grasp. I was thinking during those seconds, or minutes, of Mrs de Luth and her 'Land of Infinite Promise'. She was standing in the valley of the Orefeo wearing her beekeeper's veil and topcoat, holding a golden brooch, only a few days before losing my father. What did she know about all this? Why had I never thought of asking in Washington or writing to her family? Even in her busy lifetime a colleague drowning must have made a lasting impression.

The guide turned to me.

'He says your father was left behind in a secret place in the mountains, where the Orefeo collected plants and medicines.'

'What does he mean by "left behind"?'

There was another wait. I was shaky, like someone who has

just got out of bed after a long illness.

'He says the Orefeo had a secret place. I can't understand what he's saying really. But we never went there. By we, I mean the Israelis.'

She was disturbed by this conversation. To her it was surreal. To me it was all too real.

I told all this to my brother after lunch. He never interrupted, but kept his pale, intense face turned towards me throughout.

CHAPTER 10

'How did this happen?' asked the emergency doctor. He was Puerto Rican.

'I was mugged.'

'Punks? Black kids?'

'No, I can't say, it happened so quick.'

'You a Brit?'

'No, not really.'

'You've got a pretty funny accent.'

'I'm finding it hard to talk. Can you get the blood stopped?'

'It's stopping. Listen, this is nothing, you should see what comes in here most nights.'

'I can imagine.'

'Just lie still. I'll get someone to cement these teeth back in. The dentist don't like being called out this late.'

'Can they be fixed in?'

'Sure, they'll fall out again in ten years' time but who knows what ten years' time holds for any of us? You just lie still now.'

He shut the rubberised curtain on my cubicle. My teeth were loose, almost dropping out, holding on only by a small skein of gum. I wished I had been mugged.

Magda had hit me; her ring – a huge silver thing given to her by her lover – had struck me in the mouth, dislodging two teeth. In the next cubicle they were struggling noisily to remove the handle of a hairbrush from a complaining patient's rectum. They probably equated my problem with his. Oh Jesus. I felt a terrible sense of loss; and the loss of Magda, sliding off into irrationality, was worse than the loss of my teeth.

My childhood friend Skep back in South Africa came from a family where the badge of maturity was to lose the front teeth. His sisters lost theirs at puberty, usually as the result of drunken blows; it was thought to be inevitable and sexually inviting. Their smiles were broken and debased: they lost their innocence by having their teeth smashed out, but they gained immediate acceptance in the mysterious sexual realm. The loss of innocence represented by the reluctant hairbrush next door was a philosophical problem I was not fit to ponder.

The blood had stopped flowing. It was staunched with large pads of medical dressing inside my mouth. When the dentist arrived I was talking like Marlon Brando in *The Godfather*, with a mouth full of wadding. He was a weary man, the way New Yorkers are, elderly it seemed to me for a job like this; perhaps his record was not good.

'OK, I'll clean your mouth out and cement your teeth. Go see an orthodontist as soon as possible.'

While cleaning out my mouth he found a small diamond in the wadding. He looked at the notes and at the diamond.

'Nice class of mugger. Half a carat. It probably belongs to the state of New York but you better keep it as evidence.'

I put the diamond in my wallet.

'You're a lucky guy, they never took your things neither. Hold still, hold that tooth for me. OK. Done. It will be OK for a while but don't leave it longer than two days. OK?'

'Thanks, doctor.'

'That's OK. Rinse your mouth out with this four times a day, OK?'

'OK, thanks.'

'You can go now.'

I had nowhere to sleep except in the car, a sports Toyota, whose seats reclined to the horizontal. I slept in fits and starts woken finally by the garbage truck coming to remove the detritus of human misery from the hospital's dumpers at the other end of the car park. Surprisingly I felt cheerful. Later I mailed the diamond to Magda with a note: 'A diamond may be forever, but teeth come and go.' There was something about New York which invested me, as it had my father, with a new but not altogether convincing persona. It was as though the essential improbability of this place, the braggadoccio, the sheer bravura of it all, made the inhabitants believe they were in showbusiness, smiling through their tears, always ready with a worldly quip, always able to see the tragic and comic aspects of life inescapably entwined.

Washington DC was different. There was a spirit of graduate-school earnestness here. I knew why it had impressed my father: the broad streets, the monuments, the museums, the scientific, social and political institutions, and the imposing, elegant White House all spoke clearly of enlightenment and purpose. The National Geographic Society was itself a monument to the notion of purpose. In the courtyard of the new building was a beautiful, simple fountain of granite slabs. My father had met Cousteau and the others in the old building. I asked to see the N. C. Wyeth murals which had so captivated him. The old building had shrunk, dwarfed by the new, but I could imagine my father climbing the stairway, past these vast, meticulous paintings, so clean and colourful, so uncluttered by doubt, on his way to meet his new patrons and his new travelling companion, Mrs de Luth. There, under the pictures of Admiral Byrd and his dog Igloo (which has the Admiral's leg in an amatory embrace), Alexander Graham Bell and the other luminaries, he had found himself at last in the enchanted world for which he had longed. Had he and Mrs de Luth fallen into conversation immediately? Had he sought her out, standing as tall as a sequoia above her fellow geographers? Had he promised her his insight into the mysteries of the African interior? Had he wooed her with his talk of the psychic powers of baboons, or the uncompromising digestive abilities of the white ant, whose soul was a paradigm of the human condition (in its hopeful aspects)?

The year they had met here the Society had published photographs from the deepest known spot in the oceans, the

Romanche Trench. Darkness was being dispelled. Where better to travel than the dark continent to see a land emerging from the mystery and the shackles of its recent past, into a new era of hope? The assumptions for this transformation were based on the evidence of the recent past in America.

Magda had fallen to her knees in the elevator, undone my trousers and taken my quickly engorged cock into her mouth. We rode up to the fifteenth floor and stayed there in our depraved, centaur position until someone summoned the lift. I was just able to punch the stop button before disaster and orgasm could overtake us. We climbed out of the elevator which had stopped four feet or so short of the sixth floor. I was laughing; this was the vintage Magda for whom I had longed in the night. Her body was racked, too. I could see only her back and the top of her head. As I led her down to the fifth floor, my member preceding us, and pulled her into her doorway, I at last saw her face. She was sobbing. Her eyes were wet with tears and smeared mascara, her nipples were raised and angry with a pink rash spreading up to her throat.

'Magda. Jesus, Magda.'

'You fucker, you shit, you fucking tosser.'

She hit me.

It did not hurt but I could feel my teeth spring loose, flipping down flat like ducks in a shooting gallery. As I held on to my face she slammed the door and locked it from the inside. I could hear her harsh breathing through the door. The blood ran down and through my stubby fingers. I called the abused elevator – which had almost seen my semen and was seeing an even more vital fluid, my blood – and slipped out past the intuitive porter, who had been reluctant to let me in, to find a hospital. It would be fatal to ask a policeman, so I drove around until I came by chance to the hospital on 97th.

And that was why I was knocking on the door of Mrs de Luth's daughter Martha's house with a mouthful of dental cement crudely applied to my deracinated teeth. Magda, I guessed, was a short step from an institution. Only her beauty and her sexuality would give her some protection; protection supplied by older men who would, for a while, pay any price to keep a hold on her tantalising body, in the way that older men have always done. How our language fails us in the matter of sex: the very words are juvenile or inhibited or prurient. Magda's sexuality was so potent because it was crazy and depraved and young and innocent. I thought then that I would never see her again; she had come unglued.

'Hello, welcome, do come in.'

'Thank you.'

So here we were, the offspring of the protagonists of that far-off expedition to Banguniland. Martha de Luth Reames was tall like her mother and surprisingly old, perhaps almost fifty.

'I'm so pleased to have this opportunity to talk with you. Naturally we knew something about this accident but my mother never discussed it. It upset her deeply.'

She was her mother's daughter, with blue, washed-out eyes and fair hair turning grey, severely tied back.

'Tea? Earl Grey or Assam?'

'Yes please, Earl Grey would be fine.'

Perhaps I could recreate some of the intimacy between our parents. She went to prepare the tea.

Her living room looked out on to a paved courtyard. It was an old house, one of the modest mansions of early Georgetown above the canal, with the comfortable, domestic, English detail carefully restored. In the garden stood a giant head, glowering with Melanesian contempt from among the hostas.

'May I ask you if your mother ever wrote anything privately about the accident?'

'Nothing that I know of. Not about the accident itself. It upset her greatly, as I said.'

'What about the treasures of the Orefeo?'

'Are they still missing?'

'Yes.'

'Well, that was nothing to do with the expedition, as far as I know.'

'No, but it has been said that your mother and my father were trying to acquire them.'

'Acquire them? For what reason?'

She looked at me sternly, as if she had caught a sudden odour of impropriety.

'Different times, different mores,' I said. 'They probably wanted to put them in a museum.'

'I don't think my mother would have done that. She was a great believer in the importance of local custom and tradition. In fact in her later years she began to have serious doubts about the whole nature of her earlier work. Meddling, she called it meddling.'

'Nobody is immune to the prevailing fashions. My father, your mother, me, you. For example, where did that head out there come from?'

'It's nothing special. It's from New Caledonia and saved by my mother from a sea-captain's house that was being demolished.'

'Has she left some papers?'

'Yes. Mountains. And a sort of rambling diary or notebook. You could look through that and her files and letters, if you like.'

'I would like to. Thank you. You don't know why she failed to co-operate with the official inquest in Banguniland?'

'Who says she wouldn't?'

'The police reports in Bangunes, for one.'

As she looked at me coldly, I could see clearly what had been formidable in her mother, in the long and composed pause and the harsh blue eyes.

'My husband is a federal judge and he said something to me the other night, he said that in all his thirty years in the law he has never once heard the whole story.'

'What did he mean by that?'

'What I think he meant,' she said, 'is that the truth is more often than not too complex for the legal process.'

'I am not sure what you are getting at. Are you saying that there are different truths and interpretations of all facts and phenomena? If you are, that's not news. But if you're saying that maybe your mother knew something she didn't want to tell, then that to me is simply a fact which we could easily discuss.'

'I'm not really saying either one. What I mean is that the police in Banguniland and their reports thirty years ago should not necessarily be taken too seriously.'

'They say she didn't turn up for the inquest. Nor did she come to my father's memorial service. I can vouch for that.'

She looked at me coolly for a few moments before deciding to speak.

'She was in love with your father. I think it's as simple as that. It was too painful for her. Also her mental condition was not that good. God, it sounds crazy after all these years. In my opinion the treasures don't come into it. That's not what she was trying to hide. I remember him, you know.'

'Who?' I asked.

'Your father. He came to this house once or twice before they set off. I was at the Cathedral School then. I haven't wandered too far.'

She said it with a parched smile which caused her handsome face to crack into little drought lines. I felt that somehow we could skip the preliminaries; we were old acquaintances because of our parents.

'Do you travel?'

'Only in the conventional fashion. When I was a teenager I resented my mother. It seemed to me really selfish. She was the only mother in Georgetown who vanished for months at a time, and my father was in Europe in the army. All those great travellers were egotists. The whole notion of individuals travelling and reporting back their experiences is phoney. My mother, after her breakdown, came to realise this. There are books, classics of travel writing, based on a two or three weeks' trip. That country, these people, whatever you like, are merely grist to the ego mill. My mother came to think that her travel writing had contributed to a kind of cheapening of the American consciousness, if that's not too grand. The way that Frost did for poetry.'

'My father loved Frost. He regarded him as the essence of America.'

'So did a hundred million people, including John F. Kennedy,' she said tolerantly.

The garden outside was still, yet a few leaves floated down from somewhere. I like town gardens with their concentration and distillation. I tried to assess her daughter in the light of the information that Mrs de Luth had been in love with my mercurial father. Our age difference was probably about the same as our parents'. Where Mrs de Luth had, on the evidence, a hearty, intrepid approach to life – an Amelia Earhart or Julia Margaret Cameron – her daughter was an example of the well-informed and intelligent Washington wife, with the caution and discretion born of living in a one-industry town. I wondered if her passions ran as deep as her mother's, or Magda's for that matter. The generosity and the hatred in love are the motive forces behind so much folly. God knows what Mrs de Luth had suffered out there in the bush, in the twilight of her distinguished career, in love with my will-o'-the-wisp father, twelve or fifteen years younger than she. Her daughter, for all her careful poise, had suffered too. Our lives do not prepare us for tragedy and disillusionment, and yet you see as you grow up pain etching itself onto the faces of your friends, revealed sometimes by a blankness of expression or uncontrollable narrowing of the eyes or by little gestures of irritation which speak of innocence lost.

'She never got over it. She went crazy to all intents and purposes. A few months later she went on a trip to Indonesia, her last trip, and never left her hotel room in Djakarta, not for six weeks. She used to go round to *National Geographic* and cause disturbances. Really in retrospect it was quite funny, accusing the editor of having sex with stone-age Indian girls in the Amazon jungle and saying that the Society was building a nuclear reactor in the Congo. She accused Cousteau of being a collaborator during the war. A U-Boat commander.'

'Was he?'

She smiled, but it was not a warm smile. I had often wondered where Cousteau acquired his underwater expertise. To me it sounded as if her mother had suffered from Alzheimer's

Dementia; perhaps her daughter worried in case it was hereditary, like pale legs.

'My husband will be home soon. Will you stay for dinner? Do you like Maryland Crab Cakes?'

'I'm sure I do. Thank you.'

'Come, I'll show you the files.'

Looking through someone's personal files is a licence to invest a private life with imaginary qualities. It is an excuse to wander around the highways and back alleys of that life. And it is an opportunity to make comparisons. Mrs de Luth saw her life as a journey. Her letters and notes were full not only of her expeditions and travels, but also of the metaphors and symbols of travel. The sun was going down, she was making good mileage, the day was drawing to a close; there were safe havens or rough seas ahead, as well as good landings and calm waters. Shipmates, travelling companions, provisions, horizons, brigands, stages, camps, springs, porters, mirages and baggage – emotional and intellectual – littered her personal correspondence. This was in contrast to her actual journeys, which she saw in material terms. Her notes revealed a woman obsessed by trivial organisational detail, but with a parallel stratum of high intent and principle which seemed to be entirely artificial and unconvincing. She left carbons and those early, smudgy photocopies of her most important papers, and she had started a rambling notebook or diary in her later years to contain her cosmic conclusions. There were higher things in life, to which she aspired. In that way she and my father were alike, although his forte was identifying and recycling the big idea, rather than subscribing to it.

All this paper – her letters, essays, account books and notebooks – was neatly stored in wooden filing cabinets. There was a treasure trove here, not, as intended, of serious, highminded endeavour, but of Americana of the period of Rockwell, *Saturday Evening Post*, McCarthy and so on, and the concomitant optimistic, earnest, middlebrow theorising.

I could not find any letters to my father but it was clear from letters to friends that she set a lot of store by their expedition. She referred to it as a 'personal voyage of discovery'. 'I think we may be entering on a new, more subtle understanding of man and nature.' 'Mr Curtiz, my companion on this journey, has some interesting theories about Africa which have given me a new perspective.' 'Mr Curtiz believes that the heart, the core, of Africa is not yet understood. It is a region where perhaps some of the eternal verities may still be, in a non-scientific sense, waiting for discovery, in the way that the Leakeys have done in a scientific sense. I have this feeling that the origins of the species, the spiritual origins if you will, have been given insufficient attention. Mr Curtiz thinks that the key to this is in magic and myth, and their expression through art.' 'Mr Curtiz says that the reliance on the conscious mind has obscured a great deal of the animal intelligence which exists in humans.'

Mr Curtiz, it now transpired, was as free with his off-the-cuff theories about the species as he had been with his theories about agriculture.

'Will you come down for a drink? My husband is on his way home.'

'Thanks. This is fascinating. Have you read through your mother's stuff?'

'No. It's been looked at by researchers writing theses on *National Geographic*, but somehow I've avoided it. Do you think that's excusable?'

'Very.'

She smiled through the door, her smile autumnal, but gentle.

'You must come back tomorrow. Spend the whole day. Now, I'll fix you a drink.'

Her husband had a massive face with fine, broad features; he had the look about him of an ex-football player (which indeed he was) and the tolerant and calculating air of a man who had seen the essential crudeness of the workings of politics and government and wished to protect them from closer inspection. He was a genial man with a fund of political stories, a man at ease with middle age, success and Washington. They had no children and had never adopted any. The evidence of the eyes would suggest that he lacked nothing in potency and fertility, like a prize bull, but sperm counts obey their own laws. Magda and I had no children either, although she had had two abortions, and now we would never be able to find out if her brother's prognosis was correct. What happens to us, the childless ones? Have we broken our link with humanity, broken the golden cord like the lifeline that supported Major Edward White on Gemini 4?

'What happened to your mouth?' the judge asked me.

'I was mugged in New York.'

'Black kids?' he asked without malice.

'No. One white kid,' I said, more or less truthfully.

The lamps beside the bed in my hotel were chunky, brass-finished cubes and spheres; I was unable to turn them on without activating the television. The television seemed to be running at double speed, so that the news and the commercials fused together in a stream of inconsequence. Above the bed were prints of birds, after John James Audobon. The elevator, just down the hall, was bumping and grinding with drunken men going to bed or sneaking down to the bar, all of them, I guessed, thinking of sex – that strange eruption of love. Magda and I had been doing it in the contemporary way, in an elevator – me blithely, innocently happy, she convulsed with pain and loathing. The insensitivity of my behaviour was too painful to bear and the mystery of hers quite incomprehensible.

My mouth hurt. The cement pushed my top lip out slightly, so that in profile I imagined that I looked like a monkfish. The sense of loss was so sharp that I felt my lungs tighten involuntarily. I could understand Mrs de Luth's feelings too. It was no mystery to me that she should have gone mad for love, even on account of someone as insubstantial as my father. Love and madness are both the denial of limits.

In Mrs de Luth's study I had seen a picture taken in 1948 of Admiral Nimitz receiving the Society's medal for leaders of expeditions of merit. The Society, for all its rationality, liked the symbolism of medals. Standing with the trustees was Mrs de Luth herself, topped off by a small white cloche hat, looking like

Kilimanjaro under snow. On board the USS *Missouri*, my father too had admired Nimitz. He had rated him more highly than General MacArthur. I could see my father's legs gleaming in the oriental light of Tokyo Bay; I could see the frock-coated Japanese bent double, bowing after signing the surrender and before going home to commit hara-kiri. And then I could see Magda bowing over my cock, and feel again the shame of my gross misunderstanding of the situation. How could two people be engaged in something so intimate and be so completely at odds?

Magic, myth and their expression in art: these were the secret forces, so my father had said. Maybe he had something there. I had never believed in the magic of love, yet in losing it, in seeing its disintegration before my eyes, I had come to see that the irrational impulses are strangely powerful. Uncle Sam's scientists may well have miniaturised the turkey and tamed the atom, but they would never pasteurise the rich and turbulent blood pumped by the human heart. Poor Mrs de Luth, who had devoted her life to rationality, had discovered its incompleteness to her cost.

As I lay on my bed I could feel the undertow of this other world, like a man who has waded into a river suddenly becoming aware of the strength of the current tugging at his legs, making the next steps dangerous. It seemed to me, alive to the pull of magic, that my old dad could well be living in the remote mountains of Banguniland. Anything is imaginable, once you are aware of how little is comprehensible.

Under the unblinking, avian gaze (birds have cruel eyes) of the ptarmigan and whooping crane, I slept at last.

CHAPTER 11

Our plane landed only because the weight of the atmospheric pressure and the inertia of the water in the skies wrestled it to the ground, where it skidded and skated along the runway rudderless until it came to rest, by complete chance, near the small terminal building, but slewed round so that the exit door was facing away from the building. Our sudden arrival on such an afternoon as this from nowhere, like the Wendy bird in Peter Pan, meant that the airport was closed. We waited in the plane for an hour until an unhappy official – his uniform unbuttoned, his shoes muddy – arrived with the keys to the customs hall.

Bangunes was lashed by rain. This awkwardly packaged delivery, this unexpected gift from the heavens, this unfamiliar – well – wetness was threatening to turn the plains into a sea of muddy turbulence, in which large objects like cattle and cows would have no more significance than the barley in a cock-a-leekie, merely the chewy bits in a huge natural minestrone. People were drowned, villages were swept away, topsoil was lost in megatons. By the time we had arrived in town it was clear that the force of the rain had already been blunted on a signal from the atmosphere. God knows, after years of drought Banguniland was wet enough; from the air it had looked, as we swooped alarmingly low in search of the airport, like a vast brown lake. Not even wet-weather experts like the Swedes knew what to do with the malodorous mulligatawny which engulfed Bangunes. Once-thin cattle, now alarmingly bloated, floated serenely away across the airport road.

The Bangunes River had risen up and slopped all over the dining room of Brannigan's Hotel. Only the neo-gothic Anglican church looked completely at home in the downpour, running like some curious man-made cascade as handgrenades of water burst and bounced off its rough-hewn stone walls and red tin roof, and gushed onto the unwilling earth below. I dared not think what had happened to the nomads living at the bottom of the ninth hole.

Yet it seemed to be a good augury for the new President's rule. President Ngwenya was now installed in the Presidential Palace, his brother Frederick, my guide to the interior, his Chief Minister. I played a small part in the handover: a *Newsweek* journalist at my instigation had spent a week with the rebels and had written them up very favourably. This publicity acted as a spur to the Liberation Front and a confirmation to the government of Bangunes that their number had come up. They had left town taking as much as they could from the National Bank, which mercifully was very little, the bank having been unable to pay even the reduced interest on its loans for many years. Like all institutions in Banguniland, the bank existed only as a symbol of another life, a Platonic form, quite independent of the crushing reality. In this way people have always sought to comfort themselves. The President had invited me to dinner; there were things playing upon his mind which he wished to discuss. It seemed that the future of his country was linked to the missing treasures, and of course the treasures to my missing father. Perhaps President Ngwenya saw me as a cultural ambassador for his country, a sort of Melina Mercouri in pursuit of the Elgin Marbles. Personally I believe that the Greeks should have been very grateful to Lord Elgin, and happy to leave the marbles in the British Museum. However, the Orefeo treasures had more than mere nationalistic value: they were part and parcel of the notion of kingship, and President Ngwenya needed them to restore a wholeness to his country, wholeness of a particularly African kind, an easiness with circumstance, something that had been missing for many years in Banguniland. Without the treasures the monarchy was hollow; he would simply be a pretender if he tried to restore himself to that role without the instruments of magic.

The Presidential Palace, like many other things in Banguniland, had suffered changes in form without much change in substance. As the governor's residence it was, in Mrs de Luth's words,

> a vast, rambling, colonial, classic building, reminding the author irresistibly of Monticello, the creation of Thomas Jefferson, architect of houses and freedom.

The lawns in front of the Palace were floodlit, with small antelope standing on the higher ground away from the floods which had submerged the gardens. There was a smell hanging over Bangunes, the smell of the duck pond. Magda had once accused me of having a mind like the bottom of a duck pond, an accusation not unconnected with the profundity of her own sexual imagination. The parchment dryness, the twig-snap aridity of the atmosphere, the cow dung and woodsmoke aroma had all gone in favour of this rotting, stinking sweetness which hung over everything – even the Presidential Palace – like the mustard gas of World War One. The gardens were dotted with guardhouses and machine-gun posts. In open doors through the weakening rain, I could see the Presidential guard loitering in these shelters. They were the same people I had met out in the bush, newly upgraded. Under the huge portico of white pillars supporting a vast classical pediment, my car stopped. A servant in bare feet carried me on his back through a small lake to the front door, which caused the President's aides much amusement.

'A horse, a horse, my kingdom for a horse,' called out Frederick Ngwenya.

What a transformation! He was wearing a pin-striped suit, gold watch and crocodile shoes. His tie, of the most tasteful and rich silk, blossomed under his finely boned face. He seized my shoulders and embraced me.

'Welcome, my friend. Welcome.'

The servant, who had not fully released me from my piggyback, was briefly caught up in our embrace until he let my legs fall.

'The President has been looking forward to seeing you again.'

'How is he?'

'He's in terrific form – come in, come in. You've met most of these rascals.'

The huge hallway, with its black-and-white marble floor and a vast portrait of the President, was peopled by the former guerrillas, all besuited now, standing in two neat rows, only slightly bemused by the splendour and comfort of metropolitan life after years in the unforgiving bush. I shook their hands and stood as bidden next to Frederick. A trumpet sounded hoarsely and we all stiffened as enormous doors opened. Patrick Ngwenya, President of Banguniland, came through the doorway, shoulders clad loosely in a cape of leopard skin, and in one hand the thin white stick he had carried in the bush. He was a magnificent sight.

He embraced me.

'Let's have a drink, fellows,' he said loudly.

As his men relaxed their unnatural rigidity, servants appeared among us with trays of champagne, whisky and beer.

Patrick took me by the arm.

'What do you think of our weather?' he asked slyly.

'You don't do anything by halves, do you?'

He laughed. He was pleased to be associated with the rains.

'Now we've got to find your father,' he said.

'Are they connected, the two things?'

'Probably.'

Patrick Ngwenya moved easily among his followers, his hand guiding me occasionally. There were no women at all. Somewhere they were carrying on the bush life, the life of Africa, aided now by Magimixes and gas stoves connected to unpredictable bottles of butane, but they were still the mooring to which the vast families tied up, the calm centre of African life, the low undercurrent of reality, while their menfolk thrust themselves into the world of international finance and politics like country girls in a whorehouse, the newness and glamour of it outweighing the risks of pox, boredom and flaccid old men with absurd fantasies.

Dinner was served. I sat next to the President himself. The room was so big it would have made a respectable railway station concourse for Banguniland. The first wave of waiters brought us menus which bore no relation to what the second wave produced in the way of food. Pumpkin soup turned out to be oxtail, the fillet of beef was transmogrified into roast chicken. Nonetheless, under Patrick Ngwenya's expansive influence we were having a good time. A messenger arrived in the middle of all this and fell on his knees as he handed a note to Frederick who read it and passed it to his brother smiling. The messenger crawled towards the President expectantly.

'The debt moratorium agreed. We're on our way.'

Frederick Ngwenya, First Minister and Minister of Finance, had pulled off the big coup. They no longer had any debts to pay; in fact, the outside world had simply formalised an arrangement that had existed for years, but it was an important victory for the President in his courtship of international respectability. He made a short speech. The bleary-eyed guerrillas were drunk, drunk on South African wine and the prospects which the international community with all its velvety attraction was proffering them. Soon they would be staying in the best hotels in Europe and attending conferences with simultaneous translation of the inanities of many nations coming through the headsets. Internationalism was being brought out of the fetish hut to be worshipped. All that was needed now were the treasures, true fetish objects.

The rain whipped the windows and the lights failed a few times but our hilarity and happiness were undimmed. In watery Banguniland things had changed; the expectation was that they had changed for the better.

'We have some news for you, my friend,' said the President.

'Yes?'

'We believe we know where your father is.'

'My father. Everybody seems to have a big investment in him now.'

'You are here to find him. We want to find him.'

'What's the reason you want to find him?'

'Personally I believe he knows a lot about the treasures.'

'Why do you think that?'

His large, handsome face was lightly misted with sweat. The rain had produced a tropical closeness in the atmosphere. The President and I were in the library, sitting under a vast book-case of leather-bound British consitutional documents, last optimistic gift of the departing governor.

'How do I know that? Because, my friend, because the treasures, the spider footstool and the gold figures and so on are still missing. They have been missing ever since the expedition. Your father is probably the only person who really knows what happened.'

'Sir, if by any remote chance he's still alive after thirty years he's probably completely gaga by now. If he wasn't, he would surely have made himself known to somebody in that time; if he was even slightly lucid, he would have got in touch somehow.'

The President paused weightily before speaking.

'He was imprisoned for at least ten years.'

'*What?*'

'Yes. I'm afraid the Orefeo captured him after his accident and kept him in a hut for ten years.'

'What for, for chrissakes?'

'Difficult to know, with these Orefeo. Strange people the Jews, *les baptisés aux sécateurs*. They had their own ways.'

'So how come the Israelis didn't find him?'

'He lived in a secret place far from the village of the Orefeo; it's not even Banguniland really, but high in the mountains in disputed territory. Not that anyone really wants it,' he added.

'Can I ask you why you didn't go and find him yourself?'

'We were fighting a bush war six hundred miles away; we had no means of getting there.'

'Your father, forgive me for saying so, probably had more to do with the missing treasures than mine, as I hear it.'

'You mustn't listen to what old Monroe says, my friend. He's a good-hearted fellow but he's living in Rider Haggard's world.'

We had all slid into Rider Haggard's world, it seemed to me, a world of lost treasures, African kings, distant, magical countries and unreliable guides.

Ngwenya's personality and temperament leant towards the ephemeral. This is an alarming trait in political leaders; above all they need to be figures of substance and backbone, different from those of us who do not aspire to personify the hopes and dreams of others. I was sure that his account of my father's supposed imprisonment was simply another rabbit pulled out of a hat to keep me interested. His real cause I could only guess at. Why had he not told me this before? He seemed to be dangerously at odds with himself: on the one hand, he wanted to be seen as a liberal and cosmopolitan leader and, on the other, he was preoccupied with the myths and symbolism of his defunct kingdom. And yet Lévi-Strauss had written, 'I cannot accept the idea that myths might contain gratuitous and meaningless themes . . .' The persistence of the themes and universality of the preoccupations were, ironically, features of the derided Haggard's own writing. What did Ngwenya fear by the loss of the sacred regalia? Did he fear to enter the modern world, what Levi-Strauss called the 'hot societies' without the fallback of the old mumbo-jumbo? That, perhaps, was where his predecessors had gone wrong: they had plunged into this new world, like swimmers who had neglected to fill the swimming pool, or sky divers who had forgotten to pack the parachute. Suppose the old world, 'the cold society', had a certain stubborn value; suppose the revolution flopped badly; Ngwenya wanted to be holding a full hand of cards. My departed father was to be reanimated to help the cause. By looking for him, by publicising the events of thirty years ago, I was at the very least going to flush out the missing treasures. But what if these treasures did not exist; what if they were simply a myth too, like the myth of the white man with the shiny legs?

The President offered me an air force plane and some other unspecified transport, but my brother's money had already secured me a plane to be flown by a pilot friend of Doctor Gullikson. He was normally engaged by UNESCO to spray noxious insects and bomb the kwelea bird in various dangerous parts of the world and was still alive, so I declined the President's offer with as much tact as possible.

My interview was over. We joined the happy gathering outside on the back veranda with its huge classical pillars, watching the rain fall; it was insistent yet softer, dousing the intermittently floodlit gardens and the miserable, huddled antelope with the superfluity which would produce a new era of abundance and ease for Banguniland; or perhaps an era of milk and honey, to borrow Mrs de Luth's words. She had seen rain too, a commodity which had gone missing along with my father. It occurred to me, as we stood holding our glasses of brandy and peering benevolently across the gardens, that perhaps the secret of rain-making had been lost with my father's plunge into the swollen Bangunes River. Certainly no serious rain had fallen in the years which had elapsed.

The ex-guerrillas liked the rain. Their President, the Chief, toasted himself in their approval. It was easy to believe that things were going to be all right, standing there half pissed with the rains spattering down on saturated Banguniland. Banguniland was like a sponge or a loofah which can hold no more water. Its underground wells were full, its feeble plant life was rotting, its topsoil had washed out to sea, its scrawny animals had drowned, but after years of drought, these were merely details.

Monroe was waiting for me, beer in hand, when one of the Presidential limousines drove me home to Dr Gullikson's. In his other hand was an elephant gun. He was drunk, his broad, damp face brick red, a far cry from the prison pallor of our first meeting, and his khaki shorts and shirt were soaked. Suddenly, he raised the elephant gun and fired. A clay figure, which in a moment of recall I believed to have been holding a spear, disintegrated, in fact virtually dematerialised. The noise filled the room to bursting point; so much so that it seemed the windows and the walls might crumble with the shock, as in old newsreels of the war where buildings in Berlin and Leningrad implode gracefully and quietly. By contrast it seemed that a stick of dynamite had gone off here.

Monroe's beer was unspilt.

'How was dinner with President fucking Ngwenya?' he asked pleasantly.

'There's a hole in the wall,' I said pointing as the smoke cleared to an aperture about the size of a soup plate.

'Jerry-built, these houses. Utter crap.'

My ears were teeming with sound and there was a strong smell of gunpowder. Monroe was smiling.

'What's the food like down there now? Still the old rubber chicken and anonymous root vegetables?'

'Is this a form of art criticism?' I asked, gesturing towards the shards of clay and splinters of sideboard.

'My father paid for his fucking education, now it's goodbye Jumbo, the fat colonial. Now that he's back on top of the dung heap, I'm an embarrassment.'

'Don't shoot that gun off again, the wall might collapse completely.'

The servant arrived, the sanguine Suleiman, and gave Monroe another beer before looking sadly at the hole in the wall. He made a clicking, rasping sound like a cricket tuning up and stared at Monroe reproachfully for a few moments. Monroe was calmed by Suleiman's presence.

'Get someone to fix it, send me the bill. I hope I didn't scare you,' he said to me.

'Scared is not the right word. Terrified would be closer.'

'I'm an embarrassment all round. Look at this bloody rain. Let's hope it's drowned all the Scandinavians. Silly buggers.'

'Do you often shoot off elephant guns indoors?'

'I once shot a chandelier down in the New Stanley Hotel in

Nairobi. Great days. The governor's daughter was hanging naked from it at the time. We used to throw trifle at each other and so on. Great days. Utterly puerile, but we didn't do much harm. Now I'm an embarrassment.'

I could see that there were circumstances in which he might be thought of as an embarrassment. At the moment he seemed like a drunken maniac. My own mild drunkenness (the South African red was rather heavy) had vanished, like Gullikson's clay figure, with the deafening roar of the elephant gun.

'What exactly are you here for?' I asked.

'I'm here to find out what went on at the dinner to which I was not invited.'

'Nothing much. We drank a lot, chatted and watched the rain come down.'

'You must think I'm a stupid old cunt, mustn't you?'

'For chrissakes, don't shoot that gun off again. I'm fond of Gullikson. I do not want to have to explain to him how his house acquired the Swiss cheese look.'

'What did Patrick smarmy-arse Ngwenya want from you? Wasn't it enough for him that you got our charming little country written up in *Newsweek*?'

'What's gone wrong? Last time we spoke you were keen to see Ngwenya restored and everything shipshape and Bristol fashion with the crown jewels and so on? What's happened?'

'During the last government, if you can call the late, un-lamented President Ndongo and his murdering cronies a government, which personally I find laughable, I was a supporter of Ngwenya and his brother, the Minister of Finance. I supplied them with information, money, contacts and God knows what, and was locked up for my troubles. What have I got for it? Nothing, sweet FA. A dinner in your honour, a man I steered their way, and I'm not even invited. You're bloody lucky I didn't shoot you,' he said sadly.

'Well, I'm very grateful, I must say, for small mercies.'

'I like you, there's something about you. You'll be good for this damn country, I can see that.'

His stomach, swollen by beer, heaved as he began to laugh.

'The Swiss cheese look, that's rich. I can just see Gullikson's serious weasel face, packed with concern for the Third World, when he hears the old bastard Monroe has blown a few holes in his wall.'

'So can I.'

'What did El Presidente say about me?'

'He said that you were living in the world of Rider Haggard.'

'The world of Rider Haggard. That's no bad thing. Anyway, I'm off. I've got to see a man about a dog.'

He stood up, an operation that took some time and effort, and produced a frighteningly loud creaking of bones. He had aged. An old man was skulking uneasily under his ruddy face and strong body. This old person would soon sneak out.

'Do you think my father is alive?' I asked him.

'Is Patrick still going on about that?'

'Yes, he says he's living far away in the mountains on the border somewhere.'

'He says what?'

'On the border, a captive of the Orefeo.'

'Well, I don't know what that would be about.'

'Is it true?'

'Is anything true?'

'You've got very philosophical all of a sudden,' I said.

'When you last came to this country, only a few months ago, we were the driest country in the world. No rain had fallen in any measurable quantity for seven years and we had a murderous moron for a President. If you could see outside . . .'

'I can. Through a hole in the wall.'

'If you could see outside you would see that Baguniland has been transformed into an inland sea. Who would have thought it possible? So I'm not going to argue – if our beloved President and King-to-be says your old man is still alive – that it's impossible. How old would he be?'

'Seventy-six.'

'I'm sixty-three myself. Goodnight. You're a funny fellow. With your fading good looks and inquisitive face.'

'That's a funny thing to say.'

'This is a funny country. Night night.'

He shambled off, an old elephant returning to the bush. The gun was lying on the floor, as awkward as an unexploded land mine. Suleiman plugged the hole in the wall with sacking and swept up the bits before going off to bed himself, but he left the gun. I unloaded it and laid it on the floor again.

What did Monroe mean about my looks and my inquisitive face? There was no question that as a family we were better looking when young. My mother has a photo of me when I was at Oxford, which after all is not so long ago, and I seem impossibly young and confident with a clear gaze. And I am still younger than my father was when he disappeared.

Magda had broken with her art dealer. Now she would begin an inevitable decline; I could see it written. Yet I missed her here in Banguniland, with the rain still arriving from on high and my head hammering painfully with the report of the gun. I missed her because she was my youth which, as old Monroe had pointed out, was slipping through my fingers. My hair had lost its youthful vitality; my eyes no longer gazed confidently like a U-Boat commander's – like Mrs de Luth's – but had narrowed slightly and were sometimes dull for no reason. Magda and I had lived for a while – perhaps a year – fighting, laughing, eating, fucking, with burning intensity. If I had less of the insouciance than I pretended, still I felt blessed as only the young can be. And now it had gone.

Poor Magda, her first step on the first rung of the iron ladder to an institution was complete. Her art dealer had found her in bed with one of his painters and had thrown her out. The painter in question had disowned her completely because he had an exhibition coming up. The expensive lawyers had been throttled back and my fast dwindling supply of money was enjoying a reprieve. I had also signed a big contract with a newspaper to write about the search for my father. In a sense the search had now become the important thing, not my father. Like William Boot, I had to produce a story out of the available material.

In Washington I had spent three days reading Mrs de Luth's letters and diaries. Her last ten years were very painful both for her and her family. Her daughter's claim that she was in love, a folly of her latter years, in a deeply physical fashion, was clear from these papers. I could understand the intensity of it. After all, I had suffered myself. Surely age was no barrier to such feelings. After my father's death she wrote with a mystical bent which the Society found hard to swallow, dedicated as it was to the spread of scientific and geographic knowledge. She quoted, unconsciously perhaps, some of my father's *pensées*. His views on the social behaviour of baboons and termites, as a paradigm of human existence (stolen shamelessly from Eugène Marais), popped up frequently in her writings. The world was dangerously poised for an evolutionary regression. This was a demonstrable fact, like Uncle Sam's diminutive turkeys. Because of the unselective nature of modern life, evolution was teetering in the balance. The world had a wholeness which we must recognise. The Descent of Man might take on a whole new meaning. And so on.

Poor Mrs de Luth, shunned by the Society, pining for my elusive father, died finally in a hospital, which only money distinguished from a nut-house; she was buried quietly with her Hubbard Gold Medal enclosed in her bony hands, having repudiated everything the Society stood for.

CHAPTER 12

My father told me how strange the Japanese were. They had killed themselves after signing the surrender on board the *Missouri*. The Australian official photograph, passed by operational censor, number 19124N, hangs now in my study. What a wonderful photograph. The Japanese are in the foreground wearing tailcoats and extremely small-brimmed caps and high-necked uniforms, rigidly watching. Admiral Chester Nimitz is standing to one side. Behind the table, covered by an elegant, heavy cloth with gold piping, stand Admiral Sir Bruce Fraser, General MacArthur and various other admirals. Next to them, his legs as smooth and waxy as tapers, stands my father. Behind them are a few ranks of Allied officers waiting to sign, and behind them, stacked up in rows like the chorus from *South Pacific*, are photographers, cameramen and sound technicians all in American naval uniform. The officers stand alert and proud, conscious of their duty, the Japanese are stiff as swords, but these newspeople are busy and chaotic, like the ants that are swarming in Bangunes after the rains. The still cameras have little shiny frying pans on them for the flash bulbs. The film cameras have multiple lenses which rotate. Every face is clear. My father looks pleased to be along; his baggy shorts are fastened in a broad band at the waist, his cap (rather free of the scrambled egg that adorns Nimitz's and the British admirals') at a rakish angle. How strange to think that soon after this photograph, Chester Nimitz should have met Mrs de Luth, while my father went back to South Africa and his farming journal. General MacArthur is hogging the limelight, standing at a bank of microphones, a sort of master of ceremonies. The Japanese have their backs to the camera; is there a hint of the coming hara-kiri in their stance?

This all took place before I was born, yet it seems to have happened in another aeon in another world. Perhaps history is speeding up, the way they say it is. Certainly my father's last known years moved at breakneck speed. If he were still alive, how quickly had the last thirty years gone by? From the USS *Missouri* to this damp, stinking November in Banguniland, as I waited for my pilot to arrive from Mali (where he had been carrying a WHO delegation), I could see these years meandering randomly, but with the promise of hidden significance, like a sculpture by Christo.

Banguniland was rotting. The waters had left not the land of milk and honey, but a landscape of melted, unsavoury chocolate. In it, the remains of animal life – hardly recognisable as emaciated goats and other drought-proof domestic animals – putrefied. There were bodies of humans in the mud too; the most remarkable thing about their deaths was that they should have drowned in Banguniland. Where did all this mud come from? There was no clean water to wash in at Brannigan's Hotel, where I was having dinner with Frederick Ngwenya. The hotel was my choice; he had outgrown the seedy haunts of his days under cover. When the closer weather had set in after six whole days and nights of downpour, something odd had happened: out of the mud, plants were growing of a strange, vegetable lushness nobody could remember. Their seeds had been borne by the muddy waters from distant regions in pods, nuts and beans. These leguminous plants were in for a rude shock when the climate returned to normal.

Nobody blamed the President for the deaths of livestock and people, while they praised him lavishly for the blessing of rain. He had delivered, but he was troubled. Frederick Ngwenya seemed little concerned with his brother's preoccupations. He attached more importance to the World Bank and relations with the EEC than the return of the spider footstool and the scorpion headrest. These, he told me, were necessary but not a priority for Banguniland. They could wait. They would turn up. His aim was to avoid the creeping lethargy and indifference to which, he freely admitted, new regimes in Africa fell prey. He had a disarming quality, the same quality which had drawn me into the interior to be bitten by a scorpion and adduced to the support of the Liberation Front. (Back in London I had been interviewed by a man who was writing a thesis on scorpions.)

'I hear old Monroe tried to shoot you,' Frederick said with a laugh.

'Not really. I think the gun went off by mistake.'

'That Monroe, aai. He's a problem.'

'He simply wants recognition.'

'He wants more than that, I'm sorry, sir. He's dreaming about the Garden of Eden.'

'How's your car?' I said.

'The Pontiac? I sold it. I've got a Merc now.'

'Can the country afford it?' I asked pointedly.

'The country expects it. When are you going north?'

'When my pilot gets here from Mali.'

'Mali,' he said quietly.

Behind his sunglasses he had become thoughtful.

'Does your pilot know the interior?'

'He's very experienced.'

'I wish I could come with you. But I'm too busy now, sir.'

'Don't call me "sir" any more. It makes me uncomfortable.'

'No time for the old football, either. It's a lot of work, being in government.'

'I can imagine.'

We stared out over the dark Bangunes River. Large lumps floated by in the waters. Although the river was in spate, it seemed, because of its increased density, to be flowing more slowly. God knows what paraded by us as we sat drinking the Mauritian beer. Whole villages for all I knew. The past few days I had felt like a resistance fighter waiting in the night for an air

ines was claustrophobic in its desperate, clinging
ed a flare in the night and the thrum of distant engines.
Monroe really want?' I asked.

oe has a vision of Banguniland which is impossible.'

't mean to be rude, but what vision is possible?'

'Forgive me, but white people, sir, are trying to put this country into a new shape which they will recognise. Unfortunately I don't think our country will ever fit the bill. What Monroe wants has gone and personally I don't think it ever existed.'

'What about the President?'

'The President is seeking a wholeness for the country. The effect of the war was disruptive. There is no spiritual peace yet. A wholeness of spirit as well as a wholeness of purpose, as you would understand it.'

'Talking of holes,' I said, 'could you get someone over to Dr Gullikson's house? He's coming back soon and nobody has fixed the wall.'

'Holes. Holism,' he said whimsically. 'Are you married? I never asked you before.'

'Yes and no. I have a wife but we are separated.'

'She must be a sad woman to lose you.'

'I don't know about that.'

'I've got two wives and maybe I'll take another.'

'The country expects it.'

'That's right.'

He laughed happily. I thought of those springy girls at my party not so long ago, right here, when we had all been moved on by the army.

'Have there been many trials and so on since you came in?'

'No. Most of the important people fled in advance. All the people who stayed are on our side.'

There had been some shootings; unfit, protesting men with cardio-vascular problems were tied to posts and shot in the chest. Monroe had said that factional scores were settled. A tutor had once told me that the measure of a country's political health is the attitude of the public to the police and vice versa. Certainly in Bangunes the squads of police and army were everywhere, but there was no obvious fear and loathing.

'I have some letters for you,' said Frederick.

He took a small bundle, tied with twine, from his alligator briefcase.

'I must go now. Travel safely. Bring the old man home and give him some rest,' he said.

'Goodbye.'

He was gone, lithely and amiably. I sat alone in Brannigan's, caught in the *cordon sanitaire* his eminence had created between me and the ordinary citizens. Out in the night Frederick and his brother the President were scheming and planning. And further out, in the outer darkness, they believed my father to be waiting, sitting under a tree, or shackled in a hut, an old version of me, hairless, deranged, a barking dog of a white man, living on flying ants and millet meal, dreaming inchoately of being an explorer – half-remembered dreams of Chester Nimitz, suicidal Nips, Jacques Cousteau and the Baltic eyes of Mrs de Luth. In this dried husk, this krispie, was there any recollection of his family, of love given and garnered, of – of me? The question was, if he were still alive, did I want to meet him? Here I was setting out (could I hear the distant throb of aero-engines?) to find him. So much of my life has been spent in doing things which will turn out badly, but I have been given this role, this salmon ignorance of the purpose of all the leaping and striving. Sexual antics are no exception. Poor Magda. Her brother saw that I could not provide the warp and weft for her intricate life.

In Bangunes weaver birds had proliferated: in the past week of waiting they had been hard at work, taking advantage of the new growth to build their extraordinary nests. Gullikson knows all about the sociable weaver. I had another beer. My letters lay on the table. Reluctantly I opened them. American Express offered me their gold card, with limitless credit. How does an organisation with such poor intelligence stay in business? There was a letter from my mother. She was seriously concerned about the health of her soulmate, Mrs Orme-Watson. The Old Cyder

House, reading between the lines, was undergoing a disturbing period of change: the old folks were dying. It had never occurred to me before, but living there the turnover must be high: a constant coming, and a very final going. There was a half-hidden reproach in the letter: my 'obsession' was bound to be illusory. What she was saying was very obvious: she was definitely alive in the middle of Wiltshire, England, while my father was almost certainly not alive, in the middle of nowhere.

There were other letters, from the bank and from a television company rejecting an idea of mine for a wildlife documentary about hyena at night. I delayed opening the last letter, from Magda, until I had another beer and ordered the infamous lamb chops. Brannigan's had been passed over in the celebrations to welcome the new regime. Its status as a backwater was thus endorsed. It clung stubbornly to its old, reactionary menu and habits. I liked it. I felt proof here against anything Magda could hurl at me from that other world I had departed.

Magda's letter was a puzzle. How could someone as mysterious and unfathomable as Magda write in such a childlike and awkward fashion? Apart from short, mendacious notes left in our apartment, this was the first letter I had ever had from her. Strictly speaking, there had been other letters, but these were all too obviously drafted by lawyers, with her large, immature signature dropped carelessly on to the bottom, like a spider in repose. Her letter, written from an unnamed friend's house in Cape Cod, said that she was pregnant, and that I was the father, 'not biologically but morally'. This concept of proxy fatherhood was intriguing. Her mental state she described as 'feeling a little *moche*, as the French say'. What course of action was she demanding from me? The message I drew was that I should acknowledge the baby now that her art dealer had done with her. There was something noble and quixotic in this notion which appealed to me. She had had two abortions and presumably I was the father both biologically and morally then. So this fatherless foetus in distress deserved recognition. She said she would be going back to England, and would have the baby there. The sting had gone out of her punches – perhaps, as her brother had predicted, because of hormonal changes. She missed me, but did not expect her feelings to be reciprocated. A curious sort of cramp embraced her letter, a touchingly childish seriousness. I felt a surge of the old love, enhanced by the moonlight playing on the ominous, thick river outside. I drank another beer in honour of the baby. If I found the old man I would be able to give him news of his proxy grandchild.

Rolled over by this backwash of sentiment, I remembered the Magda I had loved: the wild, beautiful creature, the nights of unbearable imaginings, the days where time not so much stood still as ran obliquely and in reverse. Drugs played a part in this. Certainly Magda used them frequently, but she used them without moral or emotional compunction, where I had to place everything in perspective and context. I often cited experience as an excuse.

'You think too much about things. Live. Enjoy.'

'This is an old chestnut. Even the Greeks worried about enjoying themselves too much.'

'Did the Greeks have coke?'

She seemed genuinely interested.

'Probably. They had indoor plumbing.'

Stoned, I fell off a ski-lift in Chamonix. Somehow I missed the footstep and plunged twenty or thirty feet into the Panda Club, where surprised French infants were learning to ski, crouching like dwarf coalminers. Magda talked about this great feat for days. We spent money we did not have. We drank hot wine at four in the morning. We lay at night embraced tightly, our skins' dampness mingling, smearing us with a numinous wash, best applied wet for magical effect, as in a fresco.

'I love you, Magda,' I whispered, the more intensely for knowing it to be mainly a fiction.

There were shouts outside. A drowned elephant had become entangled with the end of the quay below Brannigan's. Lamps and flashlights were found and we all rushed out to see this bloated monster. It was huge, as large as a whale. The lights caught the inside of its pink mouth, freckled like the head of an old man. This elephant had floated many miles and was not to be detained long. The force of the water began to heave its great bulk round; we ran as the dock creaked and fractured; the elephant headed off into the gorged river like an ocean liner in its deliberateness, backwards now, leaving us Ahabs quiet and a little frightened. We were in Africa, but I was the only one there who had seen an elephant before this monster visited us from the interior.

I went back to Gullikson's and slept badly, dreaming that I had seen the elephant's trunk reach out to me, begging for peanuts, like an elephant in a circus. Skep and I had gone to see Boswell's Circus when it came to town, and hung about the gentle elephants for hours. We also saw a man training Shetland ponies to pirouette on their hind legs and we saw Stompie and Tiekie, the clowns, in their caravan, with old, careworn faces, the faces of full-sized men on bonsai bodies. The circus is a sinister place, the remnant of a mediaeval encampment of outcasts, freaks and mythological animals performing acts of magic and cruelty. Monroe told me of a planter who owned a huge baboon and used to tie it to a tree near the Bangunes River. He delighted in waiting for a crocodile to appear. At the very last moment the planter would shoot the crocodile, but not before the highly intelligent baboon, who loved his master despite his cruelty, was driven to a state of hysteria by the lumbering, hungry rushes of the crocodiles. The baboon decided to teach the planter a lesson. One day he knocked the planter unconscious with a rock and tied him up close to the water. The planter came round in time to see an enormous crocodile approaching at a prehistoric canter, the stuff of nightmares. The baboon, hidden in the reeds, picked up the rifle, as he had seen his master do. He aimed it carefully. Alas, he could not operate the safety catch.

*

Flying over Banguniland at fifteen thousand feet gave us car-tographers' eyes. Where Frederick and I had struggled along rutted tracks through the blind bush, I now saw watercourses, clearings and the fairy rings of what had been, in richer times, cattle kraals. From up here the bush had a pleasant aspect. The rains had brought out of the dusty scrub a verdant life. Streams and rivulets twinkled brightly far below. Large, round lakes, or 'pans' as my pilot called them, became saucers of milk as the sunlight caught them. My old friend Patel had equipped us for this journey; we had spent a pleasant afternoon under his avocado tree, discussing bourgeois living. He welcomed the new regime. His oldest daughter was betrothed. She was to live in Nairobi. Life was taking a turn for the better. I would need water-purifying tablets and the mosquitoes would be rampant after the rains. Patel was a warm man, and it added richness to our friendship that he reminded me of Tagore's postmaster with his dark, ringed eyes. He wanted me to find my father, although he was sure no civilised man would survive ten minutes at the far end of Victoria Road.

The plane's twin engines (my brother had insisted on at least two engines) were surprisingly quiet. The cabin was pressurised. It was full of equipment provided by Patel, so I sat next to Colin in the cockpit. He had none of the gung-ho qualities you associate with pilots and ex-military people, who are forced to live amongst the indifferent civilian population for the rest of their lives. He was a quiet man, who seemed weary of Africa and planes, but never complained about his lot. For an ex-RAF pilot, spraying insects and bombing birds must surely have been small potatoes. I had long since given up trying to make conversation, as the vast map unfolded beneath us. We had started at dawn to avoid the thermals; Colin was unmoved by the sunrise which was made livid by the atmospheric changes in the air. He had seen the sun rise and set on every clapped-out shanty town in Africa. All he said was 'All set? Okey-dokey, here we go.' He said this before we landed at Ngame too. By an inexplicable arrangement all of his own, three large drums of aviation fuel were waiting for us at the end of the strip. He simply handed some money to a boy in shorts and a Barcelona FC football shirt and the boy began to pump six hundred litres of gas by hand.

'Let's go and have a piss and a beer,' said Colin succinctly.

'OK.'

I followed him. He wore navy-blue shorts and a white shirt with epaulettes. His legs were hairy and brown – colonial legs. His face, too, was brown as a nut and his eyes were screwed almost closed behind his Raybans. His walk was direct, quite quick, and led us unerringly to a small store which doubled as a bar.

'I've seen worse,' he said, as we stood surrounded by curious children, who stared at us with large eyes, the eyes of people who are always hungry. I cannot remember what it is like to be really hungry. My life could be charted by a succession of meals, almost all of them excessive. I have eaten everywhere. There is almost no fruit or vegetable and no part of the animal, flesh, fish or fowl, I haven't tried, although I have eaten tripe only once, in Milan. Never again.

I asked Colin how long he thought it would take us to reach the mountains.

'Two hours and fifty minutes. Same back again unless something goes wrong. All set? Okey-dokey, here we go.'

Our plan was to recce the distant mountains, which appeared on my maps like a dangerous shoal on a mariner's chart, simply shading above the words 'Mawenzi Mountains'. The border was not marked. As we soared above the circular huts and compounds of Ngame it appeared that the bush below was infinite. It was not far from here that the accident had happened, on a ferry which served as a crossing into Orefeo country.

Of Ngame's inhabitants Mrs de Luth had written,

The local tribe, the Amabile, are a graceful, friendly people, who live on fishing and the cultivation of maize in the rich fields watered by the artery of life, the Ngame River, a tributary of the mighty Bangunes.

The artery of life had spilled into the surrounding fields and villages, and then withdrawn, leaving a choking, black silt for the graceful, friendly people to deal with. But a large picture of Patrick Ngwenya had adorned the store; at least they had a new totem. His face was radiant and he wore a general's cap with even more scrambled egg than General MacArthur's. In his hand was the delicate white stick.

Beneath us the country was more broken, with little outcrops of rock, like paving for a garden path, stacked untidily in clumps. There was still no sight of the mountains. Little was known of the mountains. For years the approaches to them had been the playground of guerrillas and dissidents; the borders between Banguniland and its neighbours ran somewhere through the mountains, but no one knew or cared exactly where this line was. Since the troubles the whole of the bush country had anyway been reclaimed by the tsetse fly. A Count Teleki had explored the mountains in 1889, remarking on the extreme cold in the high valleys but he was disappointed in his hopes of finding gold and diamonds. There were few people living in the region, and those he did meet were in a state of nervous tension bordering on mania, because their traditional enemies from the south were due for their seasonal visit demanding women, cattle and quantities of woven mats. The highly organised Count left them with a biography of Bismarck and a telescope, made by Carl Zeiss of Jena. His object was to give them an advantage over the approaching enemy and some inspiration as to how to organise themselves. Even Monroe knew little about the Mawenzi Mountains.

We circled the valley of the Orefeo. From the air the village looked almost intact, yet there was no life. The abandoned maize fields had become thick tracts of choking weed, and I could see the spring gushing furiously but unrequited. Colin believed we should overfly the mountains and try to locate from the information we had any settlements and check and update the maps before deciding on a future landing area for my expedition. At the moment we could not land because of the mud.

'What happens if we are forced to land?' I asked.

'Well that's another matter. We'll think of something.'

We saw the mountains after about an hour's flying. They appeared to have snow-covered domes like Kilimanjaro. Colin said it was lava rock, smoothed and bleached. From this distance they seemed to be set arbitrarily in the vastness around them. As we got closer it was clear that they were big – ten or twelve thousand feet, said Colin – and folded over like pastry in a bakery, each fold a valley or rift with another beyond. You could hide the whole of Bangunes in there, never mind one old man. We circled systematically; Colin checked his instruments and made notes. He had a device which kept him flying exactly to certain references so that he could scan each square mile without ever repeating himself; it had been developed for prospecting work.

Down below, the mountain domes were catching the late afternoon light, which burnished them to the colour of crème caramel. Below the bald, smooth domes were green valleys, each one dense with bush and vines and boulders. Colin flew low so that we could look into these deep gorges and into the high, open valleys above, suspended like hammocks beneath the mountain domes, another country of rolling upland blotched with muted, European colours, like the Highlands of Scotland. There was no evidence of the Orefeo.

'Okey-dokey, let's go. We've just got enough gas to reach Ngame.'

It was almost dark as we landed at Ngame. Stepping from the plane my legs felt cramped and useless. The plane looked like a beautiful and alien craft, standing there on the short, rough strip, surrounded by huts of woven reeds and dry mud. We were to stay in the government guest-house which was once the District Commissioner's residence, courtesy of the President, and an army Jeep was waiting to take us there. Whatever disasters had overtaken Ngame, they were masked by the onset of night. Fires guttered and glowed as we passed and in their light we could see women crouching, tending the flames or stirring cooking pots.

Above the duckpond smell rose the familiar scents of woodsmoke and maize porridge, and snatches of singing. Our driver, a young army lieutenant, saluted smartly as he dropped us at the guest house. The guest house was a cluster of round, thatched huts which we used to call 'rondavels' in South Africa, grouped around a rectangular dining room and living room. My room was spotlessly clean and the red cement floor had been polished with wax; the smell reminded me irresistibly of my childhood in South Africa. We were served a stew of mutton and green, leafy, wild spinach by a servant in a white jacket.

'I've had worse,' said Colin, finishing his off. 'I'll go and do my maps, if you will excuse me.'

The waiter watched me intently as I sat alone with the tinned peaches. He was eager to please, but his intense scrutiny made me uneasy; I tried to give him the rest of the night off. I pointed to the door when English failed, and he shut it. This made the room stiflingly hot so that I had to move to the sitting room, which opened onto a veranda enclosed by mosquito netting. This room had an air of expectancy: everything was ready for someone important to turn up after a gymkhana or a leopard hunt or an altercation among the natives. There were very old copies of the *Illustrated London News* in neat rows, and a drinks tray with glasses and soda siphon, but no liquor. The cushions on the heavy wooden armchairs were plumped up invitingly to receive eminent and weary backsides, and a clock ticked so loudly that it appeared to be part of the frog chorus from outside, like a metronome at music practice. I wondered if African frogs were edible; there were enough frogs raucously celebrating the rains to take care of any protein deficiency in the population.

My father and Mrs de Luth had stayed here. Perhaps there was a guest book? There were yellowed paperbacks by Edgar Wallace and Nevil Shute and H. E. Bates, and very old editions of *Country Life* and *Punch* as well as the *Illustrated London News*, but no guest book. The world which these relics conjured up was the world of my childhood in South Africa, the world that my father had been so eager to leave behind. Mrs de Luth had offered him the chance to become famous, perhaps not as famous as Cousteau, but famous enough to be recognised where it mattered and to be invited to meet the people who counted, by and large rich people with the leisure to think about the big things in life. *National Geographic* would open those doors.

I wondered if they had had dinner here with the interesting flotsam of those distant colonial days: hunters, remittance men, planters of tobacco and groundnuts, and their ladies, drunk on pink gin and the rawness of Africa. It was only a few days before the tragedy on the ferry; there was some strain in their relations, caused by Mrs de Luth's imbalance. I could see her looking at my father with the cold gaze she had bequeathed to her daughter. In my mind mother and daughter were beginning to inhabit the same body. Perhaps we all do this at the silent call of heredity.

Colin came back from his room, carrying a bottle of whisky.

'Done the maps. Fancy a nightcap?'

We sat down and Colin poured the whisky into the tumblers, which had a series of raffish etchings on them of a small, naked boy peeing into a river to the dismay of the fish; on another his little privates were in danger from an inquisitive duck.

'Colin, has anyone ever eaten a strawberry yoghurt from the end of your cock?'

'No, but there was a lady once in Dar es Salaam who could snap a Carr's Table Water biscuit between her tits,' he said helpfully.

CHAPTER 13

In the mosquito-speared night, I could not decide whether we were on an expedition or simply on a journey. When Stevenson said that to travel hopefully is a better thing than to arrive he was not talking about expeditions. An expedition is a more definite concept than a journey. It has no time for the faintly hippy notion of travelling hopefully. An expedition must have a specific object. The idea of life as a journey is a seductive notion, as attractive as the idea of the enlightenment to be found at the destination. It is a powerful myth which has sustained writers and travellers, this idea of the journey to greater knowledge and even self-knowledge. The domed mountains seemed to suggest that we were coming to the end of our particular journey. If in that vast geological disorder my father lived on, semi-animate, what purpose would be served by finding him? The truth was that I wanted to plug a gap in my own life, which had let in a nagging draft since boyhood. We had seen smoke rising in cigar feathers from a fold in the mountains. Surely whoever lived there would know something?

An armada of mosquitoes dashed themselves against the fine mesh of my mosquito net, as I lay troubled by these thoughts as well as by the sort of worries any normal person feels at four in the morning: the trivia of life rising like a tide, and unresolved questions of no cosmic significance whatever chasing themselves around and around, like a dog with an infected rear end. (Dogs no longer have this sort of thing in this day of canine antibiotics. My friend Skep's dogs were all diseased. They had lost an eye or a paw; they were as patchy as our termite-inhabited lawn, and their balls were as nacreous as an oyster shell. Naturally, I thought they were real dogs, and loathed effete King Charles spaniels and poodles.) This is the sort of thought which kept me awake. The mountains glowed in my mind as they had the first day. Nobody believed the earliest explorers when they reported snow on Kilimanjaro, yet many years later that vision of magic whiteness was proved to be snow, right on the fucking Equator. Nobody, as far as I knew, had written anything about the golden domes of Mawenzi since the sporting Count Teleki.

'Jesus, they've been sitting out here as secret as a nun's bum all these years and nobody's said anything.'

It was the longest sentence I had yet heard Colin speak.

'Were you at a Catholic school, by any chance, Colin?'

'No, I was at a comprehensive in South Wales. Why do you ask?'

'Oh, it's nothing.'

Colin and I were getting along well. I have always admired people who do something properly. Colin, as Gullikson had promised, was the tops.

One way or another these mountains were the end of the line, the interior; they were the heart of darkness. Each day we overflew them, each evening the aviation fuel gushed into the King Air's tanks. It took the small boy who pumped by hand forty minutes per tank.

'Tough little bastard,' said Colin appreciatively.

We overflew the mountains five times while Colin marked his chart with numbers and we looked for the smoke, but we did not see it again. I tried to recognise features of the landscape below. We swooped ever lower on our circuits and once we saw nervous goats grazing on a rocky slope. There were no huts although the telltale fairy rings of abandoned villages could be seen. In the evening Colin worked with his maps for a few hours and I read or wrote up my notes in a desultory fashion. The countryside around Ngame was drying fast, the mud cracking like a mirror in a horror film, the smells of decay rising and falling, a Dow Jones of putrefaction; donkeys, dogs, even unburied humans, all putrefied. Perhaps some new life form was going to arise from this primaeval mud. Yet at our guest house the tempo was not affected. The clock in the dining room, a souvenir of a great cricket match in the thirties, ticked away, as Sandile, the steward, stood nervously watching us eat; the mosquitoes hurled themselves in waves, like the kamikazes of my father's war, at our mosquito nets each night. Nobody had seen mosquitoes in such numbers. The spraying programme had stopped two years before as the fastidious Swedes refused to finance it for fear of upsetting the ecological balance, the chain of interdependence between the lowliest insect and the most evolved vertebrate, Scandinavian Man himself. The flooding had certainly tipped the scales the mosquitoes' way. By my bed stood a huge can of Doom, with which I did my best each night to redress the balance.

My father had greatly enjoyed the kamikaze raids. It was marvellous standing on the bridge, the guns blazing in every direction, waves of demented Nips appearing from all sides, skimming through the rigging, ploughing into the sea, bouncing off aircraft carriers, smashing into destroyers; it was like the Ride of the Valkyries, yet gloriously safe, magically protected by the white uniform and the shiny white legs. Magic, said Malinowski, was a response to a sense of limitation in the face of danger. No limitations here.

Here come the Nips. Here they come, the crazy wave of history, idealism gone mad, like the air suddenly released from a balloon, and here I am, a boy from South Africa standing on the bridge of Admiral Nimitz's great ship, the observer of all this history, an insider, for chrissakes, an insider. I was there, I saw it, as the Japs flung themselves against the forces of democracy.

A last defiant gesture before they settled to make Toyotas and Sonys, and conquer the world another way.

Who could blame him for thinking himself touched by magic? Who could fail to see that he was destined for better things than editing a farming newspaper for unappreciative rednecks? He had made an impression on Mrs de Luth which had been very deep. Reading her papers I had found that she suffered from a sense of guilt over his death. In a little note to one of her later philosophical writings, she discussed murder as a ritual. Perhaps he had given her some insight into the purpose of murder in primitive societies, or perhaps she had been influenced by the Sacco and Vanzetti case and its ritualistic aspects, so shocking at the time. Murder, she said, was a taboo subject in the West; its cleansing, magic, function would never be accepted as anything but a relic of past societies. Yet, she wrote, there are more murders in New York City every weekend than there are in the whole of Melanesia in a year:

'In a sense I murdered Lance Curtiz, because I wished things too violently.'

By this stage she was off her trolley, plaguing the editor of *National Geographic* with loopy stories about the great spiritual changes about to overtake society, about Darwinian evolution crashing into reverse to produce Darwinian regression, changes which *National Geographic* should explain to the world at large, unaware of the crisis to come, and especially to its readers who were only being told about the plight of the African cheetah and the depth of the polar ice cap and so on. Apart from her belief that she had murdered my father, her notes and letters were full of pathetic references to that far-off day. When he fell overboard, a lot of her sanity went with him. She renounced her previous life as a seeker after material facts, and became a seeker after spiritual truth, a hopeless ambition, and all because of him.

On day six we left the airstrip at Ngame early. The waters had receded. In the silt and dried mud the foreign, tropically green vegetable growth was beginning to wilt under the hostile aridity of northern Banguniland. Even the mosquito plague was abating. Colin felt that the time had come to attempt a landing near the mountains. He wanted to leave enough fuel and a radio beacon so that we could make longer and more accurate searches of the most distant valleys. Sandile prepared sandwiches for us each morning and wrapped them in tin foil. It was an elderly piece of tin foil and it had to be returned every evening. As we soared above the huts and the strangely mute people gazing up at us, I realised I was enjoying our routine. Colin was in charge. I peered out of the cockpit windows and distributed the sandwiches; we had become detached from the land below. Colin was marking a map and I sometimes called out references from the instruments for him, which he noted in a pad on his knee, Royal Air Force style. I had begun to believe I was working for Colin. The idea that he was employed by me – or by my brother – was absurd. The King Air was a comfortable plane and even had a radar screen; on it I could make out the mountains and various cloud formations by now. Being a pilot did not seem a bad way to make a living, although solitary. Colin never complained.

He landed the plane without difficulty on a dry pan near the mountains. A few days before it had been a gluey swamp.

'Always a good surface, these pans,' he said.

I helped him move equipment and fuel drums to the side of a small hill, a 'koppie', as we used to call them in South Africa. It was from just such a hill that my grandfather was wounded by the Boers, a natural fortress of randomly piled rocks. Colin placed his beacon right at the top, where it crouched like a frog, emitting a low, pulsing hum. From here the first defensive ring of mountains rose sharply above us. What from the air seemed to be smooth, polished rock now appeared to be slashed with crevasses. The valleys were deeper and the vegetation in them thicker than had been obvious from the flying armchairs. Just to walk to the top of the first line of mountains could take a day. Beyond that were untold folded valleys and gleaming mountain domes. The foot of every valley was clogged with huge falls of boulders, thrown down a thousand years before, I guessed.

At that moment a huge boulder bounced down the valley immediately above us, crashing like a giant marble, and with the same impact, on other boulders.

'The natives are restless,' said Colin.

'Probably the rain has loosened the soil or something,' I said.

'I hope you're right.'

In the Chamonix valley, Magda had been frightened by the strange nocturnal cracking of the Mer de Glace, and wanted to change our chalet to avoid what she said was coming. Two years later it had happened; a gargantuan piece of ice the size of the Titanic slid gracefully down the valley erasing all in its path.

'The trouble is,' she said, 'these new chalets are never built in the right places. The Alpine people know. How many old houses do you see? None. There's always a hill or a river protecting them. We've got to move.'

'OK. We'll move in the morning.'

'Why not now?'

'Because it's two-thirty am.'

'Two-thirty, so what? Time features very oppressively in your life, doesn't it?'

Even for Magda this was a classic. It was no use telling her that Alpine people, as well as having an instinctive knowledge of glaciology, also have a fondness for going to bed early. We ended up sleeping in the hired car outside the church, which had stood safely in one spot for four hundred and seventy years. I think it was the day after that I fell amongst the startled infants of the Panda Club.

The boulder came to rest, but it was followed down the mountain by a small avalanche of bushes and rocks. Then there was complete quiet apart from the torment of the pain-racked insects.

'Shall we have a closer look over the last peaks?' said Colin.

'Okey-dokey, Colin. You're the boss.'

I had called the highest of the golden domes 'Mount Magda', a *double entendre*, which Colin entered solemnly on his charts. We left this cranial peak far behind and began our routine circling in an area which so far we had hardly explored.

'Look for the water,' said Colin.

It was about half an hour before we saw it. From the far side of one of the peaks, a silver ribbon of water fluttered down into a valley. Colin banked sharply and brought the King Air low, circling and crisscrossing the valley, following the stream as it appeared and disappeared. I saw the village first. It was built of stone houses, square, exactly like the houses of the Orefeo. From the air, as we screamed low over the village, we could flush out no life. Colin rose and circled again, checking his readings. Below us was a landscape of giant tree ferns, swinging vines, dense trees and vast boulders. Some of the boulders were iridescent green, presumably from moss or lichen. The village lay above a series of terraces and beneath a wall of rock.

'Time to go back,' said Colin.

We landed on the pan for a light lunch and a map check.

'How did you know it was there?'

'I guessed; it's the watershed. Africa has watersheds. Livingstone knew that. There had to be permanent water somewhere to feed the Bangunes.'

'Nothing moved down there.'

'There are people,' said Colin. 'They were hiding. They've probably had bad experiences of planes and copters. You could tell from the paths that had been worn round the village. They quickly become overgrown if they are not used. What now, do you want me to stay a week or so?'

I had little idea what I would do next. My forward planning had not even extended this far.

'How do we get in there?'

'Your best bet is to be winched down from a copter. It would be too difficult to walk in. You'd need a proper expedition. The problem is if you come by helicopter they'll all run and if you walk in, God knows what will happen to you.'

Colin's eyes, semi-closed against the sizzling brightness, were turned towards the mountains thoughtfully.

'What about dropping a letter?' I asked.

'May work. If there's anyone down there who can read. Maybe you should drop in with a guide, say, one or two valleys away and walk the last few miles. You'd keep in radio contact in case of trouble.'

'Good idea. Now we would have to get a helicopter. Do you know of anybody?'

'Sure. It'll take three or four days to get him from Kenya. Unless you want to ask the government for a chopper.'

'I would, but to be honest I really don't know what the President's angle is. I'd like you to stay, anyway.'

'Okey-dokey. More interesting than bombing the fuck out of kwelea birds.'

The sight of the village had given me a churning sensation, a surge of peristalsis. It was the strangling sensation of *déjà vu* which is the stock-in-trade of certain nightmares. The talk of being winched down ropes into an anarchic landscape of prehistoric tree ferns and giant groundsels did not help. This adventure was taking on a life of its own. Something had gone wrong here: I was going to fall off the ferry myself in the next reel, I knew it. The strange plants, the boulder tumbling unprovoked down the mountainside, and the ghostly mountain tops – urbane, bald heads in the afternoon light – were beyond my sphere of competence.

The process of growing older is usually one of closing options, defining the topography (and topology) of life; fixing the points, playing to your strengths, blotting out childhood weaknesses and limitations. Suddenly here I was being offered a course of action which seemed completely open-ended and therefore particularly alien and dangerous. I tried to eat Sandile's crude sandwiches, carved from loaves of bread with the texture of dry cake. They had none of the springiness of bread and they were thickly spread with fish paste which made them very hard to swallow.

I was being offered the prospect of death. Normal rules did not apply down there; that was obvious from the idiosyncratic plant life which inhabited the tormented valleys – the giant tree ferns and strange, etiolated, pineapple-shaped plants crowding and jostling more conventional trees, to form dense forests, forests which never quite made it up the sides of the valleys, leaving the tops of the ridges and spines bare. And everywhere there were huge boulders, boulders, as we had seen, in a dangerously nervous condition. God knows how the original European explorers faced Africa with its vast unpredictability and boundless unfamiliarity; perhaps religion and the gun gave comfort. I began to think more seriously about a leaflet drop. It would appeal to the ex-journalist and writer, surely.

'Colin, there's something down there, but it could be anything. I mean, it could be an old village abandoned and used by hunters or anybody, or just a small, frightened family. I'm certainly not venturing alone into that.'

'I can't say I blame you. Shall we be getting off before the witching hour?'

'Okey-dokey.'

Inside the King Air again I felt calmed, like Major Edward White, back in Gemini 4 after his space walk, his 'orbital odyssey'. For those with the money, this is the age of the quick getaway. David Livingstone was almost dead after a nightmare walk of four hundred miles when Henry Morton Stanley found him; in the King Air we were back in Ngame, four hundred and fifty miles away, in just on two hours. My father used to marvel at the speed of things, the power of the jet engine and the possibilities of the obedient atom, 'tiny particles which work like genii at man's bidding'. Was it conceivable that he would allow himself like Livingstone to be mired in his own version of Ujiji?

The seats of the plane were upholstered in soft, charcoal-coloured, fuzzy material, like the seats of an expensive car. Cocktail tables in simulated walnut could be swung conveniently out. There was a flattering, seductive note in the aircraft's engines, a whisper in the air of power and possibility, the very things my father had craved. The curious thing about the mountains, I now saw as we surged upwards, was that there were no paths or tracks leading to them. Africa is stitched together with tracks, dusty scars made by game, by cattle and by man, yet the Mawenzi Mountains were approached only by trickles of stones, rock falls which anchored them to the surrounding plains like guy ropes: giant circus tents, taut crowns hiding a thousand illusions; giant mushrooms, with hallucinogenic properties, giant tombstones burying aeons of unwanted history. What a thought. All that unknown history sealed, unread, unwritten, irretrievable. There must be masses of it everywhere, history not – as in Gray's *Elegy* – mildly missed, but history of great importance and significance, certainly to the poor bastards murdered, beheaded, garotted, or crowned, deified and revered in total anonymity. Our age, whatever its fate, will be recorded to the point of banality and beyond. I have myself been on television five or six times, recognised by taxi drivers the next day, embalmed by video tape in various television companies. It is no more than a truism to say that unless it's been on television it does not exist; everything has been on television. I saw a moray eel being pulled out of a pool by a child in Greece and I recognised it at once, with its liver spots and large, malevolent eyes. I didn't need to see a moray eel for myself to know it; I had already made its acquaintance with Cousteau and with Attenborough, many times; in fact I already knew a great deal more about morays than I could possibly find useful.

Yet nobody knew much about Mawenzi. Back in Ngame we asked the army lieutenant. He had no idea; he smiled indulgently. I have found that educated Africans often have the most rudimentary knowledge of the outlying districts in their own countries. Their impulses are towards the metropolis or towards Paris and London. The remote bush to them is not a subject of interest, it is a non-place. My own theory, for what it's worth, is that Africans need to see cattle grazing peacefully to believe a place exists. The Mawenzi Mountains were definitely a nonplace; the tsetse fly, the bandits, the civil war and the sheer obstinate remoteness had all seen to that. If I was to go in there I would need help, but nobody in Ngame knew the place. Only the departed Orefeo had trafficked there. Over the Orefeo country the pall of the massacre still hung. The locals, the amiable Amabile, had not taken possession of the Orefeo village and pastures. They were not yet ready for such presumption. The distant mountains, four weeks' march, were impossibly remote, barely on the same planet. Only the Orefeo had known what to do with them, collecting, it was rumoured, sacred plants and spring water for medicinal and magic purposes. Birds lived there with long, scarlet tails, whose feathers had adorned the hair of the Orefeo magic men. The tree ferns and the giant groundsels were their special prerogative.

Ngame itself clung fearfully to the banks of the river, a cluster of huts, the church of some departed Lutherans, a school run by an aid organisation, the police station and a small army camp. Right on the bank of the river were the remains of a safari camp, a relic of more optimistic days, when tourists and hunters were expected, Now the town was digging itself out from the mud. I remember a line I had read: 'The smell of mud, primaeval mud, by jove, was in my nostrils.'

CHAPTER 14

After Ngame, Bangunes had the appearance of a bustling, modern capital. We were reviewing our situation. The helicopter was on order and the cash transfers were made from my brother's accounts. I had decided to take Gullikson with me, if he would come, and I was waiting for his reply. Monroe had volunteered his services, but his medical state was not good. The idea of climbing down a ladder from a hovering helicopter behind Monroe, his heart pumping thinly, his face becoming ever more unnaturally coloured (he now reminded me of a moray eel), with his wild, uncontrollable longings for a state of grace, frightened me. I wanted a more modern man, with some experience and scientific know-how. Gullikson was a natural scientist. Surely, in pursuit of the kwelea bird, he had met some strange circumstances. The bird life of Mawenzi would appeal to him, too. It would make a pleasant change to view exotic birds, without the need to subject them to an avian holocaust. I did, however, accept Monroe's offer of a shotgun and a pistol. Colin would be in charge of the support, taking fuel and supplies for a helicopter up ahead, establishing a base camp and maintaining radio contact. It all sounded quite professional.

While we had been away up country, Magda wrote again. More precisely, a letter from Magda found its way to me care of the President's private office. Her baby would be a girl. She had always wanted a girl. This was news to me; when I was living with her she had always wanted an abortion. The lying-in seemed to be fairly imminent. How many months had gone by since our appalling meeting in the lift? Darwin said that human beings were the only species with the ability to blush. I still felt all the symptoms he describes whenever I thought of my gross misunderstanding: an involuntary tide of shame and remorse engulfing my neck and head, stopping only as it lapped at the eyes. She must have been pregnant at the time. I tried to take some comfort from the knowledge that it was she who had started it. But I could not imagine why. I must have missed something obvious in her condition; if I could fail to pick up these signals, what else had I missed?

What is this state of antagonism, this dreadful misunderstanding, that lives on in the male and female relationship? Darwin believed women had greater intuition and perception than men, but damned himself forever in the eyes of feminists by saying these faculties were characteristic of a less evolved state. In women there lurk, as Darwin suspected, strong primal instincts. This is what Magda's fat, perceptive brother had known too. He had since married three times in six or seven years; he was obviously continuing his researches into the female psyche, selflessly.

And why had Mrs de Luth wished so actively for my father's death that she believed she had caused it? He was an amiable person, or so he appeared to us as children – eager, alert, always optimistic – even naive, it seemed to me, disloyally. Perhaps I had come by my insensitivity in his genetic legacy. Perhaps he, like me, failed to understand elemental things, things which moved other people (I mean women) deeply and obviously. What he had missed in Mrs de Luth had been gargantuan – her obsessive love for him.

It was he who had told her that evolution could easily go the wrong way, regression to the primal mud. As all naturalists know, *natura non facit saltum*, yet this obviously did not hold for the reverse process, where, if he were to be believed, there was evidence of regression bounding like a wallaby at full throttle. This thought, seriously entertained, had plagued Mrs de Luth until the day she died, heavily sedated – some said over-sedated.

157

I could imagine her daughter and the physician having a quiet, sensible word. For a start the cost of those places is astronomical. But I could not believe that my father gave any serious credence to this nonsense himself. He loved progress and science. He loved *National Geographic* with its determinedly, full-colour, WASP approach to life. Philip Roth described an organisation derisively as being 'as Jewish as *National Geographic*'. No agonising for *National Geographic* about the meaning of life. No introversion. No illness. Medical science, in its green vestments and metallic temples, was taking care of that kind thing. All was chemical, biological and geological. My father, good journalist to the last, was obviously a dealer in the popular theories and spotter of the trends which are the substance of journalism. He would never fall for the regression-to-the-mud theory himself. But God knows, you can't be sure: people will believe more or less anything. A squash-playing friend of mine, a perfectly sane man to all outward appearances, has become a Scientologist. He even presented me with a copy of a book by L. Ron Hubbard, which was so palpably absurd that I was never able to play squash with him again for fear he would ask me my opinion of Dianetics in the showers. Yet in a way Dianetics is the perfect fusion of science and religion.

I have always wanted a girl. I know it's not fair to want one or the other, but I'm so glad. You will love her just as much as if she were a boy. Will you come to London as soon as you have finished whatever it is you're doing?

Magda's marvellous, splodgy letter, full of the most grotesque assumptions about me and our relationship, a mine-field of loaded questions and unexploded answers, touched me. Her hormones, she said, had calmed her down and directed her anew. She was a madonna in waiting. In contrast to our earlier correspondence, there was no talk of money; that must have been a phase inspired by New York and orchestrated by her art dealer.

How many men had she slept with since we parted? This child, my proxy child, could be the product of a one-night stand or something worse. What a strange, casual way to introduce new life; it does not seem right that a total stranger could set this process off, in a drunken haze, in a lavatory, in a train, or on a car seat. Mercifully I had completely lost track of her movements over the months in question, so I could not, as we waited in Bangunes, try to reconstruct them. Her letter was undated but the postmark (for some reason from Geneva) was nearly two weeks old.

I did wonder why, if indeed he had been kidnapped and kept prisoner, my resourceful father had not sent a message to us. That was the most improbable aspect, that he, the great gushing spring of enterprise, should have been stilled. Surely he would have contacted us by some means? There must have been someone among the Orefeo who wanted money, a bicycle, a pen, a cheap camera or a trip to Bangunes to catch a Fred Astaire film; any number of bribes were available to a message carrier. The only conceivable explanation was that he had lost his reason. So this whole episode had ended with two mad people, Mrs de Luth – the subject of expensive euthanasia – and my father – his mind broken by disease and privation. If he were alive at all.

The President sent his brother, Frederick, to enquire about progress. I was guarded, but he appeared to know we had found something. Colin had told nobody, but the ordering of the helicopter, large amounts of fuel and mountains of supplies were hard to conceal.

'The President is upset because you have not accepted his offer of assistance.'

'Please tell him that I have no wish to waste the valuable time or the energy of his forces on this trivial matter. I am sure you have better things for them to do. How's business, by the way?'

Frederick's tailoring had taken an even more elegant direction, with a shimmering mohair suit which rested benignly on his spare frame.

'You're a diplomat, sir. You're a credit. The President is concerned about you and your father, and does not want you to take any chances. That's strange country up there.'

'Have you been there?' I asked.

'No, not really.'

'What does that mean?'

His slim face, beautifully sculpted, so that it was all angles and planes, like the face of some antelope, became serious.

'It means I have been there in my dreams. Do you have that sensation sometimes? Africans have it all the time.'

'Why is it so little known?'

'It's far. You know when your father came through here, only a few years ago really, there were still parts of the country no white man had ever visited.'

'Nobody of any colour seems to have visited Mawenzi.'

'Mawenzi. Why do you call it Mawenzi?'

'That's what it says on the maps.'

'Maps in Africa mean little. Not to us anyway. The white travellers used to write anything on their maps. Sometimes they used a native word, completely out of context. When they asked the porters the name of the place, they'd make something up, so as not to disappoint the boss. And that would go on the record.'

'You don't call it Mawenzi. What do you call it?'

'We don't really have a name for it. We don't want to have a name for it. We just call it "the mountains". To us it's more of an idea than a place. Like heaven. *Le bon Dieu sur son fauteuil de nuages.*'

'It exists. We've been there.'

'Different things exist to different people.'

'You're being very philosophical tonight, Minister.'

'Since you've been away, I've become Foreign Minister, too.'

'Congratulations.'

'Nepotism, I'm afraid.'

'I'm sure you were the best man for the job.'

'I hope so. These are difficult times. My brother is longing for a return to stability and normal relations.'

'There is one thing you could do for us. Could you recommend a guide, someone who might speak Orefeo or have some knowledge of the countryside, at least part of Ngame?'

'Difficult, but not impossible. We've hardly had time to think about that district. What's going on there? I hear from our man that the river flooded.'

'It did. It left a hell of a mess all over the town. Strange plants grew for a while in the mud.'

'The primaeval mud. We've got our own version of creation, you know.'

'Hasn't everybody?'

He laughed without his seamless face cracking.

'OK. I must be off. My car is waiting. I'll try to find somebody for you. I wish I had time myself.'

Monroe appeared as Frederick was leaving. He stared at Frederick's shirt in horror.

'Jesus Christ, look at that. Where did you get it, Freddie, out of a pimp's catalogue? Jesus, you look like a travelling johnnie salesman.'

Frederick's cheerful expression, which I watched carefully, did not change.

'I'm glad you like it, Mr Monroe. I must go.'

'Don't mind me. I'm only here to see if this explorer chappie wants to go down to the club.'

'Not tonight. I've got work to do.'

'Everybody's got work to do except me. I've got fuck all to do. Tomorrow?' he asked.

'OK. Can I bring Colin, the pilot?'

'Of course. I'll get them to lay on something other than goat. What about curried chicken?'

He gazed pointedly in the direction of Gullikson's kitchen, where the beers were stockpiled, but I picked up my papers and charts purposefully. He left, his great behind and bare knee-backs the last bits of him I saw after his head had vanished, decapitated by the African night, a night still suffused with decay. Or perhaps with the regression which my inventive father had convinced Mrs de Luth was under way.

Surely he would have sent a note, even if he had turned his back on us, a note to reassure my mother? If not, she was in her

Old Cyder House watching television after nearly thirty years, not of widowhood but of desertion. And if the mountains were nothing but an idea to Frederick, how come they existed for me and Colin? At times I thought that the unreality of Banguniland had produced myths and dreams in parched minds of a lavishness and lushness in inverse proportion to the poverty and aridity of the country. They wanted to be touched again by the magic of hope. The far-away mountains were an idea, sure, but an idea of what? This African cosmology was infinitely elastic. It lacked fixed points, it positively avoided them. The mountains did not need a name or a label. They would be robbed of their numinous qualities by such trivialities. They represented something distant and unobtainable, a bit of the African mystery which was being shown to be no mystery at all. Without the mystery where was the hope of redemption? The Orefeo went there to extract juices from roots and possibly even to mine gold, despite what Count Teleki had said about the absence of minerals. Good point. Where did their gold come from? Nobody had mentioned that. That was what Ngwenya wanted, the secret river where nuggets of gold were found and the secret valleys where the royal medicines were garnered. It seemed plain to me now: the Orefeo, the *soi-disant* Jews, had gone to the grave with the secret. There was nobody left, unless in that stone village in the Mawenzi someone lived who knew the recipes and had a map of the treasure marked with a cross. I wondered whether I should talk to the President about my insight and question him more closely about his expectations, but I decided against it. Frederick had already told me a great deal. There was, I could now see, a question of self-esteem at issue for the royal family here. They did not want to look like superstitious and credulous tribesmen while negotiating with the World Bank, the United Nations and FIFA. The country's recent past was already darkened by the shadow of brutality and ignorance. At last I could see how they were trying to use this ridiculous story, this folk memory. I was the sprat to catch the mackerel. I was the credulous one.

And yet, and yet . . . they could not have known anything about the Orefeo camp in Israel, nor the strange intimations in Mrs de Luth's papers.

The helicopter was on order from Nairobi. Gullikson was expected. He was keen to help, his message said. He had always wanted to visit the mountains, but it had been impossible during the bush war. He would be arriving within a few days. I was finding it difficult to write the copy I had promised. I could not possibly tell them of the discovery of the village, not yet, at least. I sent off some excuses with a promise of substance to come. Colin thought we should avoid the area completely until we were ready to go in, so as not to alarm anybody unduly. All we lacked now were a guide and an interpreter. We flew up to Ngame to meet a man who was going to help us, but he did not arrive. The army lieutenant laughed slyly; the missing man's wives had been bewitched. In his laugh he made it clear that he did not believe in such things, but the people up here were very traditional. His voice carried about as much conviction as a Sicilian peasant protesting that he had never heard of the Mafia. He seemed angry with the people here; the local chief was a dead loss, the food supplies were irregular and there was no television, but he promised to find the missing man for us, 'come hell or high tide'. There was more than a hint of a threat.

Travel writers and professional travellers are always anxious; the irritations and comparisons begin to obsess them. This restaurant, that view, these people, constantly scrutinised and measured. Measured against what? What is the object of travel, what is the purpose in seeing new places? Certainly in Ngame you could quickly get the sense of having exhausted the novelty and depleted the possibilities of travel. The gentle people were stunned by the ill luck visited upon them by the previous government: the fourteen-year drought, the ironically excessive rains and the near extermination of the Orefeo, whose prosperous, diligent little city-state had provided someone to trade with and someone to envy. Now they were all alone with their very own dried mud. Actually there were signs that the former mud would make a rich topsoil. The chief was fearful of provoking some new visitation by meddling with the unfamiliar, exotic-looking loam which lay all around, as black as the tip at a mining village in South Wales, where Colin came from. The traditional crops of maize, millet and pumpkins had grown within splashing distance of the river, even when the grazing had disappeared and the savannah turned to dust-bowl. There was no knowing what might grow in this rich compost. Bad medicine, bad luck for sure. We asked the lieutenant to enquire if there were any locals who had visited the mountains with the Orefeo. Taboo. Only Orefeo and only very select members of their clan had been allowed. There were a few Orefeo still living in the area, too dispirited to return to settle in their own country. They lacked conviction like unfrocked priests, debarred lawyers or politicians who have lost their majorities.

Magda's father, in his later years, had had this aura too. Life in old Prussia, which, to tell the truth, he had hardly known, had become more vivid and real to him than life in semi-decrepit England. His Continental charm and suavity began to sit on him uneasily, as though they were con-tricks he had practised all his life; his knowledge of Eastern European history and politics had become outdated; he knew no one of importance over there any longer. As his powers waned so his boulevardier's after-shave, Trumpers Extract of Jamaican Limes, appeared to me (admittedly somewhat on the look-out for family weakness) to grow stronger every time I met him. His children he acknowledged in an amused, slightly contemptuous way, as if he could hardly understand how he had given birth to adults who spoke with curious English accents. When we first moved to America, a boy at our school called Ray Cmerzyk, brother of the Congressman, woke me up in the middle of the night, with the delighted connivance of my father, to see if I still spoke funny. He and my father had had a bet. Ray was convinced that our accents were put on and that woken abruptly, we would speak like anyone else in Suffolk County.

My mother always spoke with what she thought was a perfect English accent. She believed that the highest evolutionary type was the English gentleman, a racial notion which eventually drew her to a country she hardly knew to live out her time. I have found that in Africa, and elsewhere, this notion of the English gentleman, incorruptible and brave, modest and competent, lives on, long after the model has passed on into the mythological sunset. Perhaps one of the last relics of this forgotten breed would stumble into the Old Cyder House and lighten her days. She had reproached me again for this mad expedition. It was beneath contempt now, self-indulgence with possible genetic implications. She had refused a cruise offered by my brother in favour of spending the summer in her old peoples' home with Mrs Orme-Watson. She lived there, behind a nearly opaque glass wall of prejudice, the protective growth of a troubled life. She reminded me, when I went to see her, of a fish in an aquarium, remote and incommunicado as to her real feelings, calmly swimming behind impenetrable plexiglass.

Colin, in his quiet, diligent way, had produced superb maps of the area. Unknown to me, he had taken aerial photographs of the village in Mawenzi and the Orefeo valley. While I'd been pondering, he had sent to Nairobi for prints, and now presented me with a whole package. We were able to compare the two villages. It seemed certain that they were built by the same people, unlike any of the villages we had seen elsewhere, their stonework symmetrical and pleasing, and the arrangement of the huts similar.

'Colin, you are a wonder.'

'I hope you find your dad, and if you don't, I hope you find out what's happened to him. You need all the help you can get to put him to rest.'

Colin's face, a full, rugby-player's face, with a hint of Celtic redness under the suntan, now recalled the faces of those farmers and miners in Wales, who read Celtic poetry for pleasure and write plays in Welsh on mythological subjects. So he seemed to me well qualified to talk of eternity.

'Colin, I love you.'

'Don't go mad now, you've only been in the bush a few weeks.'

'What do you think of this whole business?'

'I've done crazier jobs.'

'Do you think I'm stupid to go on with this?'

'When you look at the photos it's clear they are the same people. I don't know the background, but whatever we find it's going to be interesting.'

He was sparing with the theory, preferring to restrict himself to charts, maps, navigation and radio frequencies, yet I suspected he had an active second self. Crop spraying, map making and surveying probably induced narcosis which allowed the unconscious plenty of rope. With his practised eye he was able to see paths leading from the village, and a wall built against a cliff face, easily big enough to pen a few goats or sheep at night.

'No cattle up here; it's too mountainous and craggy. Whoever lives there leads a simple life.'

Images of Himalayan holy men sprang to mind, living alone for many years, accepting small offerings of rice wrapped in leaves left by credulous peasants. Mrs de Luth had done a story on the Himalayas called *Himalayas, Roof of the World*. She had been present when the society honoured Tenzing Norgay and Edmund Hillary with a medal apiece, even though her many talents did not include mountaineering. Mountaineering is a highly unscientific activity, serving no discernible practical purpose. The view from up there is no better than a view from a plane, and yet it seems to have attracted many eccentric and interesting people. There are mountain people, just as there are plains people. The Bangunis were plains people, understandably unsure of the mountains which, by an accident of colonial administration, straddled their northern border. The maps may have said they were in Banguniland but common sense said they were somewhere quite different. The Orefeo themselves had lived in small villages all over the region until the colonial masters tidied them up and fixed them in Banguniland. Some said they had come originally from north Africa on the Nile.

The lieutenant came to visit us. He said his men had spotted a white man on the fringes of the Orefeo country. They were nomadic people, displaced persons, with an old white man as their leader.

'He's a very old man.'

'Where have they come from?' I asked.

The lieutenant smiled. It was a silly question.

'The United Nations has banned nomads, sir, but they just keep walking all over.'

'Where is it?' asked Colin. 'Can we drive there?'

The lieutenant was unsure of the distance, but the leader of the patrol, a sergeant, was detailed to come with us. We set off immediately in the sergeant's Jeep. I tried to do some quick calculations of time and distance. They could not have walked four hundred miles from the Mawenzi in a few days, so perhaps they had already deserted their mountain village some time before we overflew it, to find help.

The ferryman lived in a small village beside the river. He was summoned brusquely from the cool depths of his hut by the sergeant. We crossed the river by the same ferry which had tipped my father into the depths. The system was now operated by a small motorised winch, courtesy of the army, but otherwise was unchanged from the descriptions Mrs de Luth and the police reports had given. It was attached to a cable that stretched across the river. Until recent times the porters or ferrymen hauled on this cable to supply the motive force. The ferry itself was no more than the sort of raft Huckleberry Finn would have felt at ease with. There were two lifebelts in faded red and white with kapok stuffing coming out of them. The river was still swollen; it was all too easy to imagine the raft tipping disastrously, or striking a submerged object, for example a putrefying elephant. Colin looked nervous as we bucketed and dipped into the torpid but insistent currents. The ferryman stared silently into the depths, apparently entranced by the deep, churning forces of the water.

'Chocks away, Lindy,' I said, manically cheerful.

'Let's hope the bloody petrol drums don't come loose,' he said.

On the ferry with us there were some herdsmen, with braided hair, wearing scraps of cloth, leather aprons and beads; they were herding bemused goats and sheep. All this and the army Jeep were entrusted to about two dozen petrol drums, lashed together and covered with sun-bleached planks, in which, I told Colin, millions of termites were living and feasting: the termite is the only one of God's creatures which secretes an enzyme, lignin, able to digest wood.

I felt nervous too, but for different reasons. There was something biblical about the notion of an elderly white man, and fitting for my father, leading a lost tribe of nomads, Jewish nomads, at that, back to the Orefeo country. Once you start to think in terms of symbols, life can become hell.

The motor coughed for a moment and the ferry plunged alarmingly, actually throwing one of the dispirited sheep onto its side, from where it took a long time (for a sheep) to rise. The sergeant shook his head in disgust: he seemed to blame the quiet herdsmen and their moribund animals for the ferry's poor performance. There were rocks, black and slimy, rising from the water on either side, rounded like the backs of hippo. For a moment I thought they were hippo, as the motion of the ferry animated them. Downstream I could see an island where the river, about a hundred yards wide, parted. The current was faster than it appeared; down there at the island it created spumes of water on the dividing rocks and vicious rapids where the water sluiced away on either side of the island in a thousand cowlicks of foam.

*

Mrs de Luth stood seized by horror, clinging to the brittle planking which served as a guard rail: as the water rolled alarmingly across the deck, the Land Rovers began to tip; at that moment the ferry struck one of the slimy rocks way under the surface. The lashing on the front Land Rover snapped. My father, vainly trying to fix it more securely, found his foot slipping into the webbing, which wrapped around his legs as the Land Rover slid forward down the steepening incline. Mrs de Luth's six feet were hurled to the deck. Two porters rushed to help my father who was being dragged towards the edge. The guard rail, designed only to deter panicky sheep, snapped like kindling.

For a moment the Land Rover hesitated on the edge; the ferry slewed round violently on the submerged rock and the Land Rover changed direction, sliding sideways and falling just before it hit the water, trapping the two porters and dragging my father with it. The windows were open; as Mrs de Luth watched – prone on the bucking ferry – it sank, cruelly slowly into the dark green depths.

*

'Jesus,' said Colin. 'Give me a plane any day.'

We were not far from the other side now, which was the boundary of the Orefeo country. Listlessly the herdsmen chivvied the sheep and goats towards the gate of sticks and wire. The sergeant shouted at the herdsmen, but they took no notice. The ferry squelched to a stop against the muddy bank of the river. The pole was pulled back and the sheep disembarked with small, fastidious hops; the two large planks were positioned for our Jeep's wheels. The rains had left the countryside green but wilting, like flowers that have been unsold in a flower shop over a long weekend. The goats began to nibble enthusiastically the moment they reached the top of the bank, but the sheep appeared confused by the lush, dying growth and followed the goats more out of habit than conviction. The Jeep was driven ashore by the sergeant, and we jumped in.

'How far is it?' I asked.

'Not far,' said the sergeant, sullenly locked in the private resentments of the sergeants' mess.

He followed a track along the river bank. At a deep pool we saw some hippo. When we stood they powered away from us, tons of protein in a country which was starving, their voices like short warning blasts on a tugboat's hooter.

The driver was silent as we set off. Colin checked his watch from time to time. Suddenly we veered away from the track towards a hill of brown rocks, casually scattered there; the sergeant stopped at the base of the hill and examined the remains of a fire. We had no idea if he had made his sighting that morning, the day before or even a week before; we had not asked. The sergeant examined the tracks in the sand.

'Not far. This way,' he said.

After about half an hour's driving over a sandy, rutted track, he pointed ahead. I saw a small gaggle of people, moving slowly with bundles of sticks. As we came closer I saw that there were six of them, walking in the direction of the Orefeo village, twenty miles distant, I guessed.

'He's there,' said the sergeant.

My chest squeezed asthmatically. The sergeant gunned the motor as if he were chasing fugitives. The poor, bedraggled band began to trot, dropping their miserable possessions, running weakly like old people from a fire.

'Stop, you stupid bastard,' I said, grabbing the sergeant by the arm. He slowed, looking puzzled, then stopped deliberately. I got out, Colin just behind me. The refugees, the displaced Israelites, stopped too and waited for us. Between us and them and their scattered possessions were a hundred yards – a hundred miles – of sand and scrub. Colin raised his binoculars. He stared at the desperate little group. The deranged insect life was stilled for a moment.

'Jesus,' he said, 'look at him.'

I took the glasses to my eyes and fiddled with the focus. I looked at the old man's shins first and then at his face. It was fringed with gingery white hair and its pale rabbit's eyes were screwed up against the light and the approaching catastrophe.

'It's an albino,' said Colin. 'I'm sorry.'

CHAPTER 15

Gullikson was delayed. He would join us as soon as he could. I wanted to see him in Africa. When we had been close friends, he was a gangling zoology student at Oxford. Since then he had lived (in symbiosis with the kwelea bird) entirely in Africa. He would appear from year to year and we would meet in a Chinese restaurant, Poons in Soho or the Hunan House in New York. He was married to a beautiful French girl by the time of his second trip, had two children (who spoke largely Swahili) by his third and had written a learned book by his fourth, about his true love, the sociable weaver. His wife, also an ornithologist, did the drawings. It was interesting catching his life in large chunks, a serial spread over many years. They were important people in the UNESCO hierarchy with an apartment in Geneva which they rarely saw.

The albino and his little band were settled with our help in the Orefeo village. It was hard to tell how old the albino was; the ravages of the nomadic life had given him and his followers a heart-rending frailty. Their clothes and their possessions could have been disposed of on a small bonfire in a few minutes leaving nothing but a handful of powdery ash. They were as slender as twigs, with round, staring eyes that did not move as flies landed on the lids. The albino spoke a few words of English; he volunteered himself as our guide, but to me he looked far too weak. Besides, the idea of an albino for a guide might appear to betray an unintended and cruel parody in our circumstances. All his life the albino had wandered over the area, heedless of borders, until the rains had drowned his remaining livestock. He was looking for help when we found the stragglers, desperate but fearful of the arrogance of power. We provided him with some chickens, purchased in Ngame, and some sacks of maize flour, to the annoyance and dismay of the sergeant. There were no young children; they had all died. One had been an albino too, a source of pride. The only surviving son, about sixteen, was delegated to come with us as an interpreter. He spoke Orefeo and Banguni as well as the language of the nomads, which was a curious collection of clicks and snaps, sounding like the Bushman language to my documentary-trained ear.

The albino, whose name was Xaloq, had three wives and two surviving children, the boy who was to be our interpreter and a girl of about sixteen. Colin produced some antibiotics and vitamins, because virtually every single one of the band had infected eyes and open sores. We visited them twice as we waited for Gullikson, and took the boy up in the plane with us. He adapted well to the new perspective, quickly pointing out landmarks which were significant to a wandering people, but from the air looked hardly more than little clumps of rock or dried, saucer-shaped pans. With the help of the lieutenant, who was glad of something to do, particularly something sanctioned by his President, we asked about the distant mountains.

'They say the mountains are not for these people.'

'What sort of people, could you ask him?'

The lieutenant smiled, embarrassed by the answer.

'Magic people,' he said. 'Sangomas.'

Sangomas were the shamans and witch doctors. Every tribe, in fact almost every village, had one, practising preventive magic and performing medical duties with herbs and roots.

'Orefeo?'

'Yes.'

'Are there any now?'

'All dead. All gone.'

The boy's name was Xai, and Colin immediately called him Guy. It was easy to see the way these things happened; just as

Ellis Island had cauterised and excised some of the more cumbersome Eastern European syllables, so the colonial travellers had tried, in simple ways, to render familiar this vast indifference. The albino was a great talker. His stories were fearful, with no happy endings. He and his little band settled into a small corner of the Orefeo village, suspicious of the gushing spring, nervous of the feral dogs and above all terrified lest the Orefeo returned, in body or spirit, to find the insubstantial nomads squatting under their fig trees, in their village. It saddened me that the nomadic life should be so full of anxiety. Tranquillity came in moving on, beyond the reach of enemies, beyond the smoke of another man's fire, as they put it. The emptiness of the country only a few hundred yards from Ngame was no threat to them; it was freedom, the freedom to wander in search of edible insects and plants, the freedom to hunt spring hares and antelope, and the concomitant freedom to get killed in any number of ways. The rains, the great augury of President Ngwenya's new regime, had succeeded where fifteen years of drought, civil war, lions and disease had failed.

I had accused Magda of having a gypsy spirit; now it seemed an honourable thing. What will the world be like when it is completely suburbanised, every family rooted to the ground? Xaloq's stories confirmed what Magda had feared about attachment: attachment is an acceptance of mortality. This was the pre-maternal Magda, the one with fig juice running down her chin and sandy creases in her thighs; I was not yet completely attuned to the picture of the new, super-tranquil Magda bathed in anticipation of motherhood. When this was all over (could it ever be over?) we – Magda, the baby and I – would go to a Mediterranean island and live quietly for a few months. We had pulled into a little island off the coast of Turkey in the day of our lemming rushes to the fun spots of the world, and anchored all days in the small cove where the water was so clear that we could see tiny, colourful fishes twenty or thirty feet down. Above, on a hill, was a small watchtower, a honeycomb of dovecotes, built a thousand years before, now inhabited by lizards and rock pigeons. I would find that island, make the watchtower livable, read, write, listen to the baby chuckle – all the time watching out to see interesting congenital characteristics developing – and Magda the gypsy could come and go, free of attachment. Acceptance of the baby as my own would be a symbolic act. My teeth were growing back firmly too, which was added proof of the healing powers of the passage of time.

With our nomads, and Gullikson and the helicopter expected any day now, our little world was growing; we were becoming a minor industry, fuelled by my brother. My father had speculated about what a world where America had never been discovered would be like, a Deux Chevaux world, a world of priests and mayors. When I first went to France and saw a Hulotesque Deux Chevaux, I understood my father's image for the first time: our aging Pontiac was a spacecraft by comparison with this mouse-trap. It was the vitality he loved about America – the brashness, the impatience, the sense of possiblity. Our nomads came from another world, a pre 2-CV world, where the height of technology was a pair of cast-off trousers with a functioning zipper. Colin demonstrated the working of the zipper to Xai, who had to take extra care as his penis was permanently at half mast. Semi-priapism was a characteristic of Bushmen, my father had once written.

Mrs de Luth loved my father because he appeared to her to be plumbed into the higher, spiritual things in life. As she watched the Land Rover roll over the edge, her unrequited love held firmly by the ankle, her physical ache for him unanswered, her guide to the higher world dragged down into the hippo world, her brain – already assaulted by the unkind chemicals of Alzheimer's disease – imploded softly, like the figs on our Turkish island, ready to expose their sea anemone interiors pinkly to Magda's probing tongue (the tongue which had an other-life all of its own). Magda, despite my warnings, had wanted to have a Turkish bath and a massage in an ancient village. The masseur, understandably overcome with lust after a lifetime of massaging elderly Turks, had suddenly offered her his own cock for attention, a role reversal which Magda found hilarious in retrospect. At the time, I remember, she ran near-naked to the little port where we were tied up, shouting, 'If you say "I told you so" I'll kill you. Quick, cast off. It's huge and it's oily and it's after me. Get moving.' Magda was at her best at moments like that. She collapsed laughing, while I fumbled with the ropes and tried to start the motor.

Mrs de Luth had written about the island below the ferry crossing:

We searched the island the following day, in the hopes of some miracle, and all the river banks. The locals say that the crocodiles have a habit of storing their victims under the banks in hollowed-out caves. I had heard of a man, in Tanganyika, who escaped from one such cave, and I prayed that Lance would miraculously appear. We were able to recover the Land Rover the next day. A brave native dove into the water with a rope to which we attached a strong chain and pulled it through the open windows. There was no sign of Lance's body nor of the courageous porters. I broke down finally a few days later; to be truthful I have never fully recovered. I have failed the trial which life has set us all. I am not one of the fit. Being tall as a girl gave the wrong impression: the tallest trees in the forest are most often struck by lightning.

Later in the same diary she wrote that she feared the world was regressing to a more barbaric state, the legacy of my father's casual theorising.

Colin had an interesting idea:

'Do you know what sort of Land Rovers they were? Are there any pictures?'

'What do you mean?'

'I mean, were they rigid bodies on the back or oiled sail-cloth?'

'I don't know.'

'Well, if your dad was caught by the leg, the only place he could go would have been into the Rover. Surprisingly he would have had a better chance if they were sailcloth which would probably balloon upwards holding a huge amount of air for hours. We used to do survival courses,' he added by way of explanation, 'with parachutes and so on.'

It certainly seemed a more probable theory than a spell in a croc's meat safe. A distraught and almost unhinged Mrs de Luth had finished the expedition, snapping away frantically with her Leica and writing furiously each evening – 'to fill the void left by Lance's death. I did not know what else to do, I had to complete the journey.'

*

As the river closed over him – the vegetable water flooding his nostrils, the dark shape of the Land Rover sinking beside him, pitching slowly then righting itself, releasing great guffaws of air – he tried to loosen his foot from the insistent clutch of the webbing. The more he struggled, the more the sisal ropes grabbed his legs. He had had the same sensation of panicky helplessness trying to unpick fishing lines. He grasped the back of the Land Rover and tried with one last pull to free himself; it was useless. His ears were pounding, his eyeballs swelling and his lungs searing. This was a banal way for an explorer to go, he thought, an accident of shattering randomness. But he had pulled himself by his efforts right into the back of the Land Rover. To his surprise his head broke the water in a dark cavern created by the sailcloth stretched over a frame of hoops, like the covered wagons that had crossed America and his native South Africa. He breathed air in great sobbing gulps. Floating around, pressing against his head, competing for space, were Mrs de Luth's wonderfully packaged supplies. The Land Rover shuddered. *It's going to turn over. The air is going to escape.* Instead it settled with its nose slightly lifted and tilted upwards so that on his leash he could just keep his head above water by holding on to one of the struts which supported the canvas. His leg, he now realised, had been badly crushed as the Land Rover fell. *The crocodiles will come as soon as they smell blood.* He started to unpick the fibrous webbing with his fingers; each time he had to submerge himself to reach his ankle; each time he was able to separate only a few strands. The sisal planters of British East Africa would have been proud of their product. How he wished he had not lost the bush knife he had worn at his waist for the first few weeks. He had no idea how deep the river was, but at the back of the Land Rover he could see light filtered through the dark green water, refracted by the movement of the current, but light nonetheless. He had the impression of seeing Mrs de Luth peering down towards him, her angular body jutting over the ferry's side, calling to him as if he were one of the Waterbabies. He thought he could hear her voice, as sharp as a corn crake's, calling his name, and it echoed slightly. Then he realised he could close the canvas flaps underwater while he was working on the webbing. Certainly the crocodiles would be puzzled by this. Nothing in their unspectacular evolution had prepared them for such intellectual effort. His left leg felt numb to the touch, yet it tingled ominously. Every few minutes he dived and picked at the thick, obstinate fibres. How long would the air last? He did not know. He tried to work out one of those cubic feet sums, which his maths master had loved. He hadn't understood them and anyway he did not know what the cubic capacity of his lungs was. The water was cold with a muddy, decaying scent, the topsoil and dead animal life in transit to the sea. He was there for hours, perhaps a whole day. Finally his leg was free. He removed his shirt, keeping only his long shorts. His hands were bleeding and his leg was dead. He undid the flaps, looked out into the murk for crocs and swam towards the fading light. It was a long swim – twenty-five or thirty feet – and an ear drum burst under the pressure. When he broke the surface he was carried downstream quite fast. It was dusk. He tried to embrace a slimy boulder for a few minutes but he was soon swept onwards. He found himself being battered on more rocks; he was in the shallows of the rapids. He could not walk, so he crawled over the stones. They were as slippery as bars of Lifebuoy. He fell and lay wedged in the rocks, lapped by the water. Suddenly hands held him gently and helped him into a makoro, a dugout canoe.

'Ngame. Mrs de Luth. OK? Very tall madam, OK?'

His rescuers were silent.

'*National Geographic* expedition. Big expedition. Lots of dash. Lots of mula. CTC,' he said, as he lost consciousness, yielding to the relief of rescue.

The makoro was poled away. Away from the direction of Ngame, into the gathering night, bearing his gleaming body through a thick bed of tall papyrus reeds, along channels made by hippo.

*

There was a disappointment for us in Bangunes. The helicopter had developed a fault and was waiting for a part from Bell. And Gullikson had been sent off on a preemptive raid against a locust plague in the Horn of Africa. The man was broadening his field of specialisation radically to include insects. He would come later.

'Let's do it together,' said Colin. 'I'll go in with you.'

He made it sound like a commando raid.

'We've got to take a local.'

'We'll take Guy.'

'But he can't speak English.'

'We understand each other.'

'You've taught him Welsh? Wonderful. Let's go. Why wait?'

'Why don't we take Monroe, just to man the radio and so on? He can stay with the plane, and he can speak to Guy on the radio, if I have any problems understanding him.'

'You'll be entering Guy in the Eisteddfod, next year. What else does he do, play the harp?'

'What about the lieutenant?'

'They won't go near the Mawenzi. None of the Banguni. That's why the guide hasn't shown.'

'Guy says only the Orefeo ever went into the mountains.'

'Are you sure that's what Guy says? Maybe the lieutenant translated freely.'

'Guy told me himself.'

'He told you himself?'

'Yes, he speaks a little Swahili.'

'Which you learnt in Dar es Salaam from a girl who could make pastry with her tits. Have I more or less got it right?'

'More or less.'

'OK. Let's take Monroe. I don't know about him but I can't see that we have much choice.'

Monroe was overjoyed, and accepted his supporting role without any signs of resenting the low billing. I decided not to tell Frederick details of our movements.

Gullikson's house became a hive of activity as we revised our plans. Xai was adapting fast to urban living, though he had to be told not to defecate on the patch of lawn, which Suleiman tended carefully with an old-fashioned push mower. The well-tended lawn was the last vestige of colonial standards, a hangover from a time when gardening had been the major employment in Bangunes, and the early evening had been alive with the sound of lawnmowers and clippers fighting a drawn-out war with the kikuyu grass. Mr Patel was a frequent visitor, bringing his quiet charm and a great deal of resourcefulness. He produced a powerful field radio, surplus from the Swedish army, snake-bite kits (two types for two different toxins), commando-style light-weight mosquito nets-cum-sleeping bags. 'You'll be delighted to know, guaranteed snake- and scorpion-proof.' He had heard of my misfortune. Monroe scoffed at these things ('All you need is an old black kettle, a box of matches and some cartridges'), but his servants were gathering together for packing in the plane what looked like a pharaoh's tented village, complete with battery-operated ice box and innumerable gas lamps. Eventually he asked if there was room in the plane for his safari cook. This old man had hunted with Monroe in the distant past, and was as delighted as Monroe to have something exciting to do. He wanted to bring his butchering and skinning knives under the impression that we were going to shoot big game. I asked if it was wise to tell him where we were going.

'Don't worry, he's a foreigner,' said Monroe. 'He's a Nyasa. The best cooks in Africa. He would love to go back to Nyasaland, Malawi as they call it now, but I won't let him. He says he's tired of cooking chicken. His name is Matenda, silly old bastard, really, but God's gift to the rude bits of a wildebeest. He can't speak a word of Banguni after forty years.'

As children we used to dread my father's cooking. He was wildly experimental and rarely successful. We were pretty happy with cheeseburgers, unknown to us in South Africa, but he wanted to try Japanese, French and Mexican dishes now that we were freed, as he put it, of the 'tyranny' of our own cook. For a time I longed for the reinstatement of our own cook, who was Skep's mother, Florrie. She had a wonderful way with roast lamb and mint sauce. 'Colonial cooking,' my father explained, cheerfully dismissive, when we asked for such things. The truth was that when we arrived in America, neither he nor my mother, outstandingly philanthropic with domestic advice as they had been, had ever seen a washing machine or an electric stove or a blender. While my father soon tired of his expeditions to the fish market to find fresh tuna fish and wearied of his searches for purple shallots and green chillies in Huntington, my mother quickly taught herself the fundamentals of plain, sensible cooking. American food is kid's food, and naturally we loved it. My father regarded the fact that he could go into an expensive restaurant and order a fillet or a turkey sandwich as proof positive of the lack of inhibition of the New World, and therefore justification, if it were still needed, of his decision to quit the Old.

'But wasn't South Africa part of the New World?' I asked.

He failed to answer this one, if I remember correctly after all these years, giving me, even then, an inkling that his powers of deductive reasoning had limits.

And Guy, the newly named Xai, reminded me very much of Skep, my boyhood friend. Their faces were similar, light in colour, and slightly – let's not mince words – simian, like a bushbaby's or a lemur's. They were both quick and darting, eager to be in on everything. The antibiotics had worked wonders on a large ulcer on Guy's leg and his pitifully thin torso was filling out daily. He followed Colin everywhere, carrying his pilot's bag, and he took special pleasure in cleaning the plane; I tried to imagine what meaning he drew from this ritual act.

'What's going to happen to him, when we leave?' I asked Colin.

'I wondered about that, too.'

'He seems to have forgotten nomadic life entirely.'

We bought him a white shirt with epaulettes from Patel's and a belt with extra holes in it to support the shorts. I wondered what Skep was doing. Still killing turkeys with a broom handle, probably. He had forgotten me, but I would never forget him. Had my father forgotten us as quickly?

*

When he woke, he was in a hut which was dark, except for chinks of light, which were so bright that they hurt his water-inflamed eyes. There was very little noise outside apart from the chicken and insect chorus of an African village; there were no voices and no children playing. He tried to stand to tell Mrs de Luth and his rescuers that he had come round and not to worry; he found that his damaged leg was unable to hold his weight. He called out weakly, puzzled by this indifference to a man who had so nearly drowned, and eager to find out what was going on. But still nobody came. He lay back on the reed mat. The rest of the day passed. He slept again feverishly. When he awoke he found a bowl of millet porridge and some sour milk beside him. His eardrum was skewered with pain and his leg throbbed; it had been bathed, leaving a brown stain on the whiteness, an irregular watermark.

He called out loudly, 'I'm here, I'm awake.'

There was no answer. Perhaps I have drowned after all, he thought.

*

We flew to Ngame en route to Mawenzi. Colin had planned everything meticulously. The boy with the overdeveloped forearms was waiting with a hand pump. Monroe drank iced brandy and soda, handed to him by Matenda, as we waited on the bumpy airstrip.

'Ngame,' said Monroe, 'always was a shit hole. In the old days the Orefeo wouldn't allow the Amabile to cross the river.'

'Did you ever see their village?'

'Yes, I did. But you had to take great care. The old king, Patrick's pater, set a lot of store by the Orefeo. Visiting them was strictly by permission only and that could take months. I was surprised when your father and the lady stringbean were allowed to visit. The American consul arranged it. Harmless man by the name of Elsworthy. Everett Elsworthy. Once dived fully clothed into the lake at the golf club for a bet. Tight as a coot. Last heard of him in 1968, a short letter from Panama, or Paraguay, one of those places, drinking himself to death. Not so much water this time, Matenda, you old clot.'

Monroe was wearing his khaki shorts and shirt and a bush hat – a soft, comfortable, well-ventilated hat, with the feathery remains of a fishing lure attached to it. He looked extremely unhealthy, but happy. We were all happy, underway at last. Xai and Colin supervised the refuelling. Despite my misgivings I was now pleased to have Monroe along. He was a shrewd man trapped in an absurd body in an absurd country; and he could shoot.

Despite the extra load, all the little things we kept thinking of piled on top of the big things, Colin launched the King Air upwards effortlessly.

'Bloody fantastic. Let's celebrate,' said Monroe, as Ngame quickly dematerialised beneath us. He held out his glass. 'Matenda, the other half please.'

Matenda struggled with his seat belt. My father, too, used to talk about the 'other half' but soon gave it up when he arrived in America. Like the cooking he had forsaken, it was a colonial expression. Or was it an Old World term? No matter, it did not fit into the forward-looking New World.

'Monroe, there's just one thing: I can't call you Jumbo,' I said.

'Why not?'

'There are enough elements of farce in this already.'

'It is a bloody silly name,' he admitted cheerfully.

'What's your first name really?'

'It's nothing to write home about. David. The oldest son is always called David in our family.'

'Have you got a son?'

'Yes. He's living in England somewhere, freezing his arse off, learning to be a doctor. I visited him once and we got thrown out of six pubs. The nice thing, to me, was that he didn't seem at all embarrassed to have his fat old colonial father with him. On the contrary, we all got on like a house on fire. We even tooted some coke, "*el snorto*", as they called it. I couldn't live there though. It's just too depressingly damp for me,' he said, answering an unspoken question.

'You've never been to Mawenzi, have you?'

'No. Firstly it was never called "Mawenzi", just the mountains, which I suppose made it more anonymous, and secondly it was accepted that it was forbidden territory, a sort of no-man's-land. The colonial chaps declared it off limits because of border disputes and so on and that's the way it's stayed. For the last ten years you could hardly leave Bangunes anyway. I wonder if there is any game up there now. Did you see anything edible?'

*

He lay in the hut for days. Food was left for him and sour milk, but his rescuers only came when he was asleep, to bathe his leg and clean up the mess. He dragged himself to the door of the hut, his swollen leg trailing uselessly. Outside three men and a woman sat in the dust around a fire. They saw him, but they did not speak. It was clear to him now that tribespeople had picked him up. His leg needed a shot of penicillin badly and resetting, for it was surely broken.

The following night he was woken and offered a drink by a new arrival, an older man who wore a gold disc round his neck. He wanted to refuse the drink but the enamel mug was held insistently to his lips. He drank.

'Oh, that's terrible,' he said, 'Do you speak English? I want to go to Ngame.'

He tried to reproduce the authentic pronunciation of 'Ngame', but the man did not respond.

'Ngame,' he said a few times, as the hut and the onlooker turned somersaults and he rolled into unconsciousness. When he woke his leg was aching almost unbearably, but it was straight and held tight in splints of wood, which were scored with the shapes of chameleons and spiders, and secured around his leg with twine made from reeds.

*

The King Air landed faultlessly on the dry pan. As we made camp, the golden domes of Mawenzi gleamed above and beyond us like distant mosques in the afternoon light. The sun set quickly behind the foothills to the west. Matenda, with the benefit of Monroe's constant advice, had made a huge fire and set up a table, while we erected three of Monroe's tents, magnificent green canvas structures with mosquito nets for windows, and heavy flaps which we pulled down over the openings and zipped from the inside. Matenda served dinner and poured sherry into our powdered oxtail soup, as though no meal could be taken without it. A gas lamp lit our table, banishing the outer world, except for the glow on the mountains which lingered above us, like sections of the moon seen close-up through a telescope. In the distance we could hear hyena calling in their anxious, loopy fashion, and also jackal yelping shrilly, as Matenda ceremoniously served chicken curry, with dried coconut and sliced bananas. From the mountains themselves no distinctive sound came at all. Xai crouched on the edge of darkness, watching this strange tableau. When we finally went to bed, he curled up on a reed mat by the fire and covered himself with a skin. I lay down on my camp bed happily after zipping up the tent carefully; but my sleep was troubled – not by the cries of the hyena but by the vision of the frightened, ravaged face of the albino. It seemed to me a cruel caricature of my lost father, the sort of vision which gives rise to nightmares. I stood up, unzipped the tent, and went round the back for a pee. When I returned I could see Xai in the glow of the camp fire watching me. He waved cheerily with one thin arm. As I clambered into my tent, he lay down again on his mat, perfectly at ease.

The nomadic life must demand an ability to live with an undertow of fear pulling at the ankles. Nomadic people must become accustomed to fear in the way that people who live by the sea become accustomed to the sound of the waves on the rocks.

CHAPTER 16

When Mrs de Luth returned to Washington DC without her coexpeditionist, she began a frantic round of meetings, organisation and writing. This activity, however, was not normal. It was hysterical. On a whim she flew to see the Leakeys' latest discovery; then she flew to Indonesia to plan an expedition to look at temples in the jungles of Sumatra and she wrote up the story of Banguniland for publication. In these months of coming and going she did not once call in at the Cathedral School to see her daughter. Now, despite the editor's strong objections, she refused to cooperate with the enquiry in Bangunes. The editor sent the American consul a sworn letter, but the district commissioner wrote back declaring it inadmissible. She refused a request to attend the memorial service for Lance Curtiz, but signed a gracious letter, written entirely by the editor. She considered spiritualism to see if she could contact Lance. But as bad as her mental state was, she saw that this would be too radical a departure from the stated and sober aims of the Society. In her diary, she wrote that she felt like a New Hebrides islander about to plunge one hundred and fifty feet from a rickety wooden platform with elastic vines attached to his ankles. The difference was that there was nothing attached to hers. She intended no humour.

Soon all these activities became confused and jumbled, so that her tall, angular body, heeling and yawing like a Baltic ketch in a heavy sea, would enter and depart the old Society building four or five times a day. Her husband, a NATO four-star general, was recalled from Europe to take charge of their daughter. He took her immediately, with the sanction of a court order, to Europe and put her in a private school in Gstaad, which was full of displaced children in similar predicaments. Mrs de Luth rampaged around Washington until the editor also sought a court order to have her restrained from bursting into his office, which she did constantly to demand that he commission a major story on the proof of regression in the evolutionary process. He found that the only way he could keep her out of his office was to have her banned entirely from the building. He did this very reluctantly, because she was a distinguished contributing editor. Eventually the men in the white coats were called. She was sedated and released a few weeks later to receive her Hubbard medal, at a ceremony which was kept short for fear of incident. In the place of the scheduled speaker – President Kennedy – one of the trustees of the Society who had known her for a long time, made a short speech and presented her with the medal. Everyone present was aware of the tragedy which had struck her, her tall crown poking out above forest canopy. She received her medal calmly but began soughing and swaying until she was led gently away by the nurse back to the home.

*

It was two days before we set out from our tented village. I had to overcome a strong urge to drop a note saying, 'It's your son, if you're down there give us a sign when we fly over tomorrow' or some simpler expedient; anything rather than walk into the unknown over six or seven ranges of mountain. As we began to mount the first rockfall, we were immediately challenged by a troop of chacma baboons which barked and screamed. My father had passed on Eugène Marais' theories about baboons – adaptation and learnt behaviour and so on – to Mrs de Luth: baboons retained an animal, indirect intelligence which man was losing through his estrangement from the natural world. Marais was not sure if this was a good or a bad thing, but for the purposes of my father's general world view it was a dangerous development. As we climbed up the unstable scree, the baboons jeered at us. Xai would have liked me to shoot one, *pour encourager les autres* (Colin translated), but furthering this petty warfare between nomads and baboons, each with their special reserves of knowledge, was no part of our plan. Anyway I was only carrying the Luger; the elephant gun was almost as heavy as a bazooka and had to be left with Monroe at base.

As Colin's no-nonsense legs climbed steadily ahead of me, I realised I was going to have to get used to his imperturbable back view. Xai skipped up the mountain carrying the field radio, relay aerials and spare batteries on his back, without apparent effort. In his right hand he carried two sticks and a spear, but he had not forsaken the shorts which flapped hugely around his skinny legs, like the generous bermudas the yachting types in the Med used to sport.

The scree was much higher than it looked from the ground. We were way above the camp, looking down on the alien, gleaming plane and the three tents, which huddled together on the endless flats, small and vulnerable. Monroe must have been watching us through his binoculars, because the radio blinked silently as soon as we paused. Colin spoke: 'Receiving, over.'

'Base here. Just about to open a cold Simba to toast your success in reaching the top of the first foothill. From here you're looking good. Over.'

'Fuck off, Monroe, don't waste the battery. We'll call you from the ridge to test the system. Over.'

'What? Oh, OK. Down the hatch. Oh, that was delicious. I may be having a nap when you call, so leave a message with Matenda. In Nyasa, of course, and only if it's urgent. Out.'

The top of the scree led into a corridor of overhanging trees and rocks, which was much cooler than the rockfall. Doves called in the trees, the gentleness of their voices like water trickling over rock, liquid and soothing. The baboons had left us and scampered away, occasionally shouting insults without conviction, like a drunk being led away by the police. Colin wanted to climb right to the top of the first ridge, a few thousand feet below the dome, both to get our bearings and to place his aerial at altitude directly above the camp. We clambered upwards, holding on to roots and vines, through the cool murmuring pipe of trees. In the fissures of the rock on either side an African fig (a relative of the fecund trees of the Orefeo valley), *Ficus sonderii*, the rock splitter, had established its strong roots giving the impression that it had actually pushed the rocks apart. If something like Dutch Elm disease ever attacked these trees, whole mountains in Africa would collapse.

After the space shuttle disaster, Mr Patel had made a bargain purchase. He had acquired a case of surplus freeze-dried space food, destined to be sold at Canaveral as souvenirs. When we finally reached the top of the ridge after about two hours of steady climbing, we boiled some water and tried some of NASA's Maryland chicken pieces with pan-fried potatoes. Miraculously, from a powder as light – and as appetising – as sawdust rose a thick, gluey, billycan full of chicken and potatoes. The chicken had the consistency of a loofah, and the potatoes were un-naturally airy, but the taste was very like real food. If I had expected Xai to do anything exotic, such as spearing a snake and roasting it, I was disappointed: he found the miracle food even more entrancing than we did.

'How are you going to describe Cape Canaveral freeze-dried chocolate turnover to him in Swahili, Colin?'

'I'm working up to it gently,' said Colin.

'Fucking,' said Xai licking his lips, under the impression, after a few days in Monroe's company, that this was a key word in the English language.

'He likes it,' said Colin, gravely.

That night we made camp by a small stream, which seeped from under the first of the onion domes of the mountain and tumbled away beneath us into one of the countless valleys and rifts radiating outwards from each crown. In the distance, over which we had flown so easily, lay many more ridges and valleys. From this height it was clear that the bowls we had seen from the air were still some thousands of feet above us. Colin had worked out the contours of the mountain and decided that we should walk along a line just below the start of the huge rock faces, which would, in theory, avoid too much scrambling up and down ridges.

'Do you think lions come up this far?'

Colin conferred with Xai. Xai mimed.

'He says mostly leopards.'

Xai was surprised to be offered more food. For all we knew, he thought the Maryland chicken was a week's ration. As we awakened some chilli con carne from the dead, Colin and I found the fire comforting. Xai sang to himself and looked down to the plain. We could no longer see Monroe's tents, but as long as we did not descend too deep into a valley, we could keep in contact with him. He had managed to bag a guinea fowl which Matenda was stewing – the only way to cook them unless they were hung for a week first, so he said. He was in good form, under the stars with his old travelling companion again. He had a message from Bangunes that Gullikson expected to be on the next flight from Somalia.

'The only problem is that he has to go via Rome,' said Monroe cheerfully.

The locust plague must have been nipped in the bud, or the larva, to be more scientific. We settled down for the night.

*

'You make such a fuss about sex,' said Magda to me, in her characteristically compendious way.

'Do you mean I should not mind if you sleep with someone else?'

'You know what I mean.'

I did in a sense. To her, sex was good clean fun, not to be confused with higher emotions. She had men friends from various other stages in her short life. From other worlds. I would hear for the first time about Serge, a great friend from California, or Wolfgang from St Moritz, or Akido from Sardinia the day he turned up to stay. I never knew precisely the nature of their previous friendship. Most of these men had the haunted look of the Euro-trash, fearful that they had missed something in Monaco or Méribel; their travel arrangements and their recreations were likely to change at a moment's notice, as word skipped through the expensive ether they breathed. Yet they were often broke; some of them borrowed a few pounds or lire or dollars, while wearing Patek Philippe or Rolex watches costing thousands. There was no staunching the steady trickle of febrile, suntanned men. I tried never to ask questions, but it was difficult not to speculate as they arrived from nowhere with only the most perfunctory introduction and slept on our sofa or floor.

Magda assured me it was all in the past. Some of them she had not even slept with, or perhaps just once after too much toot, she couldn't remember exactly. An element of morbidity invaded my thoughts. Despite the casualness of her attitude to sex, she could be frighteningly jealous of my comparatively meagre sexual past. The truth was she had banished it into a netherworld of insignificance. I had been playing in the minor erotic leagues until I met her. She was contemptuous of the kind of girls I had met at Oxford. Oxford seemed to her an insult because it was a mere fifty miles down the road. They were the sort of girls who went to bed with men to find themselves, or to write up their excruciatingly literary diaries. The girls I had known in Long Island, like Ron Cmerzyk's sister, Meredith (who had lent a dollop of ecstasy to one whole summer with her coral-snake tongue) and Mary-Anne Stafford (whose father later shot himself), were all grist to Magda's when she was angry. What had seemed at the time like innocent, even provincial confessions became in her retelling tempestuous, explosive orgies where no orifice or scruple was safe from my depravity. Oh God, she could turn things round, that girl. Also, there was a certain inevitability about the way our arguments were increasing in intensity. Once you start on that well-greased slope, there is no stopping.

Since the fateful encounter in New York, a few months ago, I had often pondered its meaning. What had she intended by it? Was it a reminder of the primal instincts I had loved, and confirmation to her of my weakness, or was it a more complex message? Maybe she was simply unbalanced, or stoned, or both. The anarchy of her emotions and actions made her innocent. Even when I finally found her in bed at midday (or more accurately, propped on the edge of the bed), with a Wolfgang casually screwing her from behind, she pleaded innocence, as the heavens crashed and the blood bounded uncontrollably around my head.

'It's not that important, for chrissakes,' she said. 'He's a nothing.'

It was so important that I believed the world was about to shatter into little fragments.

'Anyway, what did you come sneaking back for, letting yourself in secretly?'

'My plane was cancelled. I didn't sneak. I'm going. Do what you like.'

'Don't be so absurd. He's just an old friend. Jesus, it meant nothing. I didn't really want to do it, but I thought what the hell, he's keen and you're half way to Senegal or somewhere.'

I did not even need to pack before I called a taxi, although I realised that my wardrobe was unsuitably tropical.

'Go, I don't care. You make such a fuss about sex,' she called derisively after me. 'You'll see.'

*

Seen from up here, up an unknown mountain in nowhere, it had all retreated into another realm. Yet the painful memory lingered on, lodged forever where I was least able to reach it. And I could understand Mrs de Luth's madness and despair. For a nomad, death, disease and continual hunger may be bearable, but for us – brought up on the flimsiest realities, swathed in comforts both spiritual and physical, soothed with expectations and promises – there are certain things which are not bearable. To adapt my father's ideas, we have lost the animal abilities to deal with life in the raw.

How many miles was it to the upland bowl and valley where the Orefeo carried out their magic? Colin thought about twenty as the crow flies, about sixty-five as the pedestrian walks.

'Why are we doing this, Colin?' I asked.

'Because you'll never be easy until you know,' said Colin, without fear of banality.

Colin lay on his back, only his head and shoulders visible within the mosquito netting, a curious tube like a fisherman's seine, the top tied to an overhanging branch. It was cool up here, so cool that Xai had covered himself with the spare sleeping bag, although he did not like the idea of crawling into it, helpless against attack. I was more concerned that a conjugal puff-adder should crawl in with me, and zipped myself up tight.

Only twenty miles away. Who knows what my father had seen and what he had suffered? Like the nomads, he would have had to adapt to cope with such things. It was not inconceivable; during the war people had survived the death camps, even fallen in love and made love in the shadow of the unspeakable horror of the shower blocks; people who had had ordinary jobs which demanded no special accommodation to death or fear. I was puzzled, too, by a metaphysical problem. When we were in the King Air looking down, it had all appeared to be trackless wilderness, the interior. Now, were we in it, or on the edge of it? The interior was perhaps, as Frederick had suggested, a state of mind. To my father, this might be the centre of the universe, dense with meaning, rich with familiarity, the world beyond quickly thinning into incomprehensibility and menace. Why not?

'Colin, are you still awake?'

He was asleep. He could not help me. Xai sat up immediately, but I motioned him to relax, shrugging apologetically within my bug-proof reticulation. He lay down, smiling encouragingly at my peculiar behaviour. We were keeping the fire low so as not to attract attention. As we drew closer, we planned to use only gas canisters, whose pale blue light was wraithlike, yet I now thought perhaps we were labouring under a dreadful misapprehension. What if we were already there? What if they were all around us? I took comfort from the fact that Xai was sleeping calmly again, and Colin, who had had training in survival, was asleep too, making small nursery sounds of content.

I was not frightened; it seemed to me simply that we had strayed over the border of reality without realising it. The fire was all but dead, blushing gently as whispers of wind breathed on it from above.

There are dreams and nightmares from which you can consciously opt out; as they are happening you can rouse yourself and assert your waking mind to banish them. If the albino appeared in my sleep, I would wake myself.

*

His leg healed, not quite straight, but straight enough to be able to walk with difficulty. The passing weeks, flipping anonymously from the calendar like one of those film effects which indicate the passing of time, were the most acute mental torture, abetted by the pain in his leg, which had been reset by the sangoma. He no longer said either 'National Geographic' or 'Mrs de Luth'. The magic words had no effect on his captors. He had given up thinking of them as his rescuers. When he tried to talk to them they looked down at the ground and backed away. Every day they brought him food which was left at the entrance to the hut and every day the woman would come with the small hand brush of twigs and carefully brush the baked earth floor and the area immediately outside the door. He was given a drink of bitter herbs in the evenings, whose pleasantly narcotic effect he came to like. It helped him sleep and helped him forget not only the pain but the almost intolerable sense that nobody knew he was still alive. To have escaped drowning by a miracle, to have resurfaced from the reptilian depths, and yet to all appearances to be dead, was worse than straightforward drowning.

He wondered, as he lay on his mat and hobbled around just

outside his hut, whether word had reached home. Of course it had. Because he was completely isolated and cocooned, he must not assume that the world outside had ceased to exist. He thought of his wife and the two boys, who had bravely faced the journey to America and the strange surroundings, the unfamiliar snow and the new school, and how the news of his drowning would effect them. This thought was so disturbing that he sobbed as he lay on his mat, agony strumming his chest, a hollow, reverberating but useless instrument.

Ngame, he reckoned, could not be far away. He exercised his leg as best he could at night, extending and flexing the muscles, which had wasted alarmingly. The ferry was only a mile or so outside Ngame and he could not be more than a few miles from where he had been picked up. He was in the Orefeo country but not, as far as he could tell, near the capital village where he and Mary de Luth had happily posed amidst the artefacts and the cheerful, industrious people. The language they spoke was quite different from Banguni. It was, Mrs de Luth had said, a form of Ge-ez, which, she added, was a North African Semitic language, the language of the Ethiopic Church. He had tried some of his limited Zulu on his keepers, but his Zulu had anyway been of a rather debased sort; the flow of language between Zulu and master in South Africa had been strictly one-directional. He had no occasion to tell the Orefeo to mow the lawn or fetch a beer; he needed an accomplice, with a canoe. Dimly he remembered the makoro as a dark, damp tree trunk, a sort of coffin in which he had been laid by the Orefeo and floated away through the reeds. He must find the reeds and a makoro. The woman, who appeared to do much of the work, brought water each day in a clay jar from the same direction. He tried to talk to her, but she avoided his gaze. He counted carefully the seconds and minutes she was gone. The round trip to the water took her only about half an hour, walking very slowly with the jar balanced on her head. The water was therefore not far off. He started to pretend that he could not walk at all, hopping occasionally for a few yards to show that no particular vigilance was needed. Meanwhile, every night he stretched and bent his leg and walked miles around his little hut, burning with the injustice and frustration of being thought dead. The knowledge of the unhappiness that had been caused unnecessarily, and the loss of a promising career that had just started, drove him on.

*

I woke early. Below us there was a veil of mist hanging, like the smoke of the hundred thousand fires I had seen above the black townships of South Africa, completely still. There was no telling where it had come from. My back was stiff from lying on the ground. Xai was still clinging to the earth as close as a gecko to a wall, while Colin was sprawled in his sensible fashion, inside his bag.

'Morning,' he said unexpectedly. 'It reminds me of the valleys of South Wales.'

'Colin, almost everything reminds you of South Wales. I've been thinking during the night. I've come to the conclusion that we should give this whole thing up. No good – as they say – can come of it.'

'How's that?'

Xai was awake now and began busying himself kindling a fire.

'Look at it this way. Suppose he is alive, what sort of person is he going to be? And if he's dead, if he was ever here, how are we going to find out?'

'Xai will ask whoever is living there. We'll find out.'

Colin seemed faintly puzzled by my wavering and who could blame him after all his planning?

'Anyway,' he said, 'we didn't come this far for no purpose. It would be worse to quit now than if you had never started. You would never forgive yourself.'

'We could be killed ourselves; anything could happen.'

'I don't think so,' he said. 'Xai will take care of us, won't you boyo?'

Xai smiled.

'Fucking,' he said.

I was glad that my team was in such good heart. In the night I had not been troubled by dreams but by the realisation that this whole thing had started in a typically unplanned way – really from the moment when Magda's faithless soul, along with her glorious rear, was exposed to view, upended like a dinghy in a squall. This was no basis for an expedition which could get someone killed and would certainly produce pain. With that awful intensity of thought which assails you in the small hours, the dark night of the soul, I had also asked myself if I had not been a little casual regarding the President and his upwardly mobile brother, Frederick. Perhaps I had accepted their hokum too readily. If they were so keen to find my father – and incidentally their crown jewels – why hadn't they sent in a detachment of commandos months ago?

And yet Colin was right. Although I had started something I had never fully intended, we could not stop now. We breakfasted on hash browns and scrambled eggs, which popped from the sachets like genii in response to a little water. Was this what Neil Armstrong and Buzz Aldrin had for breakfast before they stepped on the moon? It certainly had a weightless feel to it, rather like my father's homespun philosophy.

Concentrating as I was on keeping up with the bounding Xai and the untiring Colin, we entered, without my realising, one of the high valleys we had seen from the plane. The air was cooler, and the vegetation between one side of a ridge and the other changed to a sort of alpine orderliness, but with curious, prehistoric plants, the giant tree ferns and groundsels we had seen from on high. The bird life inhabited the heathers which carpeted the flat parts and the branches of the mutant plants; they had dashing, energetic habits suited to a temperate climate. There was a kind of grouse which was not visible until it was almost trodden on, and it would start off at high speed, twisting low overhead and calling in alarm on frequencies borrowed from bats. In the crevices of the rocks there were little alpine flowers and orchids and the rocks themselves were covered with a red lichen, or contained dashes of colour as if crystallised fruit had somehow become embedded in them. There was a busy traffic between the orchids and the giant groundsels of small sun birds, as quick and brilliant as the humming birds photographed by *National Geographic* using revolutionary photographic techniques, their tiny wing tips beating five hundred times a minute, or was it five thousand times? No matter, the sun birds hung there in the same way, poking their curved beaks into the flowers of the outlandish plants, their wings a blur of motion, droplets of azure blue or algae green, like the spray of a waterfall, caught forever in the air. The familiar sounds of Africa were gone, to be replaced by the dreamlike sense of being in Switzerland, minus cowbells. Perhaps the altitude was having a deleterious effect. I did not have time to puzzle this out because we were soon climbing over some striated boulders, like a zebra's backside painted by a set designer, to emerge again in the familiar landscape painted in tones of brown, the landscape of Africa. And then we descended sharply into the gorges, which were hot and close by comparison, and overhung with giant figs and creepers. We called these creepers 'monkey ropes' when I was a boy. With my mother we had stayed at the Wigwam Holiday Resort, a cluster of thatched cottages in the mountains, and watched vervet monkeys swing through the trees. In fact this is almost my last childhood memory of Africa as my father was selling our house and his newspaper. He came for one week and performed his neat dive, his alabaster legs primly together, his toes pointed, into the murky depths of the Wigwam's swimming pool. A fat, green snake was pulled out of it one morning, and my brother, already showing the prudence and good sense that would serve him so well, refused to swim in the pool again. Although everyone told him it was a grass snake, he was not that easily fooled, even then.

He remembers nothing of that incident, nor of our previous life.

From the top of a ridge we called Monroe.

'Jesus, I was getting worried,' he said. 'Everything OK?'

'Yes,' I said, 'we didn't want to disturb you. Have you been trying to reach us?'

'I have, but you were out of range. Matenda's behaving peculiarly, even more than usual.'

'What's the matter with him?'

'It's hard to explain on this gadget. He says he's bewitched. He's becoming hysterical. I've been trying to find some sedatives. Have you got any?'

'There is some valium in the big medicine box in the rear hold of the plane. Is he dangerous?' asked Colin.

'Not yet,' said Monroe. 'The worst thing is I don't know how to make my own breakfast. I've got to get him right quick or it's me who'll need rescuing. I'll starve to death.'

'It's probably just shock from flying,' said Colin. 'It's not unknown for old people. Tell him to take a couple of valium and lie down for a few hours.'

'Can you boil an egg?' I asked.

'Yes, but I don't know how to get them just right, runny yoke and firm white.'

'Try cooking a few for different times, one will probably be OK,' I said.

'That's a good idea,' he replied with what sounded like real relief over the hoarse airwaves. 'I'll give him three or four pills at different times. He had better be tickety-boo by supper time, that's all I can say. What's your position, by the way? It's for the relatives,' he added, 'when they drop the wreath from the plane. Over.'

'If we go, who's going to fly you out? Matenda?'

'True, I hadn't thought of that. I'll walk. Over and out.'

'Do you still think it was a good idea to bring Monroe?' I asked Colin.

'Don't worry about him. He's lived out here all his life. He's OK.'

So I was the only one without the pedigree. Dutifully I followed him for hours, up the lizard's back ridges and down into the little gorges and up again, until eventually we reached a second alpine pasture, alive with butterflies enjoying a convention, clustered on the groundsels so that their white wings covered them like artificial snow sprayed enthusiastically on the props for a Christmas play.

'Let's have a bite to eat here,' said Colin.

'Good idea. How much further, Colin?'

'We've done well. Four days at the most.'

'Shouldn't there be some paths or something down there?'

'I don't know. They must either come in and go out by the south, by the head springs, which looks near impossible, or else they don't go into Banguniland at all, but north. They certainly haven't been this way.'

Below us on the rolling foothills there were the remains of villages, the earth flattened and a few sticks of huts still standing, but it was clear that the area had long ago been abandoned. It was not difficult to guess the reason.

'What shall we have?' asked Colin.

'Do you fancy turkey with farmhouse gravy followed by simulated brownies?'

'Not much.'

So Uncle Sam's scientists could not only miniaturise the turkey, they could reduce it to featherweight granules. My father had missed all this; I wondered what he would have thought of the world in the years that had passed. He used to play golf wearing a tie and brown brogues. The big news the year he disappeared was Cousteau's diving saucer. I have seen it and it looks too small even for Cousteau, never mind his co-*voyageur*. It looks like two large soup plates bolted together, very apt for the Commandant's *service non compris* demeanour.

Since then men have walked on the moon, the green cheese of yesteryear. And much more besides.

CHAPTER 17

What sort of child was I?

Back in South Africa my mother had tried to enroll me at the local convent. When the nuns walked towards us down a red, polished-cement cloister I legged it. To me they looked like big birds with flapping wings, only made more sinister by their pale, Irish faces. Nothing could persuade me to go back. In place of the convent I was put in the primary school, where a boy called Dennis, who had no shoes, and came only fractionally from the right side of the colour line, was beaten constantly with a ruler by the teacher, Miss Knudzen. She had massive tits, like party balloons filled with water. Dennis had a shaved head and thin, wiry legs. He was beaten at home too, and took Miss Knudzen's punishments with amused tolerance. At first I was a fearful child, and nervous of slipping into Dennis' world, a world not of right and wrong, but of random victimisation. Dennis stank, he never did his homework and his mother was too poor to make him lunch – so he was beaten. The logic of it was not clear but the possibility, arising from my father's unbounded optimism, of financial disaster leading to no lunch, no baths, a shaved head and frequent beatings seemed real to me. I befriended a cat in the alleyway outside our large Victorian house, with its waxed yellow-wood floors, and it gave me ringworm. This ushered in a shameful period of a shaved head covered with blotches of sulphurous iodine; I was convinced this was the first step in my personal Hogarth's Progress downwards, leading in the end to becoming as black as Skep and being asked to leave home to live with coloured folk in the location, only allowed into the backyard by the back gate to help kill turkeys.

The ringworm episode had its advantages: I was quickly taken away from the dreadful school, in the belief that I had caught ringworm there, and sent to Cape Town, to a private school. Here punishment was institutionalised. There was no sense of shame involved, yet I still suffered for some time from the fear of discovering that I was really an orphan, who would be abandoned again and left with strangers and forced to eat green vegetables. When I look back on it, I see that I read too many old-fashioned English children's books, in which social disgrace and disaster were always lurking for the unwary, particularly the parentless. But the new school, where I was joined two years later by my brother, had an excellent academic standard. By the time we went to America we had learnt some Latin and French and a lot of English grammar; we were so far ahead of the children of our own age that my father had difficulty reconciling his notion of a go-ahead New World with the rather rudimentary education it offered its future citizens.

Childhood time hangs as heavy as a flag on a windless day. Boredom and exhilaration are never far apart. Grown-ups are always groaning or complaining or easing themselves in and out of chairs with difficulty. The adult world seems to involve a harsh meshing of stiff gears, lacking all suppleness and joy; rather like the stick shift on our Pontiac in my father's small hands.

Xai was no more than a child really. Yet he had had a life neither of us could ever enter. He was hardened by life without being daunted. He was cheerful and eager without being malicious.

'Colin, what were you like as a child?'

'Why do you ask?'

'Look at Xai, how was he survived so well?'

'It's a question of expectations.'

'I know, but do nomad children run around shit scared from morning to night? Lions here, disease there, kids dying like flies and so on? Were you a nervous kid?'

'My dad was a miner and he wanted us to learn to swim. That scared me. This great big man, who couldn't swim an inch himself, trying to launch me in the public pool like a bloody rubber duck.'

'That's not much compared with a lion eating your sister and six more of your family dying in six years in front of you.'

'It's the rightness. Children are conservative. They want to think they are doing the right thing, the inevitable thing, they want to be reassured in that way. Perhaps it seems normal to Guy.'

'And there's nobody for him to compare with.'

'Not until we came along.'

Colin's body was always at ease, wherever we found ourselves. He was like a small bear, with no sharp edges, swathed in useful, functional flesh. I had become thinner, almost gaunt, in Banguniland, yet Colin was indestructibly solid. I've often wondered why so many professional golfers are fat when they must walk miles every week. Xai was restless, arms like tough ropes, tying and untying, his eyes quick as a bird's; tragedy had not touched him at all. This must be adaptation: you could learn to live with death and fear as a permanent condition. Xai spent hours whittling sticks, or playing a game with small pebbles, a game which he had taught Colin. I guessed neither the sense of time passing nor of time wasted meant anything to him. The two long days we had already spent in the mountains – so charged, so stuffed with expectation for me – were nothing special to him. I suspected he might wander for six months in one direction and then wander back again on a whim. His whole life could go by in this way with no regrets about unfilled time; it was quite enough just to survive with the help of the old customs. Frederick Ngwenya had told me that Africans feel uneasy about paying too much attention to time: this was belittling, and a form of unhealthy obsession particularly prevalent in Northerners. If my dad was living he would have had to acquire a lot of this African stoicism. When I last knew him he was brimming with cheerful impatience.

The Tuesday after Labor Day, at our new school, I was worried about pledging allegiance to the flag. We were not in uniform but in checked shorts and cotton trousers, bought hurriedly at J. C. Penney, which made me doubly uneasy. The old colonial education had set a lot of store by neatly tied ties and highly polished shoes. We had never been asked to stand with our hands on our hearts talking to a flag. This was idolatry, the sort of thing I had escaped by fleeing the nuns at the convent, past the deceptively meek gaze of the Virgin Mary, who adorned a crude niche just inside the front gates by the pepper trees. I stood with my hand on my chest, mumbling the only poem I knew by heart, 'If', abstaining until I had taken advice from my mother, but moving my lips so as not to appear churlish.

'Go ahead,' she said, 'it won't do any harm.'

She had ambivalent attitudes to such things as patriotism and religion.

Magda and I were soon to be parents. Exhausted and on edge, it was not easy for me to make out the threads of parentage, childhood and unease, which were entwining so intimately in my thoughts, as indistinguishable one from the other as the coral snakes at their annual meeting in Tennessee, perhaps the most pellucid use of colour devised by nature (and photographed by *National Geographic*), a sexual confusion of writhing, anxious serpents, invaders of my juvenile nightmares in their chromatic lust. It wasn't the naked breasts in *National Geographic* that made an impression on me, it was the mindless reptiles. I remember them all: the Nile crocodile, the gila monster, the sidewinder, the cayman, the mamba, the boa constrictor, the iguana, the komodo dragon, the Caribbean green turtle . . . Our childhood preoccupations all seemed now to have been tinged with vicarious apprehension; we longed for danger and fear; we wanted, like Xai, to be exposed to the elemental, but we were not. We, the fortunate few, have eliminated it from our lives. My father, on the bridge of the *Missouri*, could not believe he would be harmed. It was a game. In just this certainty of magical distance, *National Geographic* took the natural world and ordered it and coloured it and made it safe. The joke was that now we were right in the natural world, with a real nomad as a companion, but without the necessary evolutionary adaptation.

Xai was already asleep, as close to the ground as the victim of a road accident, and Colin was quiet, so I did not ask him something I had forgotten to ask before, whether or not he had children. It was anyway another instance of my glaring insensitivity: we had been travelling for weeks now and I knew very little about him; instead I was thinking only of my father and how he had been able to bear losing his family. One bite from a mamba could kill a horse within five minutes, my father had said. I checked my sleeping bag carefully for holes before shutting my eyes to the stars.

*

My father's hopping, his pained and resigned expression, and his pitifully useless leg had created the right mood of inattention in his captors. They stayed well away from him except when they had to carry out the duties necessary to keep him alive. They seemed unable to look at him for long, as if the sight of him were offensive. The sangoma visited occasionally, and they would peer through the chinks in the mud walls of the hut. They were obviously talking about him. The sangoma, whose hair was dashed with grey and whose face was very thin (so that he looked like the darkest of the wise men in a Christmas play), came to see him on the very day he was planning to escape. The sangoma spoke to him softly in Orefeo; he handled the leg, rubbed some balm into it and tried to bend the joints; then he set off again, walking all alone, carrying in one hand his thin stick and in the other a pouch, containing the useful and effective parts of plants and small animals. Around his neck was a gold disc on a thong.

The others brought him maize porridge and sour milk and his sedative drink, and went back to the fire, which was the living organ of the small camp. They slept in another hut, whose door opened towards his. At night they stuffed the doorways of both huts with branches of thick camel thorn so that the deadly white spikes created an impenetrable hedge. This thorn tree has been used from time immemorial as a fence and protection for cattle and humans against lions and hyena. To him it was in keeping with the Africa into which he had been swallowed, an existence completely without science but not without artifice. Inside his hut, whose mud walls were held in place by upright poles, he lay on his mat in a little world made only of mud, wood, grass and reeds. This was not a permanent village, simply a camp for hunters and drovers from the main stone-built village. Soon after the sun went down, the thicket was pushed and dragged across his doorway, a deterrent not only to the dangerous but to the merely malevolent animals, the honey badgers and the hyena which spent the night touring the countryside looking for trouble, the way the motorcycle gangs of Hell's Angels did on Long Island. In South Africa these gangs were called 'Ducktails' and in Britain 'Teddy Boys'. They were a worldwide phenomenon now, a sign of the looming decadence of western society. Eventually the murmur of the voices of his captors died and their fire languished. He began to dig away with a stick at the mud wall at the back of the hut. The Orefeo did not move after nightfall: the darkened landscape was full of portents – the liquid threats of the hyena, the sharp, pained cry of jackal, the shriek of cabalising owls, and unseen, but announced by sudden flurries of startled, night-blind birds, the passing of lions and elephants. At the end of each night the lions would roar somewhere in the distance, sounding like the rumble of heavy traffic.

He made a fist-sized hole in the mud walls, boring with a pointed stick. The mud crumbled easily now, dry and hard. He poked his head out into the darknes. The bush was hushed, waiting for him to move. He was frightened, but the thought of the consuming blankness of his disappearance choked him with its unfairness. It was worse than death. He pushed the mud out with his hands; it fell away in chunks, like dry dough, like unleavened bread. He crawled out through the space, feeling exactly like one of the four and twenty blackbirds escaping from the pie, spreading its cramped (and probably gravy-stained) wings.

*

The way things were going, some people in Washington began to wonder if Mrs de Luth was as crazy as they had thought. There was a worrying regression taking place. Jungle music had seized the young, there was rebellion in the air. The very word 'rebel' became something to be proud of. I tried to be a rebel, in my small way, but the bigger boys, who had sinister quiffs of hair, which terrified even the teachers, had no time for us. They told us to fuck off, while they talked about chicken runs and standing starts and laying rubber in their parents' cars. Anyway they regarded me, Wally Swarthout said, as a little Limey twerp. It was difficult, arriving in a new country and being made fatherless so soon. Like a lot of little twerps before me, I took refuge in books. We had mountains of these, some of them salty from the journey, but a lot more even than the English teacher, Mr Pinnington, who took a special interest in me after my father vanished. We acquired a certain aura of nobility and martyrdom, as if my father had been a distinguished soldier lost on service. On Memorial Day, my father's sacrifice and that of all those former pupils – many of them with very German names – who had lost their lives at Passchendaele or Nettuno and in the mysterious war in Korea became blurred in my mind. My mother absent-mindedly ordered and landscaped our lives, in what now seems heroic fashion. To her, America was a mere stopping point, or, if she had been a Christian, a station of the cross on her Via Dolorosa. Life was not disappointing, it was simply that only fools and the super-naive expected much. If she had known about it, she would have gone along with Isaiah Berlin, that the best you can expect is the absence of active repression. Many years later, I asked why we didn't all pack up and go back to South Africa. 'What for?' she asked, smiling her I-wasn't-born-yesterday smile. The equivalent expression used by Skep and his family was 'I wasn't hatched under a turkey,' which was apt, considering the low opinion of turkeys they had formed in the course of a close, professional relationship. It was a surprise to me to learn that turkeys were indigenous to America. My father knew this, of course, and at our first Thanksgiving he explained the connection between the Pilgrim Fathers and our lunch.

It seems that we, in our corner of still-rural Long Island, coped better with the disappearance of our father than Mrs de Luth did, down in Washington DC. Death brings strange secrets and emotions to the surface. When he was a young man in Madrid, Luis Buñuel was fascinated by the double suicide of two young lovers – virginal, engaged to be married and adored by their families. Buñuel concluded that there is love so intense, so overwhelming, that it is unbearable. Mrs de Luth, who had previously conducted herself with all the warmth and spontaneity of a Panzer commander, became completely deranged by love. If her problem was Alzheimer's Dementia, as I had guessed, it gave her a long period of remission. She left the hospital for three years and worked at her papers (including the diary I had seen) at home above the canal, only occasionally foraying out to berate the editor about the plans for the new building, which she saw as a monument to degeneracy and self-aggrandisement, the exact symptoms of the coming collapse that she was trying to point out to the wilfully blind.

Perhaps Buñuel's conclusion about the nature of intense love was borne out in Mrs de Luth, her brain cells already under attack from a mystery disease. And yet. ... What if she was simply tormented by her inability to live in the world she described, an insight made more painful still by the loss of the man she loved?

*

Matenda's paroxysm had passed. He was cooking again and Monroe was happy. We walked all day, up and down, from jungle to Scottish Highlands, with the biscuit domes always above us, rotating as we progressed, and below us the valleys and ravines unfolding. We were often followed at a distance by baboons; their leader, grossly swollen and overbearing like a Central American general, barked hoarse threats until we left his territory.

Xai and Colin, with their superior training, had little routines to make the long trudge bearable. Xai walked barefoot, usually just ahead, and he would catch Colin gently by the arm to point out animals and plants of interest. Sometimes he indicated the same thing, a stone or an insect, two or three times, while ignoring a view which would have given the Romantic school of painting a seismic shock of delight. Xai's cosmology, whatever its precise details, evidently started very small, with praying mantises and my old sparring partner, the scorpion, and extended all the way to the sun. They were linked in a way that I had previously recognised in the relationship between the Thanksgiving turkey and the notion of boundless space.

Colin and Xai did not talk much, but they conferred frequently; Xai looked over Colin's shoulder at the maps and watched studiously while Colin plotted our route, which he did precisely every three hours. He did it in such a way that I was always consulted and made to believe that I too knew exactly where we were. In truth, I had no idea. Once you surrender responsibility for such things, like letting someone else drive you in a strange town, you can never pick it up again. One of my biggest resentments, among many, against Magda was that she had, by her total abrogation of responsibility, cast me in the role of responsible plodder. Even her father, the implausible old *boulevardier*, began to call me on the most mundane matters, as though I was the sort of waxy concierge you find in a luxury hotel, with timetables, theatre tickets, cut-price air fares always at my command. He took to asking me these questions in a way which suggested that he could not find room in the well-furnished space inside his head for such bric-à-brac. At Oxford I had been considered a wild man, delightfully unreliable myself, but forgiven (particularly by women) for my foibles. I saw, with one of

those flashes of painful insight, that the pregnant Magda, insemi-
nated by some aspiring painter or pusher or rock musician, was
frightened by the responsibility of impending motherhood and
was making a bid for the return of her concierge – me.

Walking mutely, head down, the impact of my boots could
have provided clues to a blind man as to the terrain: crunching,
sliding, twig-snapping and sometimes splashing. Instead it provided a metronomic background to my thoughts which ranged
freely and easily like the birds on the wing above us. There were
always birds flying in the absinthe sky – falcons, hawks, kestrels,
eagles, buzzards, kites and harriers – all endlessly wheeling,
searching with their superior eyesight for rodents, snakes, rock
rabbits and lizards. What a grandiose way to take lunch, floating
on the thermal currents of the baked and tortured earth below.
There was no sign of humans until the end of the third day, when
we came upon a hut, with a small stone byre, for keeping goats at
night, said Xai. The goat pellets were old and the hut had not
been used for a long while. The walls of the byre and the hut were
made from the reddish, ferrous rocks which lay around, in the
same fashion as those in the valley of the Orefeo. Xai, too, knew
this was Orefeo work; he inspected the hut cautiously. Compared
with a nomad camp it was the Taj Mahal. He was probably about
ten years old when the Orefeo were massacred, but their powerful presence lingered on in Banguniland. His father, the albino,
had been frightened lest they return at any minute, to find him
and his worthless nomads lounging under the giant fig trees. Xai
scouted nervously around, climbing a small peak to look for the
Orefeo materialising from the ground or from a ravine or from a
rock. Their magic seemed to have left an aroma which he sniffed
nervously.

In deference to Xai's worries, we moved away from the small,
abandoned hut and camped in the open, above. Xai picked goat
hairs from bushes and put them in a pouch; I did not know if this
was for preventive medicine or to make something useful, say a
flight for an arrow or an amulet. Perhaps he was hedging his bets
with the end of our journey almost in sight. We lit the camping

stove and summoned a dinner of tuna and sweetcorn from the moribund space granules. It was lighter up here in the mountains than down in the valleys below. The dust from the plains was caught by the setting sun, which drew a veil, coloured boldly like the national flag of a Third World country, across the landscape below us, the effect you sometimes get approaching airports as dusk is falling: you're up in the clean air and they are down there, muffled for some reason in orange gauze.

Colin said we were not more than a few miles from the village, as the crow flew, of course.

*

Daily exercises and amateur physiotherapy in his small hut had not prepared the damaged leg for a long walk through the bush. Within minutes it was aching, the knee joint tightening and the crudely mended bones of his shin jarring painfully with every step. The moon threw deep shadows, a chiaroscuro which was deceptive, because it was designed for predatory animals, falsifying the topography and marring the judgment of distance and space, to give an unfair advantage to the night-sighted. At the best of times his eyesight was not good. In the navy, too, he had often been at a disadvantage, to which he never admitted, for fear that they might send him off to a desk job. His glasses, which he wore only in emergencies, were in his kitbag travelling back to America by now, or perhaps even being unpacked sadly and reverently with his other possessions by his wife and tearful children. He was wearing only his shorts, grubby and becoming frayed, and they hung loosely on his slight body. All the spare fat, the comfortable wadding of civilised life, had gone, melted away at alarming speed. His ribcage, silvered by the moonlight, was corrugated like the farm roads he had travelled in South Africa, searching for reluctant subscribers. He followed the path he imagined the woman had taken in the direction of the river, but it was soon dissipated in the deceptive light into game tracks, rabbit runs and cobwebs. He could not tell where he had gone wrong and turned back, following a familiar line of low trees, knowing that he was being watched by lions or hyena. The hyena would quickly take a reading of his poor condition, and overcome their natural scruples regarding live humans. Even as he turned back he knew he was lost. The safest policy was to climb a tree and wait until morning, but he was determined to escape the eternity of blankness and limped along, planning to walk ten minutes in each direction, counting to six hundred carefully. That way he was sure to find the river. He'd expected to come on the thicker bush, which Mary de Luth described as 'riverine undergrowth', after a few minutes' walk from the camp but now the landscape had taken on a liquid aspect; trees, rocks and animals all moved in an unstable way, prompted by the moon which was under attack from fast-moving clouds propelled by a turbulence of the upper atmosphere, independent of the heavy, expectant air on the ground. He stumbled through this floating world, frail and nearly naked. The flickering vastness produced an effect similar to the incessant firing of the naval guns at Okinawa, where the retina retained a picture which had passed moments before, causing a back-up of images to jostle the optic nerve. Eyes were caught in the unreliable moonlight, but eyes of what? He had no idea. At a distance, he saw, he believed, a herd of elephants, but it was gone before he could be sure, leaving his heart pounding dangerously in the sounding box of his chest. His chest felt frail, each individual rib liable to snap under the battering. A small sand grouse brushed his foot as he stepped on its scanty nest, and screeched in alarm before it flew blind into the scrub. He was sweating; he had lost his count, but he had forgotten at what point. He decided to start again at three hundred and to keep walking in the same direction, but he was now no longer sure of that direction. He felt as though he were drowning again – sinking slowly, and spinning. A baobab tree added to his unease because its roots were pointing skywards. He decided to climb it and wait out the night. But when he got up close to it he discovered that it had a gargantuan round trunk, with no hand-holds and no low branches. The trunk was rubbed smooth up to the height of an elephant's head; the bark was white and chafed in the moonlight. There were no other trees; they had floated away. He sat down under the baobab, trying to calm his disordered mind. He was counting out loud. He reached one thousand and three before he stopped.

In South Africa the Bushmen had held baobabs in high esteem. They were a sort of natural cathedral, vast and numinous; also they had pods and flowers and perhaps even roots which the Bushmen valued, for a variety of picturesque purposes. But there was nothing in his locker of anecdotes to remind him how the Bushmen climbed the baobab. He decided to move on, using the baobab as a beacon; it stood out from the countryside like a church spire rising above a bombed city. Yet when he looked back after a short, rasping walk, it had gone. By a coincidence the moon had gone too, dragged off and smothered by the clouds; still there was no air down here. His chest felt tight as though the nutrients in the air had been sucked out leaving only a thin mixture for the lungs to draw on, which they were doing painfully. As a child he had been plagued by fears that he might forget to breathe; one night he would wake up dead. Now he knew that his childish fears had (despite his mother's reassurances) a basis in fact. He had to force his chest to expand and close down; he could not breathe and he could not see.

He tripped and fell. As he lay he had a blind person's vision of Mrs de Luth coming into his tent at night, naked, her body all angles and bones in the lamplight, her pubic hair as fair as the beard on a corncob. She fell on him and her dry mouth began to nuzzle his flesh; he was being suffocated, but her pestle hips were grinding his sleeping, and probably comatose, privates without mercy. Finally he struck her on the head with the heel of his hand. She fell on the floor of the tent and lay sobbing. He was ashamed, but at least he could breathe again. He stood up and began to walk, trying, like the Bushmen, to smell water. All the other senses had failed him completely. Hyena called. Why did they need to jabber and whoop constantly? They were animals with a complex about life. Some quirk in the evolutionary process had left them deeply discontent. He limped and hopped on-wards, sniffing for water, an element with which he had shared a dreadful intimacy. And strangely that familiar vegetable smell, the rich, primal musk of the river and of drowning, rose to his nostrils from the dark; at the same moment the air seemed to cool and he stumbled sharply downwards; before him lay the river. He could not actually see it because it was masked by tall trees, but he could hear it beyond the reeds, calling to him seductively, an old friend, a succubus. He was buggered if he was going to try to swim. He would find a makoro, or better still the ferry, in the morning. The riverine undergrowth was a dangerous maze. He retreated up the bank and climbed the first tree he ran into, to wait for morning. He did not have long to wait. He rested his bare back uncomfortably against the reptilian bark of the tree, just in time to see the first stain of dawn spreading from below the horizon. This was a signal for the lions to start roaring and for the hippo to move clumsily back to the still inky water, calling matily to each other after their night on the tiles. The hyena and the jackal fell silent, their anxieties quelled by the light. He was tired; it was a tiredness that had sucked the marrow from his bones.

Light ruched the edge of the waters beyond the rushes, then quickly flecked the surface of the river with dabs of brilliance, and finally dyed it to an even dark green. He climbed painfully down from his tree and headed upstream. Along the banks there was a busy farmyard scene of feeding guinea fowl, ducks and small deer; the deer ran into the reeds and sedges and stood looking at him. He scanned the other side of the river in the hopes of seeing a fisherman or the smoke of Ngame; it could not be too far away. His stretch in the hut had left his legs even paler than before; his injured leg would not bend at all and he had to hop to avoid putting weight on it. He had seen men with useless limbs, limbs like sausages and pipe cleaners and vines, sliding, shuffling and skipping, scuttling like crabs from the crevices of cities and flopping, like seaweed in a swell, on the sidewalks. Now he saw that this desperate brotherhood, with their burning eyes and peculiar movements, was inviting him into their club. No previous experience, no references, no proposers and seconders were necessary. This was the quickest evolutionary regression imaginable, to a form of human low-life of the crustacean kind – mobility limited, defences nil, esteem zero. And worst of all, the nightmare not merely of anonymity but of erasure was looming. He moved on with lurches and rushes, first hopping frantically until his good leg tired, and then trying to put as little weight on the other leg as possible, which meant that he had to skip.

I was on the *Missouri*. I stood next to General MacArthur and Admiral Nimitz. I saw the Imperial Japanese Navy blown out of the water. I have two small boys. I have a wife whom (despite her reservations about me) I love. I have spoken to Cousteau (in French, twice).

And all the time the bums, the no-hopers, the cripples, the lepers and the forgotten – forgotten on a scale that not even Gray had dreamed of in his *Elegy* – were calling to him, welcoming him to their club, just as the river had tried to claim him as one of its own.

He knew his mind was not working smoothly. Eugène Marais had shown that humans, when hypnotised, performed better in the animal realm, drawing on the animal senses and memory. He was suffering from a form of narcosis. He had been given drugs. He had been deprived of conversation; that was why, he realised, his senses and intuitions had come to the fore. He went down to the river again to drink some water at a spot where the bank levelled out, and there he saw a makoro, lying like a crocodile in the reeds. In this random way he found what he had most needed. Finding without seeking. Marais was right, the animal capacities and insights had long been neglected. He felt some minor satisfaction with this first-hand knowledge as he climbed into the makoro and began to pole with the sun-bleached branch provided for the purpose. As soon as the makoro left the support of the reeds, it turned over and he had to swim it back to the bank to right it, bail it and relaunch it. Despite the makoro's instability, it was extremely heavy. Even with two good legs and no threat from crocodiles it would have been a difficult job. He started off again, positioning himself right in the middle of the craft and poling carefully. The moment it reached the deeper waters and the sharp current, the makoro spun out of his control and headed downstream. He tried to pole but the water was too deep. He tried to paddle but succeeded only in turning the makoro round so that he was racing downstream backwards, kneeling, as if praying to the river gods. He decided to try to influence the craft's choice of direction towards the other bank of the river by quick poles of the water. This was surprisingly effective. One thrust at the right moment worked wonders. After about ten minutes, he was a mile or so downstream, but half way across the river. He finally made land as the makoro plunged tail-first into a spit of black sand, sending half a dozen sunbathing crocodiles storming into the water. He was safe. It was a glorious escape. The achievement produced its own reward: there was a clear track with recent tyre marks in the light soil. They had passed this way to the ferry; this was the road. He remembered it hugging the river for a few miles before it reached the ferry. He began to hop and skip enthusiastically in the direction of the ferry. There, surely, he would find help.

The few miles seemed to be taking him most of the day. Two small boys herding goats fled as he hopped towards them. He shouted at them, calling them by his sons' names to allay their fears, but they ran fast, followed by half the goats.

'James,' he shouted after them. 'Timothy. Stop.'

The remaining goats attached themselves to him. Temporarily directionless, they were too pragmatic to throw in their lot with him. The lingering impression of the dusty little boys running in terror saddened him immeasurably.

There was a slight rise in the track and when he reached it he could see the ferry below and the small village which housed the ferryman and his family. He tried to walk the last few hundred yards with as much dignity as he could summon. The people came out of their huts to watch his jerky arrival, but they stood silently and nervously in their doorways. Only the ferryman stepped forward. He wore a pair of khaki shorts and a torn white shirt, and he carried a stick.

'Are you well, sir?'

'I'm tired. Will you take me to Ngame?'

'This way, sir.'

He followed the ferryman into a hut. He was given a kitchen chair to sit on and some maize porridge to eat. He began to weep violently, his body shaking. He had to lie down on the cool mud floor of the hut to calm his movements which were as convulsive and as uncontrollable as epilepsy.

He woke to hear voices outside the hut and rose quickly because one of them was definitely English. As he staggered into the flash-frying heat, a police Land Rover was already moving away in a nimbus of grey dust. The ferryman turned to him:

'He say you stay here, sir.'

'Who? Who?'

'The polis. You stay here. He say so.'

That night, no longer protesting, he was ferried across the river and met on the other side by the silent Orefeo. They began to carry him in a litter on a long journey to the mountains, a journey which was to last four or five weeks.

CHAPTER 18

M onroe told us that he had shot a hyena which was trying to chew the tyres of the King Air.

'Before you bleeding hearts tell me that hyenas are part of the delicate web of ecology, God's vacuum cleaners, noble hunters and so on, don't bother. They're ugly, deranged bastards. I have always shot them on sight and I always will. Over.'

'Fine. How's the plane? Over.'

'Hardly a toothmark on it. Over.'

'And Matenda? Over.'

'He's hunky-dory. He's thinking up a novel way of cooking guinea fowl at the moment, singing a mournful Nyasa folk song. He's working on me psychologically to get me to send him home. It won't wash. Now give me your exact position, if you know it. It's for the relatives when they come for the memorial service. Over.'

Xai had the radio pack ready. He was not overawed by the technology, indeed he had taken to the plane like a duck to water. He seemed to have a technological bent; he enjoyed nothing so much as changing the nickel-cadmium batteries or using Colin's compass, and he handled the camping-gas cylinders expertly. Perhaps his magic could cross the mountains on the radio to bewitch poor Matenda, like the hypnotists who used to come to our town in South Africa. A subject was hypnotised by telephone and arrived, as ordered, at the Masonic Hall with a dish towel on his head. Another stooge in the audience ('Never met this gentleman in my life before, have I, sir?') was told his chair was on fire, red hot, and he leapt up screaming, clutching his derrière.

We laughed pretty hard but Skep and his family (standing under sufferance by the exit) laughed until tears doused their faces. A singer called Johnny Ray came to town. The consensus of opinion amongst the farmers in the audience was unfavourable, probably because he wore make-up and cried at moving sections of his songs. My father thought he was sensational. We were about to leave for America so I was alarmed when Johnny Ray stepped off the stage and kissed a total stranger in the middle of a song: this was how things were organised overseas. Connie Francis would molest me at the dockside, I thought nervously, hoping Johnny Ray would not single me out next. He was so close, kissing a farmer's wife, that I could see the make-up, the sweat and the hearing aid.

Xai seemed infinitely elastic, aeriform, not the finished product of evolution but ready for any adaptation required of him, any fissure that needed filling or any interstice that wanted completion: the Ariel of the nomadic world. The idea of nomadism is buried in the race memory. It takes us back to a time when we were all free of the tyranny of geography, when we all skipped and floated on the world.

Our relationship was mute but affectionate. Xai smiled encouragement at me and was always ready to offer help as we stumbled through this strange landscape. For Xai the object of the journey seemed to have no importance; he marked his day with little repetitive actions, whittling sticks, playing his game with pebbles and looking carefully at praying mantises as if to read the expression on their small horse faces. The ethereal quality of his pastimes was matched by the lightness of his body. He rested as lightly on the ground as a dry leaf; he was like a tracery of twigs on the giraffe thorn trees which stippled the plains like needlepoint. Compared to him Colin and I were tubs of saturated fat, wobbling containers of liquid, reminiscent of Miss Knudzen's unmanageable tits. If he bled, the blood was instantly invisible, like the joke ink we used to squirt on each other from our fountain pens. He did not sweat and he drank with the pointillism of a bird. Around one ankle he wore a loose bracelet of porcupine quills and around his neck an ostrich shell necklace, the sort of thing surfers wear to proclaim their freedom from the trivial worries which oppress accountants, bank managers and dentists; in fact all the people with proper jobs.

I thought of the conversation I had had with Martha, Mrs de Luth's daughter, back in leaf-scented Washington. She said that her mother had decided that travel writing, exporting one's prejudices and preoccupations, is inherently dishonest, but this seemed to me unnecessarily severe. I was myself making notes of our expedition. It was obvious to me that I must record events and impressions. The alien landscape, the unfamiliar routines of travel and the elusive humanness of Xai, were all producing a slippage in the perceptions. I could imagine my father undergoing the same process but without the benefit of a touchstone like Colin. Alone with Xai I could see myself quickly losing contact with the realities as I had understood them and submitting cheerfully to the influence of the praying mantis and to the pull of aimlessness. Aimlessness is really only anarchism by another name. How wonderful to be able to surrender completely, a born-again nomad, washed clean of all commitments. I would even wear an ostrich shell necklace.

Mrs de Luth on her high-powered, intense expeditions had mostly been insulated from the insidious effects of travel. This was her regret. My father had sparked in her the notion that there was hidden depth beneath the surface reflection. Love refracts the light; he had become the embodiment of that notion, the living proof that there must be more to life than she had realised. Magda had induced a similar anxiety in me. Her reckless attack on life, her absolute lack of either guilt or second thoughts made me feel, like Mrs de Luth, that I had been missing a lot. The wild things, she gave me to understand, danced to another tune, an innocent and primal air, which could only be heard by the spiritually incorruptible. This was a nicely cyclical argument: the more depraved and outrageous your behaviour the greater your innocence. Naturally, I felt obliged to point out to her that poets with drinking problems have traditionally taken comfort from this belief. 'Jesus, you deliberately try not to understand. You know what the real problem is.' I did. Like a yachtsman overtaken to windward, I was becalmed. My sails were flapping as she surged ahead on a gust of innocence. In my heart of hearts I wanted to be more like her. I wanted to be aimless and innocent like Xai and like Magda.

Colin asked how we should enter the village. Did I think a few days of quiet observation or a bold entry were going to be more effective?

'What do you think, Colin?'

'Observation first.'

'OK. That's what we'll do.'

'What if you see him?'

'God knows.'

'What are your first words going to be?'

'"Hello, I'm your son," probably.'

'Do you think he will still be able to speak English?'

'I suppose so. If not, you can talk to him in Swahili.'

'That should do the trick,' said Colin, 'that'll probably bring on a stroke.'

'The truth is I haven't really thought about this. The actual moment of meeting has never crossed my mind.'

'I can imagine.'

Next morning, Colin said, we would come to the village after about an hour's walk. We listened, but from over the iguana ridges of the next hill we heard nothing to suggest that people were living there. There were no cock crows, and no faint cries carried on the wind. There was no wind. The mountains above us were still, the cornbread domes baking in the dying sun, rising to the last heat of the day, their surfaces browning as the light clotted, so that I could smell the dough of my mother's kitchen (the smell of childhood, if anything is). She wasn't much of a cook but somewhere in the memory of her Australian and Boer ancestry lurked a talent for baking. She would besiege the kitchen according to a battle plan of ancient, hand-written recipes transcribed by her from Mrs Beeton. It was a glorious war, with my brother and I as drummer boys, producing spectacular triumphs, as bananas, blueberries, caster sugar, cinnamon, nutmeg, corn flour, wholemeal flour, eggs, milk, citrus essence and dried fruits were thrown into battle. The result was always miraculously the same: a terribly beauty was born from the carnage of mixing bowls, wooden spoons, spilt milk and egg shells.

Above us the mountains darkened. I thought of Tenzing Norgay and Edmund Hillary before the final assault on Everest. It was very cold. Africa can be treacherously cold (Skep and I used to break the ice on the turkeys' water sometimes in winter), but it is a cold which travels on a false passport. Xai, for the first time, crawled right into his sleeping bag as the darkness closed. He was soon asleep. Colin was silent but waiting for me to speak, I guessed. I stared up towards the departing mountain tops. I could see the decrepit Livingstone struggling to meet Stanley, and I could see the exhausted albino magnified in an optical haze, but my father had retreated from the visual imagination. I could only summon his image as a naval officer, mummified in official photograph 19124N, standing close to Admiral Nimitz, who has an expression on his face that says: 'I wish MacArthur would get the fuck off of my ship.' If I saw him in the morning he would still be wearing the baggy shorts as I approached: 'Hello, you probably don't remember me, I'm your oldest son. Older son I mean, you've only got the two. The other is in a new business called arbitrage.'

But I could remember his warmth and good nature. All the kids at our new school liked him. He wanted us to bring them all home. They said he was 'sharp' and 'neat'. He liked them too. I realise now that he was probably soaking up the culture for recycling, but he loved their easy familiarity with the material world. He was delighted, too, that the seniors at the High School had cars and motorbikes: Americans lived in the real world, a world of obedient technology and docile atoms. He approved of school meals, cafeteria style on plastic trays. At my old school in Cape Town, we had Latin grace and table manners. The serving of overcooked vegetables and over-roasted meat was supervised by an elderly housemaster who had fought in the First World War, and brought something of the oppressive atmosphere of the Somme, a whiff of mustard gas, to mealtimes. This was all very different to the cheerful scramble at Lafayette Junior High. My father had been asked by the PTA to give a lecture on 'Africa, Cape to Cairo', which he had done with great verve; I was proud to be his son. America, I discovered, was eager to deal in love and affection. After he was gone, people still talked about his lecture so that my mother was once heard to say 'You'd think it was the Sermon on the Mount.' It was only his old journalism rehashed, but his story of the honeyguide and the Bushmen, the perfect symbiosis between man and nature, lived on in the imagination of Suffolk County. Perhaps he saw himself as the darting honey-guide, operating in a larger landscape. He was very disorgan-ised in his domestic life. He lost the keys to the Pontiac frequently, and had trouble remembering where he had put his glasses, which he wore, he said, only for the benefit of his left eye when it became tired. Yet he read the newspaper in a curious way, very close to his face, zipping through the small ads: 'Small ads tell you more about a place than the news,' he said. This is probably the only piece of his wisdom which I still use. In Sri Lanka the small ads are full of pleas for rich wives from poor men with BAs and sometimes near BAs ('BA, Colombo failed'). In Africa there are ads placed by parents of the bewitched and in California by the legion of the psychically troubled, which amounts to the same thing.

Little snatches of recollection, like tufts of grass pulled cleanly by hand, kept coming to me as we walked through the Mawenzi Mountains. This is what Eugène Marais meant by the phyletic memory, memory we don't even know we have. I remembered now that my father had tried to teach me the Morse Code and the rules of baseball. It was clear that he knew neither. Yet we went to Yankee Stadium, where he was longing to eat a hot dog and do the seventh-inning stretch, as though it were the Charleston or the Twist; we enjoyed ourselves. Wherever I am, I still look for the baseball scores in the papers. Those simple numbers bring back a sense of communion.

I had not thought about the moment of meeting because until then it had seemed completely improbable.

Colin was breathing audibly, not yet asleep. The night up here was so cold that it inhibited the insect and animal life which called out only occasionally and then in strangled, stifled voices.

*

The injustice made his chest contract asthmatically. His sense of loss was crushing. He had been robbed of everything that mattered. He had nothing; not even a sense of place. The landscape around them had lost any definition it might have had; to him it was as blank as death, as he lay for hours on end on his back, staring up at the inexpressive, cobaltic sky. There were five young men in the party as well as the sangoma who had treated him with medicines and balm. They did not travel fast but they were persistent. At first light every day they walked for a few miles before setting him down, wherever possible in the shade. They spent the middle part of the day in conversation or sleep, eating only in the evening before walking for another hour or so. In the evening they also set off to catch sand grouse or partridge, and twice they managed to snare a small deer. They brought him a piece of the liver, charred on the fire, before eating themselves. It was an honour, he knew. He began to try to learn Orefeo. On the third day of the journey one of the men revealed diffidently that he could speak a few words of English. He could say 'water' and 'meat'. When asked where they were going, he said 'too far'.

When the Orefeo rested, he hobbled around to exercise his leg, which had swollen so badly that both his ankle and his knee were rigid, held tight by the inflated sausage skin encasing them. Every evening the sangoma gave him a bitter powder to swallow or a dried root to chew, which he tried to spit out as soon as possible. He had the impression that they were heading north and sometimes he felt as if he could view their progress from high above, like the harriers and hawks which circled there constantly as he was carried. But the view from on high was not encouraging: they were tiny figures in a landscape so vast and featureless that he wondered how the Orefeo knew where they were going. There were pans of water every few miles and great herds of antelope and elephants, but no people and no villages. At night the lions roared and the hyena and jackal pleaded for release from their tribulations, but nobody was listening. One day a jet passed overhead. The Orefeo did not even pause to look up; he thought it must be the BOAC Comet. He could not make it out clearly without his glasses but he longed to be drawn up the slug trail it left in the dusty, speckled blue sky; he longed to be removed from this nightmare into the comfortable, ordered world again. The journey was the passage through purgatory: everything was being stripped from him; he was being purged. The sangoma would feel his leg and rifle through a pouch for medicines; he was fed carefully and solicitiously. One day they came upon some floating, green, bladder-like plants in a mere and the sangoma cut them up carefully and boiled and pounded them thoroughly. Only he was offered this food. He ate it, hoping it would contain some vitamins. It tasted of millet and not very nutritious. There were so many diseases he could catch. He and Mary de Luth had had shots for yellow fever, sleeping sickness and small pox, but that left dengue fever, river blindness, encephalitis, dog heartworm, cerebral malaria, bilharzia, tick fever, glaucoma and much besides which neither Uncle Sam's nor anybody else's scientists had yet discovered.

All the things that he valued most were now out of his reach. Because of the daily monotony – the passing of the unending scrub and the absence of familiar objects and sounds – he felt as if he were being radiated. The obedient atom could leach out unwanted cells. He was being prepared so that he could go backwards in evolution. Darwin had said that when he first saw a party of Tierra del Fuegans 'on a wild broken shore . . . the reflection at once rush'd into my mind – such were our ancestors'. Yet the Orefeo, for all their ease in this wild landscape, were not primal savages in Darwin's sense. Their supposed Jewishness could perhaps be detected in their evening prayers, when the sangoma would recite for a few minutes; possibly it was the Torah in Orefeo. They were obviously from a different evolutionary detour, one of the puzzling branch lines in the evolutionary network. He could only ponder the question of what they were preparing him for and wonder why they were transporting him over such a long distance. Perhaps they were going to sacrifice him in some way.

He also wondered why the policeman had not taken him immediately to Ngame. Perhaps he had been going to get medical help. His best hope at the moment was that a policeman knew that a white man had been kidnapped. His second best hope was that the man who spoke English could be persuaded or bribed to carry a message to the district commissioner or the police. First he would have to learn the language.

Days and then weeks passed. The routines of these days barely changed except in the detail of what they snared and ate. Some days the Orefeo caught nothing, and then they fed on dried worms. His leg began to get better and he was allowed to take short walks, yet despite all the space there was nowhere to go. He wrote messages on rocks with soft pebbles. He scratched his initials and made an arrow sign, the way he had done in scouts, to indicate direction. You might just as well write your name in the sand with the tide coming in, he thought. There were game paths leading in all directions but no signs that people ever came this way. Nonetheless he wrote the names of his children, James and Timothy, on the sand, as he had done on the endless beaches of the Cape; there they built dams of sand and seaweed and the little boys always expected to keep back the tide if only they scrabbled and dug fast enough with their small, stubby hands. He was too dry to weep, but he felt the wringing of his body all the same, although no tears wet his eyes. It was a feeling as desolate as vomiting long after the stomach has been emptied, the triumph of the animal reflexes over the sentient being. He stopped the dry sobbing with a big effort. He realised that what galled him most was the notion that he had been erased from the roll and declared dead. It was not a worthy reaction.

He did not know how long they had been travelling, but one day they put him down and pointed to the horizon. There, evidently, was the end of the journey. To his poor eyes it looked like nothing so much as a few cheese scones on a bread board, the sort of scones Norah produced from her tempest-tossed kitchen. Later that day he could see that they were not scones, but mountains with high, honey-coloured domes looking, in the dying sun, like the Temples of Angkor, photographed by Mrs de Luth for her story, 'Cambodia, Land of Temples and Timeless Serenity'.

*

I did not speak to Colin immediately. I wanted to ask him why it was so cold; I wanted to ask what he was going to be doing when this was all over. But I had left it late and he was asleep, sensibly not waiting for me before diving deep into the depths of his bag. It's odd the way you meet a stranger and become friends, sometimes quickly, sometimes slowly, depending on the circumstances of your meeting and the commonality of your interests. Friendship is really a form of love, but without the sexual dimension. My friends are mostly university friends, friends from before the canker fell on the rose. The friends Magda and I had in common have all gone. They were anyway not substantial people, not people you could rely on for the unselfishness of true friendship. They were people with expectations that were transparently unrealistic and perceptions of the world that were off-beam by a few crucial degrees. And they all shared a certain emptiness at the centre, a hollow spot, through which I fancied I could hear the wind whistle and resonate, like those Tibetan prayer wheels. (Tibet was another place on the crowded 'Roof of the World', its capital, 'Forbidden Lhasa'.) Magda and I had not really had time to become friends; our life had been too charged, as over-wrought as the images in rock videos with unexplained intensity.

'You don't even like me, yet you are always complaining about the way I behave.'

'Maybe I could get to like you if you behaved better. I mean, how do you become friends with someone who never bothers to get . . . ?'

'Oh, for chrissakes, put a sock in it! You're so bloody analytical. You don't "become friends" by working it all out. It happens. It's intuition, it's obvious. It's not all a question of manners, as you seem to think.'

'The trouble with you is that you don't understand the simple necessity of using words explicitly. To you words are like changes of clothes, just changes of style. To you "behave" means good manners; too suburban a notion for you. "Behave" actually is an emotionally neutral word meaning to conduct oneself. You know I don't care about good manners as such . . .'

'Oh, do shut up. You can be so fucking pompous. As soon as you say "the trouble with you" I know you're going to get very petty.'

Magda never allowed me to finish a thought or a sentence when we were in this mode. I obviously did not have whatever was necessary to hold her attention and interest. The more 'analytical' I became, the less she liked it. The less I liked it, too, to tell the truth. As we argued and wrangled incessantly, I was attacked by a fearful sense of the loss to come. I had more to lose than she had. I had the magic world to lose which she had opened to me, and which she was now discounting so fast. And yet she understood the weakness of my position clearly: I was in love with her; I was in love with her in the most basic fashion possible. Later, of course, the sex-madness receded, leaving a watermark on me like a faded winestain on a clean linen tablecloth. All part of the charm but speaking of lost innocence. Where do you go from here sexually? Towards a detached depravity? That would be even more painful than the previous loss. It would suggest predetermination and I was always quick to spot this in other people's lives.

I did not make friends quickly when we moved to Long Island.

I identified with the last Matinecock Indian, whose grave was bisected by a tree in the way the fig, *Ficus sonderii*, bisected the rocks in the gulleys around us. My father took us in the Pontiac to visit this grave. I pictured the last Indian surrounded by hostile and uncomprehending palefaces: he looked just like me with the addition of a single goose feather in his hair. Walt Whitman was born near our new home. My father tried to inspirit me with his '"boyhood's times, the clam-digging, bare foot with trousers roll'd up – hauling down the creek – the perfume of the sedge meadows – the hay boat, and the chowder and fishing expeditions." That's Walt Whitman. That's what it will be like in the summer,' said my father and: 'Look at those pumpkins. Look at the size of them, aren't they beautiful?'

How he loved it all. In those days there were farms right up to the edge of the suburbs, right up to the edge of New York City itself, it seemed, but even then the suburbs were taking great mouthfuls of the old turf. The pumpkins weighed the farmer's pick-up down; huge Americanised gourds and calabashes, warmly coloured to tone with the fall and the Dutch barns, which my father said were Rockwell red. But I lined up with the last Matinecock against all this gaudy cheerfulness. In Washington a few years ago I met the great Fred Zinneman who was protesting about colourisation of negatives. I knew instantly how he felt; it was exactly how I felt about the unnatural technicolor of our first autumn on Long Island: somebody had tampered with the negative, the pale, dusty, monochrome original of Africa. Later, when we learnt about the Loyalists and the Patriots, I knew whose side I was on.

Magda and I had had ecstasy, but not friendship. I sometimes thought that we were like miners in a narrow seam, mining the lode without placing the necessary pit props behind us. And sometimes I thought of us as mythological animals allotted inimical roles. In Africa the chameleon and the lizard, and the hare and the lion, are locked in this kind of magnetic opposite attraction. Mythology has not always been fair to women; they are often portrayed as sapping the strength and nobility of men.

Although I may have made her out that way, Magda was no succubus. My mother's analysis was more direct: Magda was a natural in bed; her attraction was physical, but who can call the sex business purely physical? I was faintly ashamed of this: it did not seem sufficiently *évolué* for someone like me. So the folly of Mrs de Luth's declining years was neither risible nor incomprehensible to me.

The mountain was not entirely silent, it was like a yacht on a calm sea, undisturbed but creaking and sighing gently. I found the quiet unsettling. I wished Colin would wake from his sensible sleep and discuss with me the nature of friendship and the idea of loss.

Ostia is a dirty place where Romans go to escape the heat and to dump litter. That is where Magda and I first made love, in the night shade of a fishing boat. We had borrowed her Italian boyfriend's motorcycle for the express trip out to Ostia in the warm air, and dawn was breaking by the time we got down to the serious business beside the fishing boat. It was light before we were exhausted and the beach, which had been magical in the crumbling oatmeal of pre-dawn, was filthy. My trousers were stained with oil and tar, and Magda's breasts had an unnatural salty film as we finally disentangled ourselves.

Later it began to worry me that she had not thought twice about taking her boyfriend's motorbike for our little effluent-strewn adventure. Such thoughts steal up at four in the morning.

CHAPTER 19

It was bitterly cold when we rolled up our bags. The Cape Canaveral breakfast had to be foregone in the interests of security. We drank water and ate dried apple slices. A mist licked the mountains wetly. Xai's pale skin had become faintly purple, bruised by the cold. He wore a woollen balaclava and a thick pilot's sweater which hung down below the level of his shorts so that his thin legs, as functional as a gazelle's, appeared to have been cut off just above the knees. As he shouldered the radio he smiled jumpily, perhaps conscious of how ridiculous he looked. His eyes were dull and the purple sheen made him seem unwell and shifty. Perhaps he was nervous; I certainly was.

'It'll burn off,' said Colin.

I thought, for a moment, he was talking about Xai's colour, but he meant the mist. It was five o'clock; after their night of muted noises, like an old contented dog's in front of a fire, the mountains were now uttering high, unsettling notes of alarm and unease. Vervet monkeys watched us and, as we prepared to march, they ran over the ridge and into some trees, their harsh calls making a mockery of our precautions.

'It's about an hour, I should think,' said Colin. 'I don't want to be dramatic, but is your pistol loaded?'

'No. I'll put a clip in, if you think I should.'

'Look, I haven't the faintest idea what's coming but this is not the time to take chances.'

'OK. I agree. Shall we go?'

We started to walk. In the cold the stiffness of my legs and the stress on the back muscles were exaggerated. Even Xai seemed to move less freely, as they say of race horses going to the post. Colin was outwardly as calm and meticulous as always. We trudged upwards into the mist, through the stubble. The brown rocks were moist and lustrous, like sea anemones abandoned by the tide. As if to back up my good opinion of Colin, whose solid back was still shrouded above me, on the slopes below us the mist was lifting as he had predicted, revealing not a sinister new landscape but the infinite and familiar folds and creases of the Mawenzi, the world – the planet – where my father had fetched up, willingly or unwillingly. The degree of volition involved was another puzzle which would be resolved. I could imagine a medium feeling the same sense of unease about communicating across the ether with a deceased relative. My feeling about the ouija board and lady mediums (not 'media', surely?) is that these are curiously suburban ways for the afterlife to manifest itself, almost as banal as the clairvoyant's ball.

The pistol in its canvas holder, now that it was loaded, was charged not only with nine stubby rounds but with a sort of electric field, which seemed to be radiating upwards, warming the top of my thigh with its potency. When Magda came into a room or a car, I used to feel this warmth, as real to me as the warmth of a person fresh from a squash court or a sauna. In a way Mrs de Luth was a medium and so was her tightly rolled daughter. To prolong the analogy, what was I? The glass that moves about at everyone's behest? The letters that form a significant word? And what was my father, that the Orefeo should have imprisoned him for years, as Ngwenya had claimed? What mantic powers had they been seeking in him? Africans are not alone in their belief that the magic world and the objective world are one. Nor is a shaman in Africa a more bizarre figure than a stockbroker on Wall Street. After only a few weeks in Africa it was easy to take the broad philosophical view in this way. You could draw your own conclusions about someone's mental state after thirty years in this wilderness.

We walked for an hour, as the mountains warmed and the mist

frazzled away. The sun eased the edginess of our departure too, although we were approaching ever closer to the village. As I had pictured it from the air, it was less a village than a small homestead, the sort of abandoned farms and outbuildings you find in the deep countryside of France. Xai shed his heavy jumper and his skin was losing its livid tinge. Eyes can change colour and so can skin under emotional pressures, as Darwin had observed. Colin paused often to use his rubber-coated binoculars while I sat gratefully on a rock or a tree root. I guessed that Xai's powers of observation and detection were on boost as he skipped airily about. Colin and I had decided that it might be dangerous for my father's safety if the Orefeo saw us and tried either to hide the evidence or make a run for it. When we discussed this, I had the feeling that we were perhaps too influenced by contemporary events – Beirut embassy sieges and so on – yet Colin pointed out that these people had plenty of experience of the world's inexplicable capriciousness, what with the late President Ndongo's murderous commandos, followed by the Israelis who had snatched away the survivors. They were not to know that the Israelis had come to save them, not those who had been stuck up here in the mountains, anyway. I had to agree with his reasoning, although rather passively. I found a tick in my navel as I dressed; perhaps I was suffering from sleeping sickness and would wake like Rip van Winkle – like my father – from all this in a few years' time. I had a loaded Luger, a Welsh pilot and a blue-tinted nomad as companions, stumbling through mountains as remote as any on this earth. The popular notion that the world is completely overrun with tourists from Stuttgart and Cleveland doesn't really hold up in many of the places I have been. Here in the Mawenzi Mountains, the last tourist was the Count Teleki in 1889.

Xai was balancing his thin spear on his hand, lightly, at the ready, as we neared the top of the hill, like the Zulus approaching Rorke's Drift, about to look down on Michael Caine.

'He's not hoping to kill anybody, is he?' I asked Colin in a whisper.

'I don't think so,' said Colin, grinning. 'What does your dad look like so I can warn him?'

'White for a start. That should be enough.'

I had not told Colin about the waxy legs and it seemed too late to fill him in on this story now.

Colin lay in the brown grass and gestured to me. I crawled forwards. Down below, at least a thousand feet, lay the village in its cup and saucer of rock. There were three main huts and some outbuildings, coops and runs. Xai whispered to Colin: above us, but across the divide was one of the alpine meadows we had crossed, hemmed in on three sides by steep cliffs. There we could see another hut and some large stone walls, which appeared to be built flat against the mountain wall, like the Indian cliff villages of Arizona and Colorado, depicted in *The Riddle of the Mesa*.

We lay with the sun on our backs, looking down at the valley and the tumbling water, which flashed like threads of silver in an Arab's burnous, through the dark undergrowth down to the plain thousands of feet below. It was a miracle Colin had found the place. We retired below the ridge and radioed Monroe, but we could not raise him.

'Are we going to move closer?' I asked Colin.

'I think we should keep watching the top hut and the village for a while. Even with my binocs, I haven't seen any movement, but there are chickens and goats in the runs.'

Xai was restless so Colin sent him up the mountain on our side of the ravine to get a closer look at the solitary hut and the stone wall against the cliff face.

'Is he all right?' I asked.

'Yes. But he's very nervous, or excited. This is no everyday little village. He has heard of this place. He says it's well known to the wanderers, although they don't come up this far.'

'Nobody does, by the look of it.'

'What do you think goes on here?'

'I think this is where they mined the gold, and collected plants and roots. That's the most sensible explanation.'

Xai had quickly melded with the rocks and scrub above us.

'I'm not sure if "sensible" comes into this,' said Colin, scanning the village below carefully. 'Here, have a look.'

I focused the binoculars. The village was dark and gloomy, still in the shade of the overhanging mountains. I saw a flash of white in one of the chicken coops and then saw a speckled chicken itself at the woven reed gate of the coop. Its head was bobbing, waiting impatiently, the way chickens do, for the daily ritual of release and feed. Suddenly the cool, still stones of the buildings were animated. I now knew for sure that they were not ruins but inhabited by real people. I felt the choking sensation of fear, the same feeling I had had when I opened the door of our apartment to anticipate the wounded animal whimpers, the little athletic noises of Magda's lovemaking. The walk from the door to the bedroom had been almost unbearable because of the certainty of what I was going to find. In just the same way, I now knew I would find my father. I handed the binoculars to Colin and lay face down to calm myself, my head resting on my forearm. After a few minutes I had to crawl back from the ridge to shit.

'Nothing yet,' said Colin, when I reached him again.

I looked down to the village. From down there, but swirling around in the walls of the valley so that it came from nowhere in particular, we heard the bleating of hungry goats. It was as resonant to my ears as the Campanile of San Giorgio Maggiore in Venice; the bells rising confidently above the tourist flux and motorboat growl with a call that crashed in my ears, vouchsafing a message of eternity, which I believed for the moment. The bleating of the goats was directed at someone, yet no one came. In films they often exaggerate one significant sound beyond all reasonable levels; it conveys the sense of what the director intends: the door's creak, the dog's bark, the wolf's howl, the water's splash, the thunder's crack, the crow's call, the bat's squeak, the rattler's susurration, the baby's cry.

The goats' demands were as painful now as an unanswered phone. Nobody came to unpen them as we lay in the warming sun. Nobody came as the morning began to gather itself from the deep, mossy shadows and the cool, moist crevices of the valley. As the goats complained, their voices were lightly underscored by the rush and tumble of water racing down, half heard, half hidden, to the vast plain and eventually via the unpredictable Bangunes River, to the sea, to join that great shard of water, which lay broken and cracked on the earth's surface. The notion which so appealed to Conrad.

Here it was easy to understand the creation myths of Africa, which concerned natural events with the direct and decisive participation of snakes, chameleons and hares. The goats were clever creatures, too, very conscious of the whimsicality of creation, not prepared to be taken for mugs. Yet what is the purpose of these myths? Do they have any expository value? The law of the excluded middle is an un-African proposition. The excluded middle is a sort of mousehole into which Africa is slipping, where nothing is either true or false. Down below, the valley was suffering from a paralysis. I could feel it setting like a limb caught in plaster of paris, or Mrs de Luth's pottery fused by the blast of Hiroshima (the unfriendly, unruly atom, this one). I wanted to roll a boulder down the cliff face; I wanted to release the chickens myself. The cries of the goats sounded like the pleading of overtired children.

Xai returned, and he and Colin had a brief discussion. Xai had lost his unnatural colour completely. Colin sent him off again, down the hill towards the valley, behind the boulders and bushes which marked the top of the ridge.

'What's he doing now?'

'He's looking to see if anyone is creeping up on us. He seems very agitated.'

'Are you serious?'

'Yes.'

I stared down at the village. Perhaps long years of suspicion and isolation had taught them to spot strangers a mile off. Yet they could not have expected us by the high route, under the golden domes. There was no movement down there except for the jostling of the caged goats indistinctly seen.

Xai reappeared suddenly. He was crouched now like a figure in a cave painting, like a figure in a modern ballet, his body tensed expressively, his thin legs bundles of fibres. He spoke to Colin in a whisper.

'Someone's coming up to the village.'

We lay, peering over the edge. Colin gave me the binoculars. I took them warily: these glasses produced nasty surprises. I scanned the valley carefully. Colin tugged my arm gently and pointed me towards a rockslide at the end of the valley. I found an old man moving slowly across the strewn boulders, and fixed him firmly in the Japanese optics. He was very elderly, shuffling slowly along the valley, like someone in oversized carpet slippers; like an elderly Chinese. He wore a short skirt of leather and around his neck, on a thong, hung a golden disc, the size of a saucer. The sight of this frail old African released me from the accumulated uncertainties of the morning. My heart went out to him; we had antibiotics and space rations. We could free him from this unnatural servitude. Yet my experience of old people told me that they are not so easily liberated. They take comfort in the accretions and deposits of age. As with oysters, the process is long and irreversible.

Painfully slowly, the old man fiddled with the lattice gate of the goat pen. (Why hadn't the goats eaten it to release themselves? Goats and donkeys, my father had written, have cast-iron digestive systems.) He drew back the gate carefully and the ungrateful goats bounded out and began to climb the hillside opposite us. Laboriously the old man released the chickens from their coop and bent to collect eggs. The goats fanned out over the steep slope. Their bleating changed to brief, world-weary goats' talk. The old man walked slowly to the second house and entered the gloom. I took the binoculars from my eyes.

'What did he look like?' asked Colin.

'Old and decrepit.'

'Who was it?'

I realised that from this distance Colin had been unable to

make out the features, while I was consumed in the straitened world in the binoculars.

'It wasn't your dad, obviously?'

'No. He's wearing a gold medal thing around his neck. He looks like an Orefeo to me.'

The sun had reached the houses below us, bleaching out the shadow and warming the cool, dark crannies. The menace of the morning had gone; the agitation of monkeys and birds calmed. Lizards appeared on the warming rocks near us. They reminded me of the Turkish island where Magda and I had anchored, an island infested with lizards; grey lizards whose tails were clearly colour-coded, the disposable bit being in a light green. These African lizards were a dusty brown but the insatiable need for warmth was something they had in common with their Mediterranean cousins. Xai had warmed up but he was still crouched, peering from behind a rock, the spear and the sticks rolling in the palms of his hands gently. Whatever magical powers resided here in this forgotten valley, they were real to him. To me the old man seemed perfectly innocuous. Yet Xai was deeply disturbed, as though – I thought – a figure from a fairy tale or a nightmare had come to life.

'Why is he so nervous, Colin?'

'I don't know. My Swahili doesn't extend to discussions of the unconscious.'

'Are you nervous?'

'Not in a physical sense. I don't believe there's any danger,' he said. 'But I feel the way I did when my father tried to launch me in the swimming pool. Do you know what I mean?'

I understood exactly.

'There are no women and children down there,' he added.

'How's that?'

'Men don't herd goats. Boys look after goats.'

I knew this. Very small boys were sent out with the goats as training for the tougher work of herding cattle, to come later. This peaceful and solitary communion with the cattle and the goats was an essential element in African life, a spiritual experience. The goats have a more pragmatic view of domesticity and tolerate it for the moment, according to African myth. Down below us all the myths of Africa were distilled into very little.

The lizards had become lustful, scuttling after each other as the sun defrosted their libidos.

'Shall we wait?' asked Colin.

'I think so. Let's see what happens.'

'How much do you want me to tell Guy now that we've arrived?'

'Just tell him that we are looking for my father.'

'OK.'

'Does he know any detail about this valley?'

'Only rumour and myth, I think. It's always been feared by the nomads.'

But I was insistent:

'Has he actually said what he thinks about it? What words did he use?'

'I get the feeling it's not expressible. It's a shock to him to find it exists at all. That's my guess, but I can't really be sure.'

Frederick had given me to understand that there are plenty of ideas in Africa which cannot be expressed. And Mrs de Luth had come round to believing that to describe and rationalise these mysteries was to debase them. D. H. Lawrence, in his New Mexico phase, had described them as the 'delicate mysteries of life'.

Xai was slumped against the rock with his head flopped forwards; he smiled weakly at our scrutiny. I had thought Xai, with his skinny arms and his inexhaustible energy, was afraid of nothing. But the sight of the harmless old man with the gold disc at his throat had drawn the sinews out of him, the way French butchers do with chicken legs.

Colin talked to Xai, and put a hand on his delicate shoulder. The old man, Xai said, was a very potent person. Xai clutched his throat to indicate the gold disc. The disc was significant. To me it looked like part of the missing treasures, the wonderfully refined work of the Orefeo craftsmen which I had seen in Mrs de Luth's cheery pictures. I had a number of theories about the cause of Xai's unhappiness, but I kept them to myself. I slept, like an animal, half awake. I woke and dozed and then slept more soundly. The tensions of the morning had drained me. When I woke again, with Colin tugging my arm gently, my shirt was moist with a dewfall of sweat.

'There's someone else. Another old man. An African,' he added gently.

I looked through the glasses. A second man was moving slowly but steadily up the slope away from the huts towards the alpine meadow above. He too wore the gold badge, over a white shirt done up at the collar. His hair was grey, like Uncle Ben's on the rice pack. Instead of the leather apron, he wore ragged trousers above his bare feet. We watched his progress for at least an hour as he appeared and disappeared among the chaotic monkey ropes and boulders, evidently following a path. It was like watching a mountaineering film on television, safely at the end of a telephoto lens. Finally he made it to the top of the path and the alpine plateau. There he turned to look back at the valley and stared straight into the binoculars for a moment; I saw him full face, so intimately that I could make out the tiny screws of grey hair on his jowls. He turned and left the optical world.

We watched the village all day long. No other inhabitants appeared. As the cold air began to creep up the mountain and the solid light of day became friable, the valley quickly lost the sunlight. The goats at the end of a long circuit were now nibbling their way back to the village. The old man who had released them appeared again, shuffling slowly with an armful of branches which he placed in their pen with difficulty. He stood waiting for the goats' return, swaying slightly. Around his shoulders he held a scrap of blanket, which hid his gold brooch. The goats filed sensibly into their pen and he closed the gate. Then he penned the chickens. The second old man was picking his way down from the high meadows, the curious, cool world of mutant plants and heathers above. Beyond that the domes of the mountains caught fire in the last rays of the sun and blazed brightly for a few minutes, while down here the light crumbled into dusk, signalled by the unsettled monkeys and late-roosting birds.

We were governed by the oldest calendar of all, nightfall and daybreak. Quickly we settled some way beneath the ridge of the hill and ate our chocolate and dried apple. It seemed absurd to guard against two or three old men, but Colin and I agreed to keep watch alternately all night. It was during my second watch that Xai left, taking the radio. I was not even aware of having gone to sleep. I woke Colin.

'I'm afraid he's gone, with the radio.'

'He loved the radio,' said Colin. 'There's nothing we can do now. Let's have a drink.'

We drank brandy from a small flask and lay half drunk waiting for dawn. At first light we discovered that Xai had taken the last of the Canaveral rations and Monroe's Luger.

'I'm sorry; I trusted him too much,' said Colin.

'Now at least we know the answer to something which was puzzling me.'

'What's that?'

'I was wondering how a nomad could survive in a state of sheer innocence.'

'He was frightened of the Orefeo.'

'It's not surprising. These old men are the priests, the rabbis of the Orefeo. Those discs are their badge of office. They are probably the last of the royal shamans. They were the Israelites to Ngwenya's Pharaoh.'

Mrs de Luth had written fancifully about the royal soul washers and photographed what she said was their sacred regalia. At the time I thought it looked rather like those little tasters sommeliers wear around their necks. I had dismissed the soul washers as crude oversimplification by Mrs de Luth in her pursuit of a colourful story, yet the medals dangling on the chests of the old men, the chests of farmyard pullets, now had a powerful significance. If these were the soul washers, in charge of purifying the King's soul, they were the Olympians of African myth and it was not at all surprising that Xai had fled. Although they were old – perhaps even older than my father – it was not their frail bodies he feared. The preoccupations of Mrs de Luth's twilit, fogbound years now also seemed to have some substance. The view from here, without a radio, without rations, without the pistol, had changed. We were the frail and flimsy ones; we were the flying ants at dusk. The soul washers had lived here for decades; they had the power of their magic, the power they had exerted over my defenceless father. It could be stated even more simply, I thought: we had lost the connections with our own world just as my father had lost them all those years ago. He had left behind a world where the latest film sensation was *Bwana Devil* in 3-D. Did the irony ever strike him? Just before he set off he had almost mastered the Hula-Hoop, he had read *The Catcher in the Rye* and he had recommended chlorophyll toothpaste for the whole family (although my mother did ask if it was a good idea to brush our teeth with extract of lawn). But he had missed the *Lady Chatterly* trial and the miniskirt and probably still believed it was OK to use the term 'coloured people'.

Colin was disturbed by Xai's defection. For the first time on this journey I felt that I had the edge over him in experience. It was no surprise to me that Xai had gone. My life with Magda had taught me that a nomad with a sense of responsibility is a contradiction in terms. The free spirit recognises no restriction. No use for someone like me to try to shuck off responsibility; the conscious effort – what Magda called the analytical approach – rules you out. I just hoped that Xai had not gone to woo the Orefeo with the Luger as a dowry. We drank some water and found a few desiccated chocolate chip cookies to share.

'Colin, let's walk straight in. Like Stanley.'

By this I meant fearlessly, discounting the local difficulties and superstitions.

'Good idea.'

Colin shaved carefully while I packed my bag. I wondered if my father would recognize me. Maybe I was frozen forever in his recollection as a small, bewildered boy with a dislike of green vegetables. It was an awkward thought, but our reunion occupied me anyway. Reunions are the stock-in-trade of advertising commercials: lovable grannies, tremulous brides, proud soldiers, graduating students, innocent children, disabled veterans and so on. Reunions are important to these advertisers; this is their version of humanness. The myth of family ties is exalted above herpes, AIDS, drugs, petty crime, tax fiddling, debasement of the language, frantic acquisitiveness and the anxious pursuit of happiness, which are the true business of our times. Maybe Xai had got a whiff of this sewer and fled towards the traditional certainties.

'What are you going to say to him?'

'I don't know.'

We started to walk purposefully down the steep hillside towards the village, which lay still, clubbed senseless by the night.

CHAPTER 20

O ld people are said to sleep very lightly. Not so the Orefeo. We had to rouse them from beneath a pile of skins and blankets where they lay, only their terracotta heads visible in the gloom. The house was dark and cold and steeped in the scents of Africa: woodsmoke, maize porridge, fermenting grain and sour millet beer, as well as the smells of old age, which are perhaps imagined: a faint, mortal, gaseousness in the air. There was no one in the other houses; we had checked quietly in the pre-dawn. The goats were clamorous. The old men stood up shakily, rubbing their faces with the flat of their hands – long, purposeful movements of their yellowing palms, as if they could rub some meaning, like liniment, into their heads. Old age, I saw, protects you from shock: they stood uncomprehending but apparently unsurprised.

I extended my hand in the respectful African way, clasping my forearm with my left hand, and said good day in Banguni.

'Good morning, sir,' said the first old man in English, holding my hand lightly between his dry fingers.

The other man was facing towards the door. His eyes were not right; milk lay on their surfaces. Cataracts? glaucoma? river blindness? I asked myself foolishly. The old men stood there, unsteadily. They were both wearing tattered goatskins, with the wool turned out at the neck (so they looked like very shabby astrakhan coats), over the things they had been wearing the day before. Their faces were pale and lined, with immense eye sockets lapped by large lids, like a chameleon's. But the first man's dark eyes were busy.

'We are friends,' said Colin. 'Don't worry.'

He said something in Swahili, which they did not answer.

'Are you from the district commissioner, sir?' asked the first man. His voice was thin but firm, and his accent unsettling, because it was not particularly African.

'No, no, I'm looking for my father,' I said.

He reached out with his hand and turned me towards the door so that he could look at my face. His touch was light.

'You are the son. You are Timotee or Jams. For a long time he said you will come. Do you want to kill us now?'

'No. No. I just want to talk to my father.'

There were tears in my eyes. The old men stood utterly helpless, the blind one swaying gently as he had yesterday, waiting for the goats to return – as Mrs de Luth had, waiting for her Hubbard medal. One day, I thought, the cynical goats will tire of his frailty and butt him to death. My mind was galloping.

'Let's go outside and talk, in the light,' said Colin. 'Come, come outside.'

It was much warmer outside. The sun had reached a spot not far above the village. The blind man walked past us to the goats and freed them. They were thin and wiry, with dirty, matted hair and pale, mullet-pink nostrils. His companion guided the blind one with a gentle touch of his arm as we all sat down on the bare earth beneath a large tree. The old men's legs were thin and bunched with excess veins and fibres, but they were working legs. Our old people seem to lose the use of their legs, while their bodies thicken out of control. The blind man did not ask what was going on. He simply sat, his hands clasped just in front of his knees, and waited. His face was serene and vacant, like a house in the country which has been shuttered.

'This man has come from overseas to find his father,' said Colin.

'I know him. He is the father's son.'

'Is he here?'

'Yes please.'

'May I see him?'

'You can see him by and by.'

There was a touch of imperiousness about the soul washer. It was of the holy variety, like Gandhi's: 'Nobody can do anything to me. I am at peace. I have nothing.'

My father would have achieved this state of grace once everything was lost. As we sat on the ground, I could see clearly how this must happen. It would be best to leave without meeting him. What could I do but disturb his serenity? And yet he must have had dreams of escape and dreams of flight. As the dreams blurred and his memories became confused, he would have begun to believe that there was no world beyond these mountains. After all, America was not discovered by the Greeks or the Romans and they got on all right without it. And then there are those familiar stories of the Japanese who lived for decades on isolated Pacific islands under the impression that the war had not ended, until they were brought out, blinking, to the new electronic Japan and honourable retirement in shoebox apartments. When my father departed for Banguniland they were still X-raying children's feet cheerfully in shoe stores. My thoughts would not slow down; they had become disorderly.

Colin was trying gently to find out where my father was kept. The old man pointed up the hill. I don't think Colin believed him. The old man had something on his mind. He said a few words to the blind man, who stood up and made his way to the house. His progress was painfully slow, his feet scuffing the earth as he walked. We watched him silently. What did they think of us, citizens of the mad anthill beyond the endless plain, beyond the metropolis of Bangunes, beyond the foetid coastal strip, and beyond, incredibly, the ocean itself? While we waited for the blind man to return, the other man sat staring straight ahead, his lips moving gently, perhaps reciting the Torah. Colin, as always, sat comfortably relaxed, but I saw for the first time that his clothes had become very shabby. Also his legs were unnaturally carrot brown, like the breasts of French ladies on the beach at Cannes.

If my father had forgotten completely his previous life – through senility or the protective processes of the brain (the well-documented repression of disturbing memories) – what purpose would be served by reminding him of who he really was? Memory reassures us that we are the same person as in the high-school photograph or the playpen. But what if we don't want to be the same person? There must be many people – war criminals, murderers, reformed alcoholics, twice-born Christians – who want to forget their previous lives entirely. For these people memory would be painful and even harmful. Surely the brain's inclination to blot out these destructive memories is Darwinian? And surely – I couldn't stop – there was a relationship between memory and imagination. They are entwined as intimately as the writhing heap of lurid snakes which, thanks to *National Geographic*, inhabited my adolescent nightmares. What if my father had reworked certain aspects of his previous life and then adopted them as memory? What chaos would I cause in his unconscious by straightening out his memory for him?

If I could. My own experience showed that memory and imagination were often hopelessly indistinguishable. There were times when I believe I imagined entirely the incident with Magda in the lift. Then I have only to run my tongue over my poorly aligned front teeth to feel the shame rising again. Memory may be great, but sometimes forgetting is better.

The blind man was returning. Round his neck he now wore the medallion of a soul washer, gleaming in the sunshine which had newly arrived on the valley floor. He had discarded the cumbersome goatskin. In his hand he was carrying what I took to be a small writing case in rococo leather. He gave it to his companion, who showed it to us. It was a radio, dating from the pre-Japanese era, a Roberts from England, made to look like a cigar humidor or desk ornament. Carefully he opened the little brass catch at the back. The woodwork behind the leather veneer was suffering the effects of the climate.

'Look please,' he said.

There was nothing to see, except an empty space the size of a hamster's nesting box.

'We need a battery, sir,' he explained.

There were no batteries that shape any more, but I remembered them as clearly as cars with fish tails. Those batteries were square and bulky and leaked acid.

'Our supplies are in the plane,' said Colin apologetically. 'What did you listen to, before the battery went?'

'On the wireless we listened to the BBC. We like very much the news. Unfortunately we have not got a battery for too long.'

This information made a shambles of my speculations about my father's memory and the old man's understanding of geography. Why was I surprised? In the 1930s, St John Philby, the father of the spy Kim Philby, carried a radio with him into the deserted quarter of Arabia, not for the news but the cricket scores. Radios were commonplace in every nook and cranny of the world.

As well as a little imperiousness, the old man had a sense of decorum: he had his own agenda for discussion, and it could not be rushed. After the battery, they were anxious to know about Prince Charles. Had he become King? Colin was on firm ground here, as a Welshman. He was able to explain that the Queen had made him the Prince of Wales. This was not news to them. President Ndongo's overthrow was. They were delighted. They were surprised to hear that Patrick Ngwenya had taken over as President. This was something of a drop in status, it seemed. They had a long discussion, unconcerned with our anxieties and preoccupation. I told them of my visit to Israel. The blind man was particularly interested and the whole story was repeated for him in Orefeo, although he appeared to understand English. Later I wondered if they saw some symmetry in my visit to the Holy Land.

'Could we see my father now?' I asked after perhaps an hour had gone by.

'We go now.'

We stood up. The first old man, whose name we later learnt was Rantung, went into the house.

'Do you really think they've got him up there?' asked Colin.

'I'm sure of it.'

'They seem very casual.'

'I don't suppose it seems strange to them.'

Rantung reappeared wearing his medallion and carrying a stick; he began to walk purposefully up the hill towards the temperate zone. The blind man, Oryema, returned to the gloom of the house. I could imagine that his blank eyes might be sensitive to sharp sunshine, the milk in danger of curdling. Rantung did not speak. He walked slowly but his breathing was even. It was a steep climb. When we stopped to look back, the village was far below, but the plateau above was no closer. From here there was a clear view all the way down the ravine (the *couloir*, as mountaineers say) to the plains below. The flat earthers, however, would not be able to see the village lying on the saucer of rock with its pattern of trees and vines. We walked on upwards, disappearing behind huge boulders for a few minutes into tunnels of rock and overhanging branches. My lungs were rasping with each breath.

Africa did not make clear distinctions between the real and the imagined world. That is what I could have said in answer to Colin's question. I knew that my father in order to survive would have had to drop these artificial distinctions. Perhaps I had lost them too; or perhaps this distinction is just a conceit of our times. The altitude, anyway, made my thinking very volatile, like the darting flight of the sunbirds which were now plundering the strange plants beside the path to the uplands.

Rantung led us up over the lip of the plateau. We walked towards the cliff face and the little square hut which stood in a clump of tree ferns. Suddenly Colin began to run. From the direction of the cliffs, Xai was loping towards us. The old man stood stock still and I could only think that Colin and Xai were pleased to see each other as they drew closer. But Xai began to fire the pistol; sharp cracking noises reverberated around the steep cliffs and out over the meadows of the Alpine wonderland; great clouds of doves rose from the cliff face like puffs of grey smoke. I did not realise that Xai had shot the old man because at that moment he and Colin met and embraced. When I saw that Colin was holding him pinioned tightly and speaking to him urgently, I ran at last to the old man. He was lying face down on the heather. I rolled him over gently. Xai had hit him only once, in the face; for a moment I thought the bullet had gone right into his head, but it had passed into his open mouth and come out through his cheek. I fumbled in my bag for the first-aid kit, my hands palsied. Xai was bent almost double in Colin's arms, shouting threats at the soul washer in the strange Ge-ez language. I staunched the blood with a swab and placed my sleeping bag under his head. The day was cool up here and the heathers were scented, unobtrusively in flower.

Colin had released Xai, who sat hunched, gulping air noisily. I saw that his hair was elaborately braided and that around his head he wore a thong to which he had attached swatches of goat hair and the dried bodies of little birds. Under his eyes he had painted half moons of white, with clay. His face was unbearably young and formless with confusion.

Colin was holding the pistol as he came over to look at the old man's wounds.

'That doesn't look too bad, thank God,' he said.

I wondered what horrors he had seen elsewhere: the exit wound was nearly as big as the old man's mouth. Colin placed some wadding inside his mouth and dressed the wound with antibiotic powder before closing it with surgical tape. I looked towards the cliffs where the pigeons were still circling in alarm, and towards the hut, but no one came.

'Your father, he's that side,' said the old man through blood-painted lips as he caught my glance.

'I'm sorry,' I said, squeezing his wrist lightly. It was dry and scaly.

The history of exploration is the history of disaster. The suddenness was shocking. Who could have guessed that Xai would try to shoot the soul washer? After we had made the old man comfortable in the hut, we discovered that Xai thought Rantung was going to kill us or worse. Instead of being grateful for his solicitude, we were angry with him. He was deeply distressed and stood up to walk jerkily round in a circle; agitation convulsed his expressive body. He was muttering and shaking his head, but his anger was not convincing; we had kicked the props out from under the fragile construction he had built to accommodate our unpredictable ways.

Rantung was silent as Colin injected him in his thin arm. He went to sleep very quickly.

'He's OK,' said Colin. 'Go and see what you can find.'

I walked towards the cliff face. The wall which we had seen the day before was of dry stone; it followed the natural contours of the rock face like the walls of Great Zimbabwe. I found myself thinking of Mrs de Luth, but the picture I had in mind was of her daughter's scrubbed blue eyes. Our expedition was a disaster, just like hers. I could feel the chaos rising. I could picture Mrs de Luth (equipped with her daughter's eyes) peering into the swift, vegetable currents of the river, trying to make out the elusive figure of my father, hoping to see his alabaster legs scissoring the depths vigorously as he pushed towards the surface, waiting to see his head break the water cheerfully. I understood her anguish.

The stone wall gave off a breath of cold before I reached it, like the frozen food display in a supermarket. In the wall, topped by a large, flat rock, was a narrow entrance. I squeezed through into intense cold and deep gloom yet the gloom was pierced by rods and cones of light sliding through the loosely fitted rock walls. The cavern in front of me was dry and cold, so that I was shivering violently both from the cold and the morning's confusion.

Seated on wooden and gold stools in the near dark was a group of elaborately dressed men, holding ornaments. Among them was my father, wearing a leather apron above his gleaming legs; on his bald head was a single band of gold thread, and on his chest a gold medallion. Even in the dark his face was unmistakably my face, and his legs, my legs. He appeared to be smiling, and with reason because he was sitting on the spider footstool beside Patrick Ngwenya's father, holding on his lap a book.

I was calm at last, the calm of a penitent in a cathedral. I wished

I could reassure Mrs de Luth about the smiling figure. He had achieved what she had desired most: he had lived the story. And by a meaningless coincidence, he too had received a gold medal for his efforts.

CHAPTER 21

Magda has little lines beside her eyes now, only detectable in strong light. They are the legacy of giving birth, I think. Her nomadic days are nearly over, although (like my mother's) her eyes are often fixed on the horizon. The horizon in this case is across a cold, green sea, where, as I write, ice is aggregating on the water's edge, a rhinestone necklace between the grey of the snow on the shore and the green of the bay.

In another room the baby is waking: her gurgles and cries arouse mixed feelings in me. I resent the demands which never slacken, but I also feel privileged to be their focus. Magda has gone into Bridgehampton to do the shopping. I leave my writing to get the baby's bottle.

The Turkish island, on inspection, was not practical; babies have very specific needs. Her legs have creases not only at the top of the thighs, but behind the knees and at the ankles. When I go to lift her, the baby aromas, like my feelings, are mixed: there is a pleasant, herbivorous, dairy smell, but it is laced with the sharper, chemical smell of urine. I am adept at removing the Pampers, swabbing her down, dusting her fat little crevices and bundling her up again; I can do this with one hand while holding the bottle in place with the other. So far she looks like no one I have ever met, not even Magda. But her smile is friendly.

I am working on a biography of my father based on the account he left of his capture and life among the Orefeo. I have decided to interpret it freely, because the story is full of contradictions. 'Conflate' is the word for what I am doing.

*

After he was taken to the Mawenzi, it seems his mind was cracked, in the sense we would know it, by the years of isolation and deprivation. There was no initiation or training for his role. His appearance in the rushes, gleaming and near-naked, to which he refers, I have interpreted as proof that the Orefeo believed he was the long-awaited messiah. Rantung more or less confirmed this. But the text left by my father talks of the creation. The first man, he says, came from a split reed. This is also a Zulu myth, which he perhaps remembered. His story makes few distinctions between the real and the imaginary worlds, but there are clues that this is mystical writing rather than an actual account of events. At least one of the Orefeo, as we discovered, spoke English; they would all listen to the radio together. This happened until the Orefeo massacre dried up the traffic in batteries in 1984. From Rantung we learned that my father had died soon after; in fact, kings and their prophets do not die. They move to the anteroom in God's house where they are bathed in herbs by the soul washers and seated with their peers. The cold and the dryness, and perhaps the scented Nilotic balm of the Orefeo, keep them preserved. On close inspection they are not perfectly preserved; they bear the same relation to their former selves as bottled fruit to fresh fruit.

Time rests lightly on the face of an Inca boy who froze to death in the Andes five centuries ago.

The famous *National Geographic* picture shows that the little boy's skin has certainly puckered and coarsened, but his expression and posture are intact. This is very similar to the condition of the figures in the cave. As I write this, the cave sounds gloomy and even eerie, but the atmosphere, despite the cold, is warm; it is cheery and domestic. In the past, qualified Orefeo were able to drop in for a chat and advice. Sometimes the King would send messengers via the soul washers to his ancestors and receive practical and sensible answers. After the arrival of the prophet, this practice was forbidden by the Orefeo, who were proposing to return to the promised land under my father's guidance.

*

Patrick Ngwenya has restored the monarchy in Banguniland. Naturally it is assumed that he has no time for the superstitions of the past. The treasures are used on ceremonial occasions simply as a reminder of the past.

I think of my father often. We had to move him to retrieve the stool. He was very light, almost weightless, like the space meals. But I am always cheered by the vision I have of him sitting, smiling, in the gloom. Rantung told me that my father spoke of me often; he said I was his favourite. Naturally I have not told my brother this. But we did agree that my father should stay in the mountains.

*

The baby is crying; she has finished her drink and wants to leave the crib; I reach her just as I hear the crunch of the tyres of our car on the snow outside. Magda has returned. Like all fathers, I lift the baby quickly and pretend I have been playing with her for hours so that I can hand her to her mother. They both smile, pleased enough with my deception.

Magda brings a letter from my mother. Mrs Orme-Watson has died. My mother is going to prospering Banguniland to spend a month, at least, with Monroe. She writes:

Jumbo (bloody silly name) is a true gentleman. Thank you for introducing us.

Colin is now Chief Instructor in the Royal Bangunes Air Force. He and I never saw Xai again after that day. We never saw the radio again either. Sometimes, as I watch the icy waves licking the shore, I imagine Xai, still in his outsize shorts, sending a message over the endless scrubland:

'Fucking. Over.'

It is tempting to draw a facile conclusion about the significance of this. But I will resist the temptation. I have miles to go.